GAME CHANGER

KELLY JAMIESON

THE WYNN DYNASTY

Bob Wynn, owner of the California Condors. Originally married to Grace Rogers (deceased), parents to Mark and Matthew with Grace. Parents to Everly, Asher, Harrison, and Noah with Chelsea Wynn. Grandfather to Jean Paul (JP), Théo, Jackson, and Riley.

Chelsea Wynn (formerly Clark), married to Bob Wynn, mother of Everly, Asher, Harrison, and Noah.

Matthew Wynn, owner of the Long Beach Golden Eagles. Son of Bob Wynn. Married to Aline Gagnon. Father of Théo and Jean Paul (JP).

Mark Wynn, coach of the Long Beach Golden Eagles. Son of Bob Wynn. Divorced from Victoria (Tori) Kendall. Father of Jackson and Riley.

Théo Wynn, general manager of the California Condors. Son of Matthew Wynn and Aline Gagnon. Grandson of Bob Wynn (with Grace).

Jean Paul (JP) Wynn, son of Matthew Wynn and Aline Gagnon. Grandson of Bob Wynn (with Grace). Plays for the Long Beach Golden Eagles.

Jackson Wynn, son of Mark Wynn and Victoria (Tori) Kendall. Grandson of Bob Wynn (with Grace). Plays for the Chicago Aces.

Riley Wynn, daughter of Mark Wynn and Victoria (Tori) Kendall. Granddaughter of Bob Wynn (with Grace). Goalie coach for the San Diego Hawks, affiliate team of the Long Beach Golden Eagles.

Everly Wynn, daughter of Bob and Chelsea Wynn. Executive director of the Condors Foundation.

Asher Wynn, son of Bob and Chelsea Wynn. Sports reporter for *Playmaker* (hockey blog).

Harrison Wynn, son of Bob and Chelsea Wynn. Plays for the Pasadena Condors, affiliate team of the California Condors.

Noah Wynn, son of Bob and Chelsea Wynn. Plays for the San Diego Hawks.

JAX

"What are you looking for in a relationship?"

I eye the woman across the table from me in the restaurant where we just had dinner. I'm pretty sure "a way out" is not the correct answer here.

It's the honest one, though.

I met Kiera at a club the other night and asked her out. I keep doing that. I just want to have fun. And hot sex. Is that too much to ask? I don't want commitment or—Jesus!—the M word.

"I'm not looking for a relationship," I say, smiling to soften the message.

Why are we even talking about a relationship the first time we've ever gone out?

Her bottom lip pushes out and she gives me sad eyes, but then smiles. "You just haven't met the right woman."

"You could be right." And I still haven't.

I repress a sigh. Kiera's beautiful—tall, great rack, fantastic legs. All male eyes…no, let's go with *all* eyes in the restaurant turned to her when we walked in. She's wearing a dress that's wrapped around her like an ACE bandage and heels that could cause a serious ankle injury if she falls off them. She picked this uber trendy restaurant, with dim lighting probably designed to hide the tiny portions of mystifying food. They can't fool me, though, because I'm still hungry. Her conversation has been limited to how much she hates her job at the bank, what a dick her ex is, and how much money hockey players make. (I'm a hockey player—that didn't just come up out of the blue.) And the biggest turnoff? She talks to the waiter as if he's her personal servant. I fucking hate that.

"I'd love to be your date for your friend's wedding this weekend."

Sweet buttery Jesus on a breadstick. That is *not* happening.

"I'm sorry." I smile again. "I RSVPed a long time ago and I didn't include a date. It would be rude to show up with one at the last minute."

"The groom is a hockey player. I'm sure they can afford one more dinner."

My eyebrows rise. "I don't think that's the issue."

"Oh, come on." She leans forward and actually bats her eyelashes at me. I don't think I've ever seen that done before. "I'm sure they don't expect you to go alone."

"I'm sure they do, since that's what I told them I'd be doing."

My teammate, Steve Shevchuk, is getting married this weekend. I'm going stag to this event. I absolutely could have replied to the invitation saying I was bringing a plus one; I'd have no trouble getting a date. Does that sound douchey? Don't mean it to, it's just the truth. Anyway, taking a woman to a wedding is the worst idea. They get all emotional and damp-eyed and start thinking about their *own* wedding, which leads to hurt feelings when I tell them I'm never getting married. Also, when you bring a date to a wedding, only about a hundred people will ask "When are *you* two getting married?" It makes me nuts.

A few of the other guys are also going solo, and we'll have fun at the open bar generously provided by Steve and Molly.

"Would you like to see the dessert menu?" Our server pauses at the table.

"Ugh, no," Kiera say dismissively.

I resist the urge to roll my eyes. "Just the check, please," I say with a smile for the server.

"Are we going somewhere else for a drink?" Kiera asks. "Maybe dancing?"

"Sorry." I tilt my head. "I have an early meeting with my agent tomorrow."

"I thought your season is done."

"It is." We were knocked out of the playoffs a few weeks ago. "But I'm a restricted free agent and we need to talk about my next contract."

"Oh." She blinks.

I take care of the check, adding a generous tip to make up for having to deal with Kiera, and I usher her out of the restaurant and onto North Lasalle Drive. It's a beautiful June evening in Chicago, the sun setting and twinkling lights coming on around us.

"We could go for a walk," Kiera suggests, taking my arm. "On the Riverwalk."

She's persistent. I'm starting to feel like a jerk for turning her down. "Sorry. Can't. I'll take you home."

I parked in a parking garage a couple of blocks away, so we set off down the sidewalk. I keep talking, mostly so Kiera can't suggest something else for us to do that I don't want to.

Once I've dropped her off at her apartment in River West, I let out a sigh of relief. I like women in general and I'm usually a helluva lot better at picking someone to have a fun evening with.

I know it's a dick move, but instead of going straight home, I stop by the Irish pub where I know my buddies Heart, Rico and Gander are having beers. Just for one. I really do have a meeting with Paul in the morning.

"Hey! Jax!" they all great me as I approach the table.

"Hey." I pull out a wooden chair and drop into it. "How's it going?"

"Excellent. Where's your hot date?"

"Just dropped her off at home." I grimace and shove a hand through my hair.

They all make a low sound of understanding.

"Welp, have a beer," Rico says, lifting a hand to attract the waitress's attention. She speeds over with a big smile, and I order a Goose Island Belgian Ale.

The White Sox are playing the Royals on the big screen TV I'm facing. I check out the score—White Sox leading five-three.

"Ready for the wedding this weekend?" Heart asks. His name is Brian Erhardt, but we call him Heart or Hearts.

We all groan.

"I'd rather stay home with a case of beer, a bag of Doritos and the remote control in my hand," Rico says.

"I'd rather rotate my tires," Gander says.

We all laugh.

Rico sighs. "Flowers, decorations, finger foods, frilly female clothing, missing sports on Saturday afternoon. So much fun."

"Women love weddings," I say. "This girl I was out with tonight was trying to get me to bring her as my date."

"Jesus. She doesn't even know Chucky and Molly."

"I know." I shrug. "I don't get it."

"She'd get to buy a new dress and shoes and cry during the ceremony," Rico says.

"We're so cynical."

"Yep."

"If men planned weddings…" I rub my chin. "They'd be different."

"Oh hell yeah! We'd wear sweats and our old T-shirts and sneakers."

"Serve beers and pizza," I add.

"We'd crack open cold ones as soon as the minister pronounces them husband and wife," Rico says.

"We'd walk down the aisle to Led Zeppelin," I add, grinning. " 'All My Love!' "

"Yeah! Perfect!" Rico and I bump fists.

"And the reception would be a big party with beer pong and boat racing." I lift my ale in a toast as we all guffaw in delight at planning our dream wedding. "No speeches," I add.

"Hell, no."

"Somehow I don't think that's what's happening this weekend," Rico says with a sigh.

"Nope. But you know, Molly's pretty down to earth. It probably won't be crazy over the top with doves flying around and fireworks and a rose petal cannon." I nod.

"Rose petal cannon? Is that a real thing?" Rico's mouth hangs open.

"Yeah, I went to a wedding last summer that had that."

"Jesus. But, yeah, I agree, that's not Molly's style."

Molly Flynn, the fiancée of our teammate Chucky, is a sweetheart. She and Chucky have been dating for a couple of years so we've all gotten to know her pretty well. I feel like I know her better than most, because we discovered a mutual love of trivia one night at a bar. We ended up on the same team, and we were goddamn unbeatable. She's a schoolteacher, so she's smart and she knows a lot, as do I, so we started going to trivia nights together since Chucky hates it.

"I trust there will be no crapping doves," I say again. "To Molly." I lift my beer, and we all toast the bride even though we all want to go to this wedding as much as we want to have our butt cracks waxed.

2

___

MOLLY

I am seriously going to vomit.

All over this gorgeous dress that cost me a fucking fortune.

I'm standing in the Metropolitan, on the sixty-seventh floor of the Sears Tower. Well, Willis Tower, but I don't know anyone who calls it that.

I'm in a curtained-off area behind guests seated in rows facing the big windows at the far end of the room. A pale runner lines the patterned carpet up the middle of the rows of chairs, candles and flowers bordering the runner.

My mom and dad are with me, their faces lined with concern.

"Are you okay, honey?" Mom whispers to me.

"Fine." I grit my teeth and straighten my shoulders.

Music wafts from the front of the room, the songs I carefully chose months ago for this occasion. Right now, it's "Don't Stop Believin' " played by Vitamin String Quartet.

Yeah, I stopped believin' last night.

I press a hand to my stomach. I can do this.

Steve's best man, James, appears, ready to take Mom down

7

the aisle. She gives me a shaky smile and a kiss on the cheek, then takes James' arm.

I turn to Dad. Our eyes meet. "I'm sorry, Dad," I say inexplicably.

His forehead furrows.

The song changes to the "Glasgow Love Theme" from the movie *Love, Actually.* I've always loved that movie. Yes, I'm a total romantic. Or, I used to be.

The music is beautiful and evocative. Dad takes my arm, and we move into the opening. The crowd stands, all heads turning toward us, beaming.

A shaky breath lifts my breasts beneath the off-the-shoulder dress. I raise my chin and stare straight ahead at my fiancé as Dad and I slowly walk down the aisle.

Steve smiles, standing next to his groomsmen. My three bridesmaids are on the other side of the aisle in their champagne-colored sequined dresses, holding small bouquets of white peonies. My own bouquet is bigger, with soft pink roses and peonies among the white ones, and sprays of pale greenery.

Steve's so handsome. Clean cut, with short, dark blond hair, his athletic body perfect in the black tuxedo, he stands with his hands loosely clasped in front of him, his eyes focused on me.

My heart hammers against my breastbone and my knees wobble with every step I take. I feel like this isn't real.

The music reaches a crescendo as we arrive at the front of the room. The officiant we've hired for the ceremony smiles benevolently at me as Dad releases my arm, kisses my cheek, and steps away. I swallow and stand next to Steve.

Damn, this song! Pressure builds behind my eyes and cheekbones. Why couldn't this be the moment I'd imagined when I chose this beautiful music that I love so much? The piece ends with tinkling piano notes and soaring violins, and I nearly lose it.

I catch my best friend's eye. Grace's mouth is tight, her eyes shadowed. She gives me a tiny nod, and I know she's telling me she's with me whatever I do.

"Friends, we have been invited here today to share with Molly and Steven a very important moment in their lives. In the years they have been together, their love and understanding of each other has grown and matured, and now they have decided to live their lives together as wife and husband."

I don't hear much more over the buzzing in my ears. My hands are sweaty, my skin clammy. Then I'm called on to say my vows.

Grace hands me my phone.

With shaky fingers, I unlock it and reveal the screen ready for me to read. Facing Steve, I begin. "I'm supposed to say something now about our love and the promises we make to each other." I suck in a breath. "But I'm not going to do that. Instead, I'm going to read the text messages that Steve has been exchanging with a woman named Claire."

Stunned silence falls over the room. I feel Steve tense, and I flick my eyes up to his. He stares at me, his eyebrows pulled together, his mouth open. I lift my own eyebrows then resume my reading. " 'I can't wait to be with you again. After the wedding, things will settle down to normal and we can be together again.' " I scroll up. " 'Your body is incredible. I love making you come.' " Another one…'I love you. I can't stop thinking about fucking you.' "

Shocked gasps fill the air.

"What are you doing?" Steve whispers, trying to grab my phone.

I step back, set my jaw and keep going. " 'I only w-wish Molly could give a blow job like you do.' " I pause. "This one's from Claire. 'Baby, you know I love your big cock.' Then there are the pictures. A selfie of the two of them. A topless photo of Claire. And a lovely dick pic from Steve. Also from Steve: 'I want to smack your ass and fuck you hard from behind.' "

I'm really shaking now. Grace steps closer and slides her arm around my waist.

I look up at Steve again. "Obviously, I can't marry you today." I turn my head toward the guests. "I'm sorry, everyone, there isn't going to be a w-wedding."

Pandemonium breaks out, a muted roar rising as everyone starts talking, some rising from their seats.

I turn to my parents, who had no idea this was coming. "I'm sorry."

The shocked expression on their faces nearly takes my knees out.

Grace holds onto me. "We're with you, Mol," she whispers.

"I need to get out of here."

"Of course."

We bolt down the aisle, threading our way through people. I vaguely register shocked, concerned faces but I try not to look at anyone, my humiliation complete. We make our way to the dressing room where we prepared for the ceremony not long ago.

My other two bridesmaids, Allison and Brielle, follow us, locking the door behind us.

I head straight for the champagne bottles on the counter, picking up one we were drinking earlier that's still half full. I lift it to my lips and drink straight from the bottle.

Grace is beside me, rubbing my shoulder. "Attagirl," she murmurs. "You did it."

"I did." I swipe my fingers beneath my nose. "Why do I want to cry?"

"Because your heart is broken." She leans her head against mine. "I'm so sorry. That ratfucking bastard."

"I want to throat-punch him," Brielle says fiercely. "In fact, I think I might go do that."

"I'm coming with you." Allison scowls. "Motherfucker."

Before I can tell them not to bother, they've disappeared. I grimace at Grace and sink into an armchair, clutching my bottle of bubbly.

"I'd like to castrate him," she says, grabbing another bottle and a flute. "But I don't want to do jail time."

I guzzle more champagne, the bubbles pleasantly stinging my nose and throat. "He's not worth it."

I lean my head back and close my eyes. Only twenty-four hours ago, I totally thought Steve was worth it. Worth marrying. Worth loving.

What a fool I was.

And what a fool I've been, not to know what was going on behind my back.

"How could he?" I whisper, my throat squeezing up.

"I don't know. I'd really like to hear his explanation. Because there is no explanation that's good enough for cheating. For fuck's sake." Grace shakes her head and sips her champagne, more ladylike than I am right now despite her language. "That's just bullshit. And who the fuck is Claire?"

"I don't know." My bottom lip quivers. "She's pretty and she has great boobs." I look down at my modest chest.

"If that's all he cares about, then he really is a dickhead."

Someone knocks on the door.

We look at each other.

"Molly? Are you in there? Open this door!"

Steve.

I frown. "I thought Allison and Brielle were dealing with him."

"I'll fucking deal with him." Grace jumps up and stalks over to the door in her spiky heels. "Get fucked, Steve!" she shouts through the door.

I actually snort out a laugh.

"I love you," I whisper to her.

We hear more voices—female voices. Another male voice. My parents. There's a lot of yelling and I catch a few swear words.

Grace rolls her eyes and sets down her glass. "I'll be back."

She disappears out the door, and I leap up to lock it again.

I'm alone.

I hear Grace telling everyone to go away and give me my space. "Especially you, asshole," comes quite clearly through the door. I hear more male voices. Maybe Steve's friends. They won't break the door down, will they? They're all hockey players, big and strong, and have been known to get into the odd fisticuffs.

The voices fade away as my girls take care of things. I feel bad about Mom and Dad. Luckily, they didn't pay for much of the wedding; Steve did, since he's loaded. That's *not* why I was marrying him, just to be clear. I don't care about money. I thought I was marrying for love.

My heart contracts sharply, the pain stealing my breath.

Love.

What. The. Fuck.

I lift the champagne bottle and finish it off.

Standing in the middle of the room, I can see my reflection in the full-length mirror on the wall. I love this dress. It's a princess dress, with a full skirt and beaded bodice. I felt like a princess when I tried it on, and I couldn't wait to feel like a princess wearing it in front of Steve.

I look down at the ring on my hand. I love my ring, too. I slip it off my finger and tuck it into my little beaded purse.

I'll give it back to Steve. Maybe he can give it to fucking Claire.

I'd like to give it to Claire. Right between the eyes.

Another knock on the door startles me. I turn and regard it suspiciously. It better not be Steve again.

"Who is it?" I ask.

"Jax."

I blink.

Jax Wynn is one of Steve's friends and teammates. But he's also *my* friend. My tequila-drinking, trivia-playing buddy. Biting my lip, I cross the room and unlock the door. I crack it open and peer out. "State your business."

His lips quirk. "Are you okay?"

"Are you kidding me? Of course I'm not okay!"

He winces. "I know. I'm sorry. Can I come in?"

"Did Steve send you?"

He frowns. "No."

"Okay." I open the door wider to let him in, then lock it again.

"I saw your bridesmaids ripping into Steve," Jax says. "I can't believe what just happened."

I sigh and move to the counter where the champagne bottles are. The open ones are all empty. I pick up a full one and peel off the foil. Then I turn to Jax. "Can you open this?"

He takes the bottle, grabs a small towel and easily removes the cork with a pop. He looks for a glass, but I seize the bottle and take a swig.

He scratches the back of his neck. "You look beautiful. If that helps at all."

"It doesn't really, but thanks."

"Yeah." He sits in one of the chairs, resting his elbows on his knees. "How did you find out?"

"Someone sent me screen shots of the texts last night."

"This Claire girl?"

"I don't know. I don't know who else would know or be able to do that. Unless someone got Steve's phone. It doesn't matter."

"That was…gutsy."

I nod slowly. "Probably stupid. I wanted everyone to know what an asswipe he is, but now everyone knows what a loser *I* am." One corner of my mouth dips.

"What? Loser? You're not a loser. He cheated on you."

"Because I don't give blow jobs as good as Claire."

"Christ." He rubs his face.

"Also, my boobs aren't as big. In fairness, though, he may love making *her* come, but he wasn't that good at it with me."

Jax chokes.

I drink more champagne. Feeling a little woozy. That's good though.

I sit again, my skirt spread all around me. "Did you know?" I ask quietly.

Jax's mouth pinches up. "No," he says shortly.

"I just don't understand."

"Me either. Hand over that bottle."

I comply with a wry smile, watching as he lifts the bottle to his lips. His throat works as he takes several swallows.

"I need to get out of here." I stand and look around the elegantly appointed dressing room.

Jax stands too, looking faintly alarmed. "Where are you going?"

"I don't know. I can't go home. My apartment's empty." My lip wobbles again. "I just moved in with Steve last weekend. And I can't go there. I don't want to see him again."

"I think you're going to have to see him at some point."

"No." I firm my lips and cross my arms. "Well, maybe. But not now."

"Want me to go find your bridesmaids?"

"No. I just want to disappear." Then I sigh. "I don't even have a car here."

"Uh…"

"Can you give me a ride?" I meet his eyes pleadingly.

"I don't have a car either."

"Shit."

"We can get a taxi."

"I guess."

"But where? Your parents' place?"

"I don't want to face them either. Oh God." I close my eyes briefly. "Can we go to your place?"

His eyes bug out. "What?"

"That's perfect. Nobody will find me there." I grab onto his arm, distantly noting the size and firmness of his biceps. "Please, Jax."

3

———

MOLLY

Jax's eyes shift around, but then he nods. "Okay. Sure. Let's go."

I want to escape so badly I don't even take the time to change back into the clothes I arrived in. All my other things are already at the hotel where we were supposed to spend our wedding night. Shit.

Oh well.

Jax opens the door and peers out. We can hear faint voices but nobody's in the corridor. He leads me out toward the elevators. I don't know what's going on, if guests have left, or stayed, and I don't care, but I just don't want to run into anyone.

But Jax takes me on a convoluted tour that ends up in the kitchen where my wedding dinner is being prepared. We meet stunned faces. "Is there a freight elevator?" he asks.

A woman points.

"Thanks." Jax smiles and nods, takes my hand and rushes me through the kitchen.

In the empty elevator, I lean against the wall. "Wow. Great idea. Thanks."

The elevator makes a rapid descent to the main floor.

"Hopefully we can find our way out from wherever we end up," Jax says.

We emerge into a deserted loading area. We both scan the space and spot an exit door. We find ourselves in the loading dock area on Lower Wacker Drive.

It's dark and desolate down here. "Great." I look around at all the concrete. "Lovely."

"We need to get a taxi," Jax says. He leads the way to a narrow sidewalk.

Cars roar past us, the sound echoing in the enclosed space as we walk a dark incline leading up to street level.

Near the top of the incline, a man sits against the wall with a big bag beside him, no doubt containing all his worldly possessions. He eyes us as we approach.

I'm glad Jax is with me.

"Beautiful bride," he says.

"Thanks."

"I was married once." He chokes on a sob.

Oh my God.

"That cheating whore…I got six kids with her." He wipes his face. "She was fucking everyone in town behind my back."

"Wow." I drop down into a crouch next to him, my skirt spread all around me. Vaguely I realize this sidewalk isn't exactly clean, but whatever. "Same. My fiancée was cheating on me."

"Him?" The man eyes Jax suspiciously.

"No. *He's* rescuing me. I didn't go through with the wedding."

"Good for you." He pats my hand, tears still in his eyes.

"I'm sorry that happened to you."

"Yeah. My life went into the shitter after that."

"I'm sorry to hear that." I have no cash whatsoever, or I'd give him some.

Jax digs into his pocket and pulls out a bill that he hands to the man. "Here you go, man."

"Thanks. Good luck, pretty lady."

We emerge onto South Wacker. City lights glitter around us. Jax spots a yellow cab and raises his hand to hail it.

I see the driver do a double take at my wedding dress, then jerk the wheel and screech to a halt at the curb.

"This doesn't look weird or anything," I mutter, hoisting my skirts and clipping after Jax in my high heels as he jogs over to the taxi.

"You wanted to leave," he reminds me over his shoulder.

We jump in, me wrestling with the multiple layers of my dress. Jax helps me deal with it, tucking fabric under my thighs, then I pull the door closed.

"Newlyweds!" the driver says. "Congratulations!"

Jax and I exchange glances. I widen my eyes at him, and the corners of his mouth lift.

"Uh, thanks," Jax says.

"Where to, lovebirds?" the cabbie asks.

Jax gives his address.

The driver chats all the way to Jax's place, although I don't say anything, lost in my misery until we pull up in the driveway of Jax's building. I've been to his place once before when he had a party; he lives in a new, super modern high-rise on North Lake Shore.

Jax pays the driver and then leads me through the elegant lobby to the elevators where we take a ride up to the fifty-fourth floor. I'm hanging on by a hair at this point. Also, my feet hurt.

Inside Jax's condo, I kick off my pointy-toed shoes and wiggle my toes on the hardwood floor. As I was the first time I came here, I'm mind-boggled by the incredible views out his floor-to-ceiling windows. I drop my tote bag and toss my purse onto a couch as I pad on bare feet over to the windows, mesmerized. Far below us, streaks of light curve along Lake Shore, with other skyscrapers twinkling around us. For a moment, I stare out at the city, feeling lost and despondent.

"Here." Jax speaks behind my in a low voice.

I turn and he hands me a glass of clear liquid.

"Gran Patrón," he says.

"Perfect." I take the glass and sip the tequila, savoring the smooth feel and the hint of citrus. Jax taught me to like tequila, which we often drink while we're kicking ass at trivia contests.

With a glass in his own hand, he moves over to sit on one of a pair of long couches. "The beaver is the national emblem of what country?"

I tilt my head, a smile tugging at my reluctant lips. "Come on. That's way too easy, my Canadian friend."

He grins.

I wander over and sit on the couch opposite him, a big cocktail table between us. I take another sip of tequila. "What is the name of Batman's butler?"

He shakes his head. "Alfred."

"I guess if we're going to practice, we need more challenging questions."

"Yeah." He drinks. "What are you going to do?"

I know exactly what he means. "I don't know."

I become aware that my purse is buzzing. "Shit. My phone."

I lean and stretch out my arm to grab the purse. With my nose wrinkled up, I pull out my phone. It's blowing up with about a thousand text messages and missed calls. I sigh. "I guess I should let some people know I'm okay."

"Some people, meaning not Steve."

"Yeah, I don't give a shit if he's worried. He probably doesn't care anyway."

"I'm sure he does."

I shoot Jax a dark look. "Why?"

"He loves you, Molly."

"Apparently not."

He winces.

I ignore the messages from Steve. I don't want to read his lies. Fucker. I send a message to our wedding planner, Katelyn Bennet, apologizing for what happened. I tell her to call me if she needs me. Then I tap in a few quick messages to my bridesmaids and to my mom and dad, not telling them where I am, just that I left and I'm fine.

I'm not really fine, but I have to say that.

"This is nuts." I lay my head back. "I'm supposed to be celebrating right now."

"Yeah." We fall silent for a moment, then Jax says, "You should have seen the look on the officiant's face when you read those messages."

" 'I can't stop thinking about fucking you?' "

"Yep." He chuckles. "Holy shit, I thought his eyes were going to burst out of his head."

I grin. "Well, I'm glad I provided some entertainment."

"You had to know that was going to be crazy."

"Oh yeah. I nearly changed my mind about doing it, but I was just so *pissed*."

"I get it."

"Don't worry, I won't tell him you bailed me out tonight."

Jax lifts a shoulder. "Whatever."

"I know he's your teammate and your friend. I'm sorry I involved you in this."

"It's okay." He meets my eyes. "I'm *your* friend, too."

"Thanks." My throat constricts.

"Uh…you want to stay here tonight?"

"Could I?" I bite my lip.

"Sure." His voice sounds like he swallowed sand.

"I might need to borrow a few things."

"Yeah. We'll figure it out." He pauses. "You hungry?"

"Not really. But I am kind of drunk, so I should probably eat something."

"I don't have much here. I'm leaving for California tomorrow."

"Right." I remember him mentioning something about traveling.

"I can order something in, though. Any preference?"

"It doesn't matter to me."

"I'll get a pizza." He pulls out his phone.

"Sounds good."

He orders the pizza, then disappears into his bedroom. When he returns, he's dressed in pair of well-worn jeans and a gray Chicago Aces T-shirt. He's carrying some clothing. "Here." He sets them on the couch next to me. "I know they're not going to fit, but at least you can get out of that dress and be more comfortable."

"Thanks." I scoop up the clothes. "Is your fireplace gas or woodburning?"

"What?" He glances over at the wall. "It's gas."

"Damn. I was thinking we could have a dress burning."

He laughs. "Guess not."

I trudge to the bathroom where I study my reflection. My mascara is a bit smudged, but otherwise my subtle smoky eyes and blushed cheeks are still perfect. My hair is in an elaborate updo of loose loops and twists, with small white flowers and pearls woven through it. Gripping the marble vanity, I close my eyes as a wave of pain washes over me.

Since I got those texts last night, I've been a wreck. A

nervous, heart-broken, nauseous mess. But I was also determined not to be a victim. I wanted to make a big, bold statement, and I did it. I hadn't thought through the aftermath, though, and what would happen next.

Jax has given me a pair of plaid pajama bottoms with a drawstring waist I should be able to tighten, and a huge, soft T-shirt. He's such a sweetheart.

Big problem though—I can't get the little buttons on the back of my dress undone. I peer over one shoulder, then the other, nearly breaking my arms trying to do it.

I really don't want to ask Jax for help. I mean, we're friends, but he's a guy, and this is…awkward.

Finally, sweaty and frustrated, I give up.

I walk out the living room where Jax still sits. "Sorry to bug you with this, but…I can't get my dress undone."

He looks over at me. "Oh." He sets his glass down and rises.

I present him with my back. "The buttons are really small."

"Yeah." He clears his throat. "They are."

The dress is off the shoulder, so the top of my back is bare. He moves up behind me, and his fingers brush over my skin as he starts to work on the tiny studs. I can feel his warmth and his focus as he opens each button, from the top down to my waist. The bodice loosens around me and I lift my hands to hold it in place.

Finally, he says hoarsely, "There you go."

"Thank you."

I hasten back to the bathroom, the dress now loose, my back entirely bare. I step out of it, leaving it in a pile on the tiled floor. I'm not wearing a bra, and my panties are white lace. The white lace that was supposed to be sexy for Steve when I first planned to wear them but which I knew he was never going to see when I put them on earlier today.

"Fuck him," I mutter, pulling on Jax's T-shirt. I tighten up the drawstring on the pants and roll down the waistband, then roll up the hems so I don't trip over them. Jax is a lot taller than me.

I bundle up the dress and shove it in the corner. Then I pull out the pins and pearls and flowers in my hair and shake it out with my hands. There. Now I'm comfortable.

Back in the living room, Jax has some music playing quietly and he's looking at his phone.

I sit again and pick up my tequila. "Are you getting texts about the wedding?"

"Oh yeah." He tosses his phone onto the couch. "I told the guys I bolted since it seems the wedding wasn't happening and I'm leaving tomorrow."

"Do you need to pack? Don't let me keep you from doing what you need to."

"I'm mostly packed. My flight's not until three o'clock, so I have time in the morning."

"Okay, good."

Our pizza arrives. I manage to eat a couple of small pieces even though I didn't think I wanted any.

"So you're going to see your family in Los Angeles," I say to Jax as we eat.

"Yep."

"You don't seem thrilled about it."

His jaw tightens. "It's not going to be fun. Family stuff."

His family is pretty famous. His grandfather is a hockey legend. As a Chicago girl, I've always been a fan of the Aces, but I learned a lot more about hockey when I started dating Steve. I've heard the stories about Jax's dad suing Jax's grandfather over money, but I've never really talked to Jax about it.

"Well, they're still family, so it's good to go visit."

"It's not just a visit. My grandpa has Alzheimer's."

"Oh no." I gaze at him sympathetically. "I didn't know that."

"They haven't really gone public with it yet."

"That's awful. But it's good that you'll go spend some time with him."

"The thing is, I haven't really seen Grandpa for a long time." He sets his empty plate on the coffee table. "The last time was a family wedding and I pretty much avoided him."

"Oh. Why is that?"

"It's a long story. My family is complicated. But now… knowing what's happening to him, I need to make sure he's being looked after."

I frown. "You don't think he's being looked after?"

"His wife is…let's say, a trophy wife. I worry that now Grandpa's health is failing, she'll bail on him."

My eyes fly open wide. "That's terrible!"

"Yeah. So I need to go see him and…shit, it's probably too late." He rubs the back of his neck. "Anyway, I'm not really looking forward to the trip. But it's just ten days, and then I come back here, then head up to Canada for the rest of the summer."

I nod, recalling he mentioned this. "That'll be nice and relaxing."

"Yeah. I'm going to stay at the lake where my grandparents —my mom's parents—have a cottage. It's really nice there."

"What will you do?"

"Swim. Golf. There's a great golf course there. Fish. And take lots of pictures."

Jax is an avid photographer. "Oh, you'll love that."

He smiles. "Yep. Can't wait." His smile fades. "What did you have planned for the summer?"

I'm a third-grade teacher. We planned the wedding for June when we knew school and hockey season would be done. "We were going to go to Europe for a few weeks." I pout and poke at the pizza crust on my plate. "I guess that's not happening now. Then I was going to spend the rest of the summer redecorating Steve's condo and settling in."

"Don't you want that crust?" Jax asks.

"Here." I hand him my plate. We've done this before too. He loves pizza crust and I don't. "I don't know what I'll do now. Go into seclusion, I guess."

He snorts, then chomps on the crust. "Don't do that."

"I don't want to face anyone. I don't want to see anyone I know. And I sure as hell don't want to deal with the media." I throw myself back into the couch cushions. "My life is ruined."

"Drama queen."

I lift my head to glare at him. Then I sigh. "Yeah. I know my life isn't over. But it feels like it right now."

"I know. I'm sorry. This is shitty. You should do whatever you want to do."

I mull that over. I wasn't lying when I said I don't want to see anyone. This wedding was a big deal, since Steve is an NHL player. He'd invited guys he used to play with, even some media people he knows. It's going to be in the news that I left him at the altar because he cheated on me. He's going to be humiliated too. And he's not going to be happy about that. Steve's a great guy, but he has a temper.

Getting out of town for the summer sounds amazing. If only I could do that too.

I could.

I study Jax. "You know what I'd like to do?"

"What?"

"I want to come with you to California."

4

———————

JAX

Holy snapping eyeballs.

I can't take Molly to California with me. What the hell is she thinking?

I swallow a sigh. She's upset. She's not thinking clearly. She'll realize in the morning we can't do that. "I don't know," I finally say. "That doesn't seem like a good idea."

"Why not?" She commandeers the tequila bottle and pours herself another.

Okay, she's also toasted. Again, she'll have more sense in the morning.

"Well, for one thing, Chucky would have my balls in a vise if I take off with his fiancée."

"I'm not his fiancée anymore." She sets her little chin stubbornly.

"Still, he'd be pissed."

"Probably true. But I don't really care at this point." She lifts one shoulder dismissively.

She can dismiss that, sure. I'm the one who'll have to deal

with Chucky's ire. Jesus. I can only imagine how incensed he'd be.

"Also, you don't have a flight booked."

"That's easy to solve." She picks up her phone and waves it in the air.

"Or a hotel room."

"Please," she scoffs. "These are not real obstacles."

"You don't know my family."

"That's okay. I'll do my own thing while you have family time. I can lay on the beach or by the hotel pool and drink margaritas for a few days. It'll give me time to process things. It sounds perfect."

She's not giving up.

"Let's talk about it in the morning," I suggest carefully.

She purses her lips. "You think I'm drunk."

"You *said* you are." She's exasperating as hell, always has been, but for some reason it always just amuses me.

"Right. Okay, I am. Fine. But I really want to go with you. I'm not saying that because I'm drunk."

"We'll see." I stand. "I'm going to check the guest room and make sure the bed's made up."

She needs a good night's sleep and hopefully in the morning she won't even remember this conversation. I march down the hall and into one of my extra rooms. My cleaning lady makes sure it's kept up, since some of my friends often spend the night if we've been drinking. This room is the bigger spare room and has its own bathroom.

Yep, there are clean sheets on the bed and a basket of toiletries on the vanity in the bathroom. All ready for Molly to sleep it off.

I stop in the room for a moment before going back to her, to regain some equanimity. This runaway bride thing has knocked me for a loop. Totally not how I expected the day to turn out.

My gut aches for Molly. I damn near died when she was up there reading those dirty text messages, looking like a beautiful, virginal princess in that frothy dress. I could see how distraught she was even though she was holding it together. I couldn't even make sense of what was happening.

I'm also pissed the hell off at Chucky for what he did.

I may not believe in marriage for myself, but I do expect guys who get married to be faithful. And when they aren't…it pisses me off.

I've seen what happens when men cheat. Men who seem like decent guys. I've experienced the pain that a divorce causes because of infidelity. It makes me want to puke.

Now Molly's sitting on my couch wearing rolled-up pajama pants and a loose T-shirt that doesn't hide the fact she's not wearing a bra, her face sad, on the verge of tears. I fucking hate that she's hurting. I also fucking hate that she thinks Chucky screwed around on her because of…her oral skills and, uh, lack of boobage. Not that I have any experience with Molly's oral skills. I close my eyes as an image of her on her knees in front of me pops into my head.

Jesus! What is wrong with me?

I swipe a hand across my forehead.

Onward.

I return to the living room. She's turned around on the couch so her chin is resting on the back of it, facing the windows. Her red-gold hair is a tousled mess of waves, just brushing her shoulders.

The bare shoulders I saw earlier tonight, undoing her dress. She has faint golden freckles there and a tiny mole on her left shoulder blade.

I shake my head. "Okay. The guest room is ready for you, whenever you want to go to bed."

She flips around to face me. "Thanks. I think I need more tequila, though."

What the hell. I pour myself another glass and top hers up. "You might regret this in the morning."

"I've never been hungover from tequila."

"So you say."

"You don't believe me?"

"Let's say I'm skeptical."

"Tell me about your family."

"Ugh. Why?"

"I'm curious. Why are they 'complicated?' "

"It's a long story." I swirl my tequila and take a sip.

"Fine. You can tell me on the plane tomorrow."

"Jesus." I shake my head, fighting a smile.

She grabs her phone.

"What are you doing?" I'm ready to snatch it out of her hand if she's trying to book a flight.

"I'm Facebook-stalking Claire."

"You know who she is?"

"No, but I bet Steve is friends with her."

I watch her swipe and tap at her phone, a little notch between her eyebrows.

"Ha! This is her!" She holds up the phone, then stares at it again, nibbling her bottom lip. "Well, her profile is locked up so I can't tell much about her. Shit."

"Probably for the best."

"I'll google her."

"Do you really want to do that?"

"Yes." She frowns at her screen again. "No." She lowers her phone. "She knew he was getting married. She probably sent me those screen shots. What kind of woman does that?"

I sigh.

Molly drops her phone. "Ugh. Maybe I should go to bed."

"Sure."

"Thank you, Jax." She meets my eyes. "I'm really grateful for letting me escape the crazy."

"Any time, Flynn."

She almost smiles. Then she stands.

I show her to the guest room. She takes it in. "Nice decorating."

I know the room is sparsely furnished. The guys who stay over here after a night of drinking don't care about matching pillow shams. "Hey, you said you were grateful. Did you expect the Waldorf Astoria?"

"No. The Peninsula. That's where I'm supposed to be tonight."

"Fuck. Sorry."

"Don't. I was joking. I don't care what this room looks like, just that nobody will find me here."

"Your secret is safe with me."

"I know." Her lips curve into a sad smile. "Thanks again. Good night."

"Night."

I close the door behind me when I leave.

I should hit the sack too, I guess. I go shut off all the lights and load our tequila glasses and pizza plates into the dishwasher. I better run it tonight so they're not sitting in there for weeks. Then I trudge into my own room, which is bigger but not much more decorated than the guest room. My suitcase is on the floor, half-filled with clothes for my trip. I'll throw a few more things in there in the morning and I'm set.

I sit on the side of the bed and think about what just happened.

Holy shit.

I'm harboring a fugitive.

Ha ha. And I called Molly a drama queen.

The good thing is, I'm leaving tomorrow. When I come back in ten days, things will have settled down. A lot of my teammates who were at the wedding will have left town for the summer, although some stay here in Chicago. I won't have to face any awkward questions or comments about Molly.

She can go to her parents in the morning. I have time to take her there. She can stay with them while she and Steve figure things out. Maybe they'll even get back together.

Ugh. Weirdly, I hope that doesn't happen. She deserves better than that. Not a cheating liar who cheats.

I change out of my jeans and tee, leaving my boxers on. I usually sleep naked, but with someone else in the condo, I should probably be semi-decent just in case.

I turn on the TV in my bedroom and prop myself up on the pillows to channel surf. Nothing holds my interest and I leave it on the golf channel playing a rerun of some tournament, dropping the remote to the bed.

I hope Molly's okay.

I surface from sleep, gradually becoming aware of noises from the living room. Or maybe kitchen.

I stare up at the ceiling in the dark. Molly is moving around out there.

Should I go see if she's okay? If she needs anything?

I don't move.

I'm sure she's fine.

Aw, fuck.

I throw back the covers and roll out of bed. Running a

hand through my hair, I stumble across the room and down the hall.

She's standing in the dark, staring out the window at the city.

She's still wearing my T-shirt and it hits mid-thigh. Her legs are bare.

"You okay?"

She jumps and whirls around, pressing a hand to her chest. "Oh my God! You scared me."

"Sorry." I slowly walk closer. "I heard you out here. Just wanted to make sure you're good."

Now I'm closer I can see her face is tear-streaked, her eyes puffy. Dammit.

"I'm sad," she admits, leaning her head against the window. "This was supposed to be my wedding night. But it's not just that. The whole life I thought I was going to have is gone."

I guess that's true.

"Everything I dreamed about and imagined…" She closes her eyes and another tear squeezes out.

"Your life's not over." I lay a hand gently on her shoulder and squeeze briefly. "You'll have all those things."

"Maybe." She presses her lips together, then opens her eyes and swipes her fingertips beneath one. "I'm sorry. I didn't mean to disturb you. I'm fine. Go back to bed."

"You sure?"

"I wouldn't mind some tea…if you have any?"

"Uh…I'm not much of a tea drinker." I head to the kitchen to check the cupboards. Miraculously, I find a box of some kind of herbal tea with candy canes and gingerbread men on it. Someone must have brought it over at Christmas. I fill a mug with water and set it in the microwave, which is probably the wrong way to boil water, but it's easy.

Molly followed me. I turn to see her leaning against the

raised ledge between the kitchen and dining room. I catch her gaze roving over me and I become aware that all I'm wearing is a pair of boxer shorts. My skin heats as I hold up the box. "This is all I have."

"That's fine. Thanks." She takes the box and pulls out a tea bag. "Smells nice." Her shoulders slumped, her hair a mess around her face, she sighs. "I really don't want to be such a downer. Just feeling sorry for myself right now."

Seeing her hurting is no goddamn fun, let me tell you. Anger at Chucky spurts hot inside me. He's a friend, but I'm pissed. "I get it. You have a right to feel that way. But someday this will all make sense."

"You think?"

"Yeah. Everything happens for a reason. Sometimes not getting what you want can be a good thing."

She eyes me. "Doesn't feel like that right now."

"I know. But you'll get through this."

"Thanks." The corners of her mouth lift. "You're a good friend, Jax."

The microwave beeps and I take out the mug. I set it on the counter and she drops the tea bag into it.

The condo is mostly dark, quiet, the feeling intimate and sequestered. This is a first for me; when I have women here, the most romantic thing I whisper to them after is, "Hey, go home." We don't usually have middle-of-the-night conversations about the meaning of life.

I just want to make Molly feel better. I'm spouting bullshit I know nothing about, trying to help.

She sips her tea. "I'll take this and go back to bed."

"The tequila didn't help you sleep?"

"I did sleep for a while. Then I woke up and started thinking. Why is thinking in the middle of the night the worst? Everything seems terrible and hopeless."

"I guess I don't usually do that." I rub the back of my neck.

"Lucky you. Okay, see you in the morning."

I watch the T-shirt twitch over her ass as she walks away. She may not have big hooters, but she has a spectacular ass.

Okay, yeah, I've noticed that.

Hopefully I can get some sleep too.

I didn't set an alarm, and I'm shocked when I grab my phone and see I slept till nearly ten.

I bolt up in bed.

Molly.

The condo is silent.

I throw back the duvet and once more go searching for her. Her bedroom door is still closed, the rest of the place deserted, so I guess she slept too. That's good.

I'm not a tea drinker but I like coffee, so I make myself a cup in the Keurig, then carry it into my bedroom. I need to shower, finish packing and take Molly… somewhere.

After I'm showered and the beard stubble is tidied up, I toss my toiletry bag into the suitcase, along with a few more T-shirts. I add one pair of dress pants and a shirt, but I don't plan on doing anything that requires dressing up. My camera gear is already packed.

Molly appears in my bedroom door, now wearing the plaid pajama pants again. "Morning."

"Hey. Good morning. You must have gotten some sleep."

"Yeah."

She's washed her face and she looks so different without all the dark stuff on her eyes, kind of pale and soft and vulnerable. "Good."

She holds up her phone. "What airline and flight are you on?"

Jesus. She's still on this? "Seriously?"

Her little chin is firm. "Yes. Seriously. I won't be a bother. I just want to get out of town."

"Molly. Wait." I cross the room to stand in front of her. She tips her head back and meets my eyes. "I think you should go to your parents' place. I think you should call Steve. And I think you two should maybe go for some couples' counseling and see if you can work things out."

Her eyes widen. They're a light green, almost the color of a pear, with a dark ring around the iris. "What?" She sounds like I just jabbed a stick into her belly.

"Maybe you can work things out. Let him explain, apologize, grovel."

"Explain what?" Her voice rises.

"I don't know." I swipe a hand over my mouth. "Maybe he has some kind of explanation."

"There is no explanation for cheating!"

I sigh. "I know." I totally agree. But I feel I have to give this a shot. "But people make mistakes. Maybe you can move on from this."

"Are you fucking kidding me?" She plants her hands on her hips and gives me a glare that could ignite a bonfire. "I saw those texts! I know what he was doing! And who he was doing it with!"

Shit. Shit. I hold up my hands and make a calming motion. "Okay, I get it."

"I want to move on, alright. But not with him! Look, I'm not saying I hate him, but I hope his next blow job is from a shark."

After a stunned beat, I burst out laughing. I fall against the wall, I'm laughing so hard. "Jesus, Flynn."

She gives a lopsided smile, her anger dissipating. "It's true." Her eyebrows slope down. "Why are you saying this stuff? You really think I should go back to him?"

"I'm not saying that." I shake my head. I don't even know what I'm saying. "I just feel like you shouldn't bail on a relationship without making an effort."

"I made an effort. He didn't."

Honestly, I don't blame her. Like I said, she deserves better. "Okay. It's your decision."

"Good. I'm coming to California with you."

"You could just stay here. If you want to hide out for a while. The place'll be empty."

She pushes out her bottom lip, considering this. For a few seconds I think she's going to go for it, then she shakes her head. "I want to be far away. This is going to be all over the internet."

I exhale slowly. "Okay." I grab my own phone and find the boarding pass I downloaded yesterday when I checked in. I give her the flight number.

She sits herself down on my bed without being invited. After a moment, she says, "What's your seat?"

"3C."

Her head snaps up. "First class."

"Yeah."

"Jesus," she mutters. Her fingers move on the screen.

Maybe a thousand bucks or more will deter her.

Then she lifts her head and smiles. "Wow, I can't believe seat 3A was available."

"You didn't."

"Yup. I'm booked."

I shake my head. "Okay, then. What are you going to do about clothes?"

She looks down at herself. "I guess I can't get on the plane like this, huh?"

"Wouldn't bother *me*."

She laughs. "You know I won't. Can we stop at a Target on the way to the airport?"

I can't say no to her, goddammit. I never can. I hope she doesn't realize this, or I'm fucked. "Sure. Why not."

5

JAX

Several hours later, we're at O'Hare, checking my bag and Molly's newly purchased suitcase filled with clothes and girl stuff from Target. Molly spent most of the drive to the airport on the phone with Katelyn Bennet, sorting out wedding-related issues. Katelyn is a wedding planner and she's married to another one of our teammates, Tanner.

"Flying first class is nice," Molly says when we're in the first-class lounge. "I've never done it before."

"I need the leg room." At six-two, sitting in the main cabin is pretty damn uncomfortable.

"I guess you do. I gather the charter plane you guys use has more leg room.

"Yeah. It's all customized for us."

We order drinks.

"Do you miss hockey?" she asks.

"Not yet."

"When will you miss it?"

"In about a month." I grin. "That's usually how it goes. I

love it, but the season is long and hard. My back's hurting, and summer off gives it a chance to heal."

Her lips pout in concern. "Are you okay?"

"Oh yeah. Nothing serious. I've had some physical therapy —tight hip flexors apparently pull things out of whack. I have some stretches and exercises to do."

"Oh, that's good."

"After a while away from the game, though, I get antsy and anxious to get back on the ice."

She nods.

I guess she knows this stuff since she was engaged to another player.

Molly leans across the small table. "That girl is eye-fucking you."

I shake my head.

"Over there. The blonde."

I roll my eyes. "I'm not looking."

"Why not? You're single. She's hot."

"I'm a little occupied at the moment."

"Damn. I'm cramping your style, aren't I? You'd probably buy her a drink if I wasn't with you." She slumps back in her chair.

It's a possibility. Passing the time in an airport with a hot blonde is never a bad thing. But I have a cute little strawberry blonde sitting with me, so that's not happening. And I don't really care.

"I love people watching in airports." Molly leans back in her chair to look around. "That couple over there?" She moves her head. "Sugar daddy and his sugar baby."

I follow her gesture and study the couple. Yeah, the guy's older, well-dressed, neat gray hair. The woman wearing high heels, tight, skinny black jeans and an expensive looking silk blouse has her hand on his arm, laughing at something he just said. "Nah. That's a father and daughter."

"Are you kidding? They're flirting like crazy!"

"I don't see it. And look—they have the same eyes and nose."

Molly squints across the room. "I don't think so."

I grin. I have no idea and don't really care but she seems into this. We start making up stories about everyone else in the lounge.

"That guy's a Russian oligarch," I tell her, motioning to a man sitting alone.

"Ooh! That's good. I think you're right. He's probably en route to Washington to meet with a scammy politician."

We finish our drinks and stroll out to our gate. It's nearly boarding time.

"I need to use the ladies' room," Molly says. "I hate using the bathroom on airplanes."

She disappears and I pull out my phone to pass a few minutes. Things have died down about the wedding, it seems. Or maybe not. Rico sent me a link to a gossip blog that has a whole thing about Chucky being left at the altar. Ugh. I won't tell Molly about that.

We're first to board and settle into our seats. Molly's all smiles checking out the space we have and the little menu. "We get food!" she whispers to me.

"And booze," I add.

"We can drink our way across the country."

"Don't get too carried away. I have a party to go to tonight."

"What? A party?"

"My cousin JP just got engaged. My aunt and uncle are throwing a party for him."

"Oh, nice!"

"They don't know I'm coming."

"You didn't tell them?"

"I told them I was coming, just not exactly when. They planned this party the same day I arrive, so I'm just going to surprise everyone."

"Fun! Okay, now tell me about your family and why you and your grandpa don't get along and why you don't trust his wife."

"It's long and complicated."

"We have about four and a half hours," she says, fastening her seatbelt.

I laugh. "True." I fasten my own seatbelt as people file past us, filling the aircraft. "Okay. You know my grandpa is Bob Wynn."

"King of hockey."

"Yeah. My grandma—his first wife—died a few years before I was born. She came from a wealthy family in Toronto."

Molly nods, shifting a bit to face me, leaning her elbow on the small table between us.

"Grandpa remarried about two years after Grandma died. His new wife is a lot younger than him. He was living in Los Angeles then, and my dad and my uncle both thought this woman married him for his money."

"Ooh. Is she young and beautiful?"

"Yeah," I admit. "I mean, she's a lot younger than Grandpa. It caused bad feelings between all of them. They never liked Chelsea, and that pissed off Grandpa. Then Grandpa and Chelsea had a bunch of kids, which was around the same time I was born. And my sister and cousins. So it's kind of weird that we have an aunt and uncles who are basically the same age as us. Dad and Uncle Matthew didn't like that, either."

"I'm kind of feeling sorry for your grandpa and Chelsea."

"Huh. Really?"

"Yeah." She gives a firm nod.

"Well, I grew up with my parents and Uncle Matt and Aunt Aline all telling me that Chelsea was the devil and Grandpa was stupid for falling for her conniving, money-grubbing scheme." Another reason why marriage is for suckers.

"Oh my God."

"And then there's the money part."

"This is like a soap opera."

"Yeah." I grimace.

I pause the story while announcements are made and we taxi out onto the runway for takeoff. I watch Molly's fingers clench together tightly as the plane lifts into the sky. Her eyes are squeezed closed, her lips rigid.

"Nervous?" I'd like to reach out and cover her hands with mine, but I'm not sure if that's appropriate.

"I don't want to die," she says through clenched teeth.

I swallow a laugh. I fly so often I don't even think of it anymore. "You're not going to die."

"You don't know that."

"Okay, let's say the odds are very, very small. Minute. Infinitesimal."

"It's one in five point three million."

"Of course you know that."

"But I don't care about odds. Even one in five million means it's possible."

I can't help my smile. "You need another glass of wine."

"Yes. Yes, I do."

It's not long before the flight attendant comes by to ask about drinks. Molly is distracted by having a choice of wines. "You don't get a choice when you fly coach," she whispers. "I mean, your choice is white or red." She selects a Pinot Grigio, and I ask for a beer, which also has several choices.

"Okay, back to the Wynn family soap opera," she says once we have drinks in hand. "The money."

"Well, like I said, Grandma came from a rich family and she left my dad and Uncle Mark a bunch of cash. I don't know how much. Just over a year ago, Dad and Uncle Mark sued Grandpa because he stole their money."

Molly gasps. "Oh my gosh! I heard about the lawsuit. Did he actually steal it?"

"Well, we thought so." I rub my forehead. "That made Dad even more pissed at Grandpa, which made *me* pissed at him too. I've…been avoiding seeing him ever since."

Her eyebrows lift. "Ohhhh."

Now she's getting why this trip isn't going to be fun. I don't have much of a relationship with Grandpa, but I need to try before it's too late. "We found out later about the Alzheimer's. I blamed him for stealing money when it was probably his disease. I feel guilty, and I need to make sure he's okay."

"That's…very honorable of you."

Is it? Mostly I feel like a knob. "After Dad and Uncle Matt sued Grandpa, Grandpa fired my dad."

Molly's eyebrows fly up into her hairline. "Your dad worked for him?"

"He coached the Condors."

"Oh my God."

"Yeah. And Dad and Uncle Matt were so pissed, Uncle Matt bought a team—the Long Beach Golden Eagles, which have a huge local rivalry against the Condors."

Molly chokes on a laugh. "Wow. Not many people can buy a hockey team to piss off their dad."

I grin. "True. Then Uncle Matt hired Dad as their coach. So that really got Grandpa riled up. If they thought that was going to make him pay the money back sooner, they were wrong."

Molly rolls her lips inward on a smile. "Again, wow."

"But recently, the whole younger generation of Wynns—except me, because I live so far away—decided to try to do something to reconcile Dad and Uncle Matt with Grandpa. And especially because now we know he has Alzheimer's." I stop and clear my throat. "Apparently they've all been getting together and figuring out a plan. They discovered that Grandpa didn't actually steal the money, he borrowed it, with their agreement. But he hasn't paid it back like he was supposed to."

"He probably forgot." She pauses. "I don't mean that disrespectfully. But if he's ill…"

"Yeah. Could have something to do with it. It sounds like Chelsea has figured out a way to repay it—"

"I knew it!" Molly pumps a fist. "She's not a sugar baby!"

"I'm not so sure. It could have been her who made him take the money, and now that Dad and Uncle Matt are fighting back, she knows she has to repay it."

She gives me the side-eye. "You really don't like her. I can't wait to meet all these people."

I freeze. "Wait, what? You want to meet them?"

"Sure! I'll bet this party is going to be lit."

I hadn't thought of bringing her to the family party. Although ditching her in a hotel room all alone as soon as we get there doesn't seem very polite.

I knew this wasn't a good idea.

"You're kidding me." I stare at the clerk at the front desk of the Tarragona Resort in Rancho Palos Verde.

"I'm sorry, sir." She gives me a sympathetic smile. "There are a few weddings being held here tonight, and tomorrow visitors are arriving for a big conference."

"You have no rooms at all."

"That's right. We can let you know if we have a cancellation, though."

Molly's hovering beside me anxiously. "I'm sorry," she whispers. "It's a big resort, I didn't think it would be all booked. I can go somewhere else."

There isn't anywhere close by. The resort is on a large property on the coast. I sigh. "We'll just share a room. Something will open up after the conference, I'm sure."

Molly bites her lip. "Well, okay."

I finish checking in, and we go to our room on the fourth floor.

"Ocean view!" Molly whisks straight to the big window and draws back the curtains. "Oh, this is beautiful!"

The resort sits atop a bluff next to the ocean, so the view is panoramic. The sun hangs low over the Pacific, gilding the blue with glints of silver and gold. It really is nice, but I almost enjoy Molly's delight more than the view.

She unlocks the sliding door and opens it to step out onto the balcony. I follow and inhale the soft, fresh air. A couple of wicker chairs and a small table sit in the corner.

"Did you know the Pacific Ocean is the biggest ocean in the world?"

I grin. "Yes, as a matter of fact, I did know that. Also the deepest."

"Yes. The Mariana Trench is the deepest ocean trench, deeper than the height of Mount Everest."

"Which is…?"

She turns to me. "The height of Mount Everest?"

"Yeah."

"Twenty-nine thousand, twenty-nine feet." She rolls her eyes. "I can't wait to get my feet wet in the ocean." Eyes warm and soft, she adds, "Thank you for letting me come with you. For a while, I forgot about what a mess my life is."

My heart softens. "Your life isn't a mess. But good, I'm glad we've taken your mind off things. Now, we need to get ready for the party."

"Oh! Are people going to be dressed up?" She sinks her teeth into her plump bottom lip, a small divot appearing between her eyebrows.

"Nah. Well, Chelsea will."

Her eyebrows shoot up.

"I don't mean that in a negative way. That's just her."

"Okay. I guess I can wear that sundress I bought earlier."

"That'll be fine." Except the idea of her changing into a sundress in the room we're sharing has every nerve ending in my body on alert. What the hell was I thinking?

Molly turns back to the room. "The room is lovely too."

This resort is five stars, so yeah, it's pretty nice. I picked it because it's close to Dad's place and to Matthew and Aline's home where the party is tonight.

The king-size bed takes up a lot of space.

One bed.

What the hell are we going to do about that? There's a sort of couch—a chaise, I think it's called—but there's no way in hell I'll fit on that. But I'd feel guilty making Molly sleep there.

Again, what the hell was I thinking?

Well, we'll worry about that later. "I'd like a shower," I say. "Traveling makes me feel gross."

"Go right ahead. I'm going to call my parents and let them know I'm okay. And Grace."

I find my toiletry bag and lock myself in the huge bathroom, all marble and stone tiles. The shower is fantastic. I could stand under there for an hour, but there's someone else who might want to use it.

My mind drifts to Molly in the shower…

Shit! What am I doing? She's Chucky's fiancée. Ex. But no matter. She's still not someone I can be having wet, soapy fantasies about. Ever. We're friends.

As I dry off, I realize I should have grabbed a change of clothes. I wrap a towel around my waist so I'm decent and open the door to release a cloud of steam.

"Next," I announce, stepping into the room.

Molly's already changed into her dress and is brushing her hair in front of the dresser mirror. Her eyes shift to me and widen, then blink rapidly. "Um…"

Her gaze tracks over my chest, the towel, then back up. I swipe at a water trickling down my shoulder.

"Right," she says breathlessly.

Damn. I'm having shower fantasies about her, and she's ogling me. This is a disaster in the making. I'm going to have to be on my best behavior. Not something I'm good at when it comes to women.

But this is Molly.

She looks so pretty in that dress—a flowery print in shades of orange and gold, a fitted top with tiny straps and a ruffled skirt.

She picks up the pink makeup bag she purchased earlier and disappears into the bathroom.

I dress at rapid speed in case she emerges from the bathroom, but she's in there for a while. I unpack a few things into the drawers Molly has left empty for me. She's filled a few with lacy lingerie I'm tempted to snoop through. I was a gentleman and left her alone in the lingerie department at Target, but now I'm curious what she bought.

Jesus! Here I go again, thinking about Molly's underwear.

I rub my face and check out the mini bar. I better not drink anything though; we had a few on the plane, and I'm driving the rental car we picked up at LAX.

Finally, she reappears, her hair in messy waves that look casually stylish, and makeup on her eyes again. And lips. They shine with a soft peachy gloss.

"I'm ready."

"You look…great." I attempt a casual compliment. She smells good too, like pink grapefruit.

"Thanks. You too." She smiles at my khaki pants and navy shirt I left loose, sleeves rolled up.

"Okay. Let's roll."

She picks up her purse and a sweater. "Let's make like a rock."

I frown, holding the key to the car. "What?"

"Let's make like a rock and roll."

I drop my head forward in amusement. "Right, right. Sorry."

She smacks my shoulder. "Keep up, Wynn."

I grin, a sense of fun fizzing in my chest. I'm not even dreading seeing the family, which I should be. It's been a year, other than a few quick meetups when playing against the Golden Eagles when I can see my dad and play against my cousin JP, or when we play the Condors and I see my my other cousin Théo, who's the manager of the Condors.

One thing I didn't tell Molly about was the tense relationship I have with my dad.

My parents divorced when I was fifteen. It was a brutal time. I blamed my dad for it. It had to be so hard for Mom. I know the fact that I hated Dad really bothered her, but she never once criticized him. To my face, anyway. She was a single mom, and a hockey mom for both Riley and me, which is extra hard. As a teenager, I didn't appreciate how difficult it had to be for her, and I probably still don't because I've never been through that. And I never will.

So on top of seeing Grandpa, seeing Dad tonight isn't something I'm all that stoked about either.

But Molly's happy anticipation of this party where she knows no one is infectious.

Not sure how I'll explain who she is and why she's with me. Could be awkward, but we'll figure it out.

The twenty-minute drive to Uncle Matt's place in Rolling Hills is scenic, almost rural, winding through palm trees and scrubby hills with the odd mansion tucked into them, then through a more residential neighborhood. I pull up in the big stone driveway of the house, a low ranch-style, which is full of cars, but I slip the rental car in behind a Beemer and turn off the engine. "We're here."

Molly slides out before I can open her door, but I close it for her, lock the doors with the fob, and lead the way through the white picket fence and up the paved sidewalk to the front door.

I take a breath. "Okay, if this gets too much for you, just let me know."

Molly regards me skeptically. "You mean if it gets too much for *you*."

"Ha. Maybe."

Unexpectedly, she reaches for my hand and squeezes it. "It'll be fine."

"Famous last words." I ring the doorbell.

A moment later, it opens. Aunt Aline peers out, her expression first blank, then her mouth opens into an O and she stares. "*Oh mon dieu!* Jackson!" She opens her arms for a hug.

"What?" I hear my sister's voice from inside. "Jackson?"

"Come in," Aline says, stepping aside. "What a surprise!"

I motion Molly inside first, catching Aline's curious look at her, then lead the way to the entrance to the big living room.

Riley rushes across the room toward me. I grin and hold my arms wide. "Surprise!"

Riley throws herself at me, and I wrap her up in a big hug. "Oh my God! I can't believe you're here!"

I squeeze her, affection swelling in my chest. "Hey, little sis."

I lift my head. Jesus, the room is full. The family seems to have grown.

Dad makes his way across the room toward me, smiling. "Holy shit! What are you doing here, son?"

My gut clenches, but I shrug casually as I release Riley. "Thought I'd surprise you all by showing up a little sooner than I planned. Uh…" I glance over my shoulder, turn and gently draw Molly forward. "Hey everyone, this is Molly."

The room goes silent, staring at her. Of course they think we're "together."

Molly lifts a hand, beaming. "Hi, Wynn family. Nice to meet you all."

6

MOLLY

Well, I got what I wanted. Here I am, surrounded by the legendary Wynn family. Yikes. What was I thinking?

Everyone's staring at me, and I am acutely aware that they may know who I am and that I just jilted my fiancé. And now I'm here with Jax.

Maybe I should make a run for it.

Nope, nope, can't do that. Nothing for it but to make the best of this situation I got myself—and Jax, for that matter—into. So I smile and wave and don't bother waiting for introductions.

"Hi, you must be Riley," I say to the woman Jax just hugged. "Nice to meet you."

She shakes my hand, bemused. "Um, yeah, hi Molly."

"My dad," Jax says. "Mark Wynn."

"Mr. Wynn." I shake his hand too. He smiles, and I see the interest in his eyes. He glances back at Jax.

"Call me Mark," he says. "Pleased to meet you, Molly."

Jax continues the introductions, and I start to lose track of who everyone is. Jax greets Taylor, whom the party is honoring, with a friendly hug and says, "Last time I saw you, two guys were fighting over you." He slides a sly glance at JP, her fiancé.

What? I'm so curious I could burst!

Taylor laughs. "Oh yeah."

"Welcome to the family."

"Thank you."

But there are more. I keep smiling and shaking hands. Finally he introduces me to his grandfather, Bob Wynn, and his wife Chelsea.

Jax was right. Chelsea's stunning, her blonde hair in a wavy bob, her makeup impeccable, and her slim black pants, silky tank top and heels are all killer.

"It's Jackson," Chelsea says to Mr. Wynn in a low voice.

Oh God. What if he doesn't even remember Jax? I cast a quick look at Jax and bite my lip.

Bob Wynn eyes Jax. "Haven't seen you in a while, Jackson."

"No, sir." Jax clears his throat.

Okay, at least he recognizes him.

"Surprised you've lowered yourself to join us."

"Ouch," Jax mutters.

"Or maybe it's just me you haven't wanted to associate with."

My insides tighten as I watch the exchange.

"Pretty much," Jax agrees.

Mr. Wynn barks out a laugh. "At least you're honest."

"I *am* honest." Jax tips his head to one side. I can see he doesn't know what to say. He clears his throat. "I'm sorry, Grandpa."

Bob Wynn nods.

Jax looks at Chelsea. "We need to talk."

She tilts her head, clearly surprised. "Of course," she murmurs.

"We'll talk more while I'm here," Jax adds to Mr. Wynn.

"Huh. You assume I want to talk to you after all these years," Mr. Wynn says gruffly.

Eep. Mr. Wynn's a little salty.

Mr. Wynn turns his attention to me. "New girlfriend," he says. "Or are you two gonna surprise us and tell us you're married, like Théo did last year?"

I shoot Jax an alarmed glance.

"She's not my girlfriend, Grandpa. Just a friend."

I hear someone behind me choke. Great. They know.

"Uh huh." Grandpa frowns. "Sure."

"She's not his girlfriend, Dad," someone speaks up.

I turn to see one of the guys…Jax's uncle Asher, I think?

"She's engaged to Steve Shevchuk," Asher says, giving me a narrow-eyed look. "He plays for the Aces."

"Jesus Christ!"

I jump at Bob Wynn's shout and whirl around, wide-eyed. Nervously I edge closer to Jax as Mr. Wynn glares at him. "You kids! You can't keep stealing other men's women!"

My thoughts freeze with confusion and I blink rapidly.

Everyone starts murmuring. Asher's comment has clued everyone in that I'm the runaway bride they heard about.

Jax speaks up. "No, Grandpa, that's not it."

"I'm not engaged to Steve," I say firmly, loudly. Then I add glumly, "Not anymore."

"You *were*?" Bob Wynn snaps.

"Er, yes." My gaze darts around the room, and heat washes up my throat and into my face.

Bob slaps a hand down on the arm rest of the chair where he sits. "Dammit! Jackson, you should be ashamed."

I suck in a breath and turn to Jax. "I'm so sorry," I whisper.

He shakes his head. "Grandpa, we're not together. She wanted to get out of Chicago, so she came with me. That's all."

Bob Wynn frowns. "Well, that's as stupid as a screen door on a submarine."

"It was my idea," I speak up. "I begged him to let me come. He didn't want to do it."

Jax rolls his eyes and sighs. What's with that? I'm trying to help him out.

"Interesting," Asher comments.

I resist the urge to scowl at him.

Crap. Jax was right. His family *is* nuttier than squirrel shit.

I turn back to Bob Wynn and smile. "Mr. Wynn, your grandson is a knight in shining armor. He saved me when I needed help. I'm very grateful to him, and I apologize for showing up uninvited at your family party. I'm a little intimidated by all the hockey talent here."

His frown eases and he slowly smiles. "Well, aren't you a sweetheart. Jax, get this girl a drink."

I catch Chelsea Wynn's eye. She grins and gives me an approving nod. I smile weakly.

Jax and I make our way to a bar set up on the sideboard in the dining room. He pours us each a glass of red wine and we rejoin the party.

"So when is the wedding?" I ask JP and Taylor.

"Not until next summer," Taylor replies. She makes a face. "We have to work around the hockey season."

"Of course." I smile. "I get it. We…had to do that too…" My voice trails off.

Her expression shifts to concern. "So what happened?"

I heave a small sigh. "I discovered he was cheating on me the night before the wedding."

"Oh my God! That's awful."

Somehow the group around us has altered to include Lacey and Everly, separating Jax and JP.

"That must have been hard," Everly, Jax's aunt, says. Her

expression is neutral, her voice impersonal. She's very cool and composed.

"I probably shouldn't be sharing all my personal woes with strangers," I say apologetically. "Let's just say it was a disaster and move on."

They all exchange glances. "Sure," Taylor says. "Any wedding-planning tips?"

"Hire a wedding planner." I laugh. "Seriously. We hired Katelyn Bennet. She's married to Tanner Bennet, who plays for the Aces?"

They all nod.

"She's amazing. It was so good to have someone who knows the best places and people to hire, and makes things run smoothly."

"That's a good idea," Everly says.

"I don't know," Taylor says. "I'd kind of like to plan things myself."

"Oh, you totally can!" I nod enthusiastically. "You can be as involved and hands-on as you want, if you have a good planner."

"We should check out some names," Everly says.

"Or *you* could plan my wedding." Taylor bumps Everly's shoulder with a smile. "You love planning."

"I do." Everly grins and her face warms and softens as she smiles at her friend and future…in-law. I can't quite remember how she'll be related to Taylor. This family *is* complicated.

I spot appetizers on the low cocktail table and excuse myself to step over and get food. I'm starving. That meal on the plane was a long time ago. I load up a small plate with skewers of tortellini, salami, cheese and olives, some nuts, and crackers. I rejoin the women. "I'm so hungry," I say, then pop an almond in my mouth.

"We're having dinner shortly," Everly says.

"Aline's an amazing cook," Lacey adds.

"Er, what was Mr. Wynn talking about when he said 'you can't keep stealing other men's women?' "

Taylor grimaces. "He was talking about JP. He, er, dated a woman who was his brother's girlfriend."

"Remember that night they were all here?" Everly says to the others. "It was only a little awkward." She rolls her eyes.

Lacey laughs. "Oh my God, it was terrible! You were all picking on JP."

"He deserved it," Everly says. "And yes, I did tell him that to his face."

I watch this with fascination. "Jax didn't mention that when he told me about the family drama. Wow."

We're joined by Jax's sister at that moment. Riley seems hesitant, which is how *I* should be feeling, not her, so I give her a warm smile and shift to make room for her. "Hi."

"Hi. Aline said to let everyone know we'll eat in about fifteen minutes."

"By then, I'll have cleaned every plate on that table." I nod to the appetizers. "I need to try those little bruschetta things." I fill my plate again.

"Those are balsamic blueberry and goat cheese," Lacey tells me. "So good."

"Yum." I hope I'm not making a pig of myself, but damn, I like food and I'm hungry. I try one. "Delicious."

Jax detaches himself from the family he's been talking to and slides over next to me. "Okay?" he murmurs in my ear.

I nod, smiling. "Yeah. Getting to know these amazing women."

"Need more wine?" He gestures at my glass, which is nearly empty.

"Yes, please."

He takes my glass and crosses to the dining room.

Four other pairs of female eyes follow his movements, then turn on me. I blink back at them. "What?"

They all smile.

"So," Riley says. "How did you happen to end up here with Jax?"

I roll my eyes. "Well. Let me see if I can make a long story short. I jilted my ex at the altar. I needed to get the hell out of there, so I asked Jax to drive me. We went to his place." I hold up a hand. "Jax and I are friends. We're a team at trivia nights at some local bars."

They all nod slowly.

"I didn't want to face anyone, so I stayed there. He was leaving today, and I begged him to let me tag along so I could get out of town." I shrug. "That's it."

"You left your fiancé at the altar?" Riley asks, wide-eyed.

"You didn't hear about it?"

"No!"

I suck my bottom lip briefly. I could say more, but I don't. "Well, it's probably on YouTube."

They all burst out laughing.

"You're probably right," Everly says, amusement glinting in her eyes. I like that much better than the detached looks she gave me earlier.

Jax returns with my wine. "So, what are you up to for the summer, Rye?" he asks his sister.

They chat, eventually getting to the things they want to do while Jax is here, and Riley, the sweetie, tries to include me.

"I don't want to interfere with your family time," I tell her. "I'm going to lay around the pool at the resort. Maybe go for a hike and find the beach."

"We should get together, the 'young ones,' " Everly says to Jax. "You missed all the fun of the family meetings." Her voice has a bit of an edge.

Jax shoots his grandpa a concerned look. "How's he doing?"

Everly's eyes shadow and her lips droop. "Okay. Sometimes good, sometimes…not."

Right. It had slipped my mind that her dad has Alzheimer's. "I'm so sorry about your dad's illness," I say quietly.

"Thanks. It's been hard."

"Yeah, we should get together," Jax says. "We need to talk."

"You sure?" Everly eyes him skeptically. "You didn't seem to want to have much to do with it."

"I was on the other side of the country," Jax replies, with a hint of defensiveness.

I touch his back to show my support.

"Uh huh," she says skeptically.

"You're here now." Riley defends him, narrowing her eyes briefly at Everly.

Hmmm.

"Yeah," he says shortly, then sips his wine. "We can get together any time."

"I'll arrange it," Everly says tersely.

Dinner is served then, so we all move to the gigantic dining room with a table as long as a runway. I pause next to Aline. "I didn't realize this was a sit-down dinner. I do apologize for showing up uninvited."

"It's fine." She's so gracious and sweet. "We're happy to have you. Here, you can sit next to Jax."

She probably had to reconfigure her entire table setting because of me. Oh wait—she didn't know Jax was coming either. Nonetheless, shame curls inside me at my selfish entreaty for Jax to bring me here. Well, actually, I didn't need to come to the party; I would have been fine exploring the resort. *He* was the one who insisted on not leaving me alone my first night.

Still, I feel a bit ill-mannered. I resolve to leave Jax to his family visits for the rest of our stay here. There's a lot to do at the resort and I'll keep busy.

"So, has my family convinced you that I'm right about them?" he asks in a low voice.

"They are…a lot," I admit. "But I like them."

"Ooookay."

I nudge him with my elbow. "Come on. You like them too. You love your sister."

"Yeah, *she's* okay."

I laugh.

Conversation buzzes around us. I find myself watching Bob Wynn, how he doesn't seem to pay attention to the conversation, noting how Chelsea sticks close to him, and the determinedly cheerful expression she wears. Sadness swells in my chest for both of them. Well, for the entire family, but right now I'm imagining what it's like for a husband and wife to be losing half of their relationship.

I look down at my plate. One more reason to never have a relationship.

I'm an outsider for much of the talk; there are family reminiscences, some of them a bit snarky, stories and jokes. But I listen and laugh and occasionally Jax leans closer to explain something to me.

After dinner, Jax and I take seats in the living room near Bob Wynn, and listen to the conversation he's having with Mark and Matthew.

It's…heartbreaking.

And I can tell Jax is hurting too.

They talk about the Condors' season and Bob nods and smiles and makes a comment that's completely unrelated. He tells a story about someone, I don't even know who, which goes on for a good two or three minutes, but makes no sense whatsoever. It's words, and he sounds clear and confident, but they're not put together into anything meaningful.

I sense Jax's frustration, but somehow I know it doesn't help to tell Bob he's not making sense, or ask him if he remembers the first time Jax scored a goal. He can't remember and it's not fair to ask him. I don't have experience with Alzheimer's, but I smile when Bob smiles, and make appropriate comments during the story as if it makes sense.

I meet Chelsea's eyes. She's used to this, I can tell. She gives me a faint smile, almost apologetic but tinged with sadness, and I return the smile with a minute shake of my head to say it's okay.

Ash is leaving, so people stand and mingle about to say goodbye.

"You and Harrison live together. Why didn't you two come in the same car?" Everly asks Ash.

"First rule of Wynn family gatherings," JP says. "Always bring your own car so you can leave when you want."

Everyone laughs.

Ash points at him in agreement.

"It's true," Jax says in my ear. "You ready to go?"

"Any time you are. I'm just tagging along."

"I'll have lots of time to visit with everyone," he says. "I think I need to…go for a walk."

I nod, and we take our leave too, with lots of hugs and intentions to make plans. I'm touched when Riley says, "I hope I'll see you again."

I shrug and peek over at Jax. "I hope so too. We'll see."

Everly, Lacey and Taylor make similar comments, suggesting a girls' night while I'm here. It sounds fun and amazing, and I could use some girl power support right now, but I'm not really part of this family. I'm only Jax's friend and

I'll probably never see them again, but I make non-committal comments and then Jax and I head out.

"Holy shit," he says.

"You okay?"

"I don't even know." He rubs his mouth and pulls out of the driveway. "There's dysfunctional, and then there's whatever the fuck we are."

7

———

JAX

I find my way back to the resort with the help of my GPS. Spotlights illuminate the palm trees around the grounds, white lights twined around their trunks. I park and we walk into the lobby. The bar on our right is open and lively. "Let's have a drink," I say, jerking my head toward it.

"Okay."

There's a huge fireplace at one end and the bar is open to a terrace. We find a table near the fire and a waitress approaches right away with a smile.

Molly studies a cocktail menu. "I'll have a watermelon margarita, please." She smiles back at the waitress.

"Of course. And for you, sir?"

"Have you got Gran Patrón Añejo?"

"We certainly do."

"Great, thanks." I turn back to Molly. "I couldn't drink enough at the party since I had to drive back here. And I needed to drink."

She smiles and rests her chin on one hand. "Your family is interesting."

"Interesting? I assume that's a euphemism for fucked up?"

She laughs. "They're not that bad. I feel so sorry for Chelsea, though."

I snort. "Yeah, you said that earlier."

"Well, now seeing her with your grandpa…and it's only going to get worse." Her eyes shadow. "Can you imagine? The person you love most in the world, your partner in life…deteriorating like that right before your eyes, and there's nothing you can do?" Her voice catches. "It must be so hard for her."

"Yeah," I say slowly. "You're right. I noticed that everyone seems a lot warmer toward her than they used to. I guess I have some catching up to do."

"You will. Everly's going to make you." Her eyes glint.

"I see you have Everly figured out already." I smile.

"She's kind of scary."

"Yeah, I was always scared of her when we were kids."

"Get out."

I laugh. "Sort of. But part of that was probably the feud between Dad and Chelsea and Grandpa. Everly always knew we didn't trust her mom, and that made things awkward."

Our drinks arrive, and I relax back into the comfy chair with my tequila and let out a sigh. "I hate it that Grandpa's not doing well. And I've missed so much time with him."

"I'm sorry." Molly's voice is soft. "It must be hard."

I nod but don't say anything. She's…pretty great. She's just been through a hell of an ordeal herself, and she's sitting here all sympathetic for me and my family.

"I'm sorry I caused some trouble by showing up with you." She picks up her drink. "I never even thought that they would know about the wedding, but I guess I should have. I'm sure it's all over social media."

"Probably. Also, probably good to not know that. Don't look."

"I don't think there's any way I can stop myself." She grins crookedly. "I'll try."

"You were going to marry a hockey player. You know you can't look at all the shit they write about us. And about the WAGs. Especially about the WAGs." I've seen some cruel shit online.

"True."

"Especially someone as soft-hearted as you."

"Soft-hearted?" Her eyes widen. "Me?"

I laugh. "Yeah, you. You cry at any TV commercial with a dog in it."

"I do not."

"Yeah, you do. It's not an insult. But…"

"What?" She eyes me with eyes as big as hockey pucks.

"It's easier to get hurt when your heart is all squashy."

She snorts. "Squashy-hearted. Got it." Then she lets out a short puff of air. "I may have been squashy-hearted in the past, but no more. I'm never going to let a man fool me or take advantage of me again."

I don't believe in love and marriage either, but it makes me a little sad hearing her say that. She's always so happy and vibrant, and I hate to think that Chucky's bullshit has turned her off men and relationships. Because she's made for love and commitment and probably a family. I, on the other hand, am not.

I take a gulp of tequila, which slides warmly down my esophagus.

"So, what's up tomorrow?" Molly changes the subject.

"I'm going to go to Grandpa and Chelsea's place. I want to find out what's happening medically. How he's managing."

"Checking up on Chelsea?"

"Well, yeah."

"For what it's worth, I don't think you have to worry. She's pretty attentive to him. I think she cares. And…I think this is really hard on her."

"You decided that in a few hours?"

She tosses her hair back. "You know I'm always right about stuff."

One corner of my mouth lifts. That is true. "Well, I guess I'll see."

"What about your dad?"

"Eh." I gaze into my amber drink. "I'll see him at some point."

When she says nothing, I look up at her. She's regarding me with her head tilted, lips pursed. "What's that about?"

"What?"

"You and your dad." Then she nibbles her bottom lip. "Sorry. Not my business, I guess."

"My dad and I have never been close. He and my mom split up when I was fifteen. He left Winnipeg and took a job in Hershey, Pennsylvania. My mom and my sister Riley and I stayed. We didn't see much of him after that."

"Oh. I'm sorry."

I hitch one shoulder. "Not a big deal. Lots of couples divorce these days."

"Then why do you seem like you hate him?"

"I don't hate him."

"Okay. Sure." She eyes me and clearly recognizes this isn't something I'm eager to talk about. Turning her head to survey the lounge, she says, "This resort is way nicer than I expected."

"Yeah, it's pretty good. We should go for a walk, explore the grounds."

"Okay."

So after we finish our drinks, we do that. The night air is fresh and calm, carrying the scent of the ocean. The rustle of palm fronds above us is the only sound as we stroll a dark path past bungalows, around a wing of the hotel, and into one of the pool areas.

"Oh my gosh, this is amazing!" Molly gawks at the luxurious pool with cabanas and loungers. The pool glows turquoise in the dark, the water still. "I can't wait to get down here tomorrow!"

"That's your plan, huh?"

"Hell yeah."

I chuckle.

"I'll need to buy some sunscreen," she adds.

"Pretty sure they'll have that in that shop in the lobby."

We keep walking. The dark sky is streaked with pale blue clouds. We follow a path to the edge of the bluff and gaze out over the navy ocean. The muted rumble of waves onto the shore carries on the ocean breeze.

Molly lets out a soft sigh.

"You okay?" I ask.

"Yes. Suddenly I'm exhausted."

"That's understandable. You've been through a lot. Want to head back to the room?"

"Yeah."

Great. The room we're sharing. That's not going to be awkward at all.

Now I'm tense.

We've circled back to the front entrance of the hotel and enter the lobby, cross to the elevators and ride up to the fourth floor. The air in the elevator is thick. I try not to look at Molly, and I get the feeling she's doing the same.

In the room, I flick on a light.

Molly walks over to the dresser and pulls out some clothing, pajamas, I guess. She looks directly at me. "I'll sleep on the lounge," she says.

I eye it doubtfully. "I don't think it's going to be long enough."

"I'll make it work. I just need one of the pillows. Since there are about ten on that bed, you should be okay."

My lips twitch. "Yeah, I guess I can spare one."

"I noticed an extra blanket in the closet."

I don't feel right about this, but I know it's ridiculous for me to offer to sleep there. "We could share the bed." Holy shit. Did those words just come out of my mouth? "I mean, not…it's a big bed. We can, ah, put pillows down the middle."

She frowns and scrutinizes the bed. "Well, let me see how the lounge works. If it's terrible, we can try that."

She disappears into the bathroom.

Sighing, I find the blanket and spread it out on the chaise, then settle a pillow against the back of it. Then I pull back the fluffy duvet on the bed, on the side away from the chaise longue. I sit on the bed and plug my phone in. Guess I should have packed some pajamas.

I scroll through news and social media until Molly reappears. Aw, fuck me. She's wearing a long T-shirt that shouldn't be sexy, but totally is. It's gray cotton, short-sleeved, the hem almost down to her knees, but she looks hot.

"I know this is weird," she says, not looking at me, stuffing her clothes into her suitcase. "Let's just try to ignore each other."

Bahaha. Yeah, right.

I stand. "Okay if I use the bathroom now?"

"Of course."

I wash up but keep my clothes on. When I return to the room, the lights are out except the small lamp beside the bed. Molly is a blanket-wrapped ball on the chaise. I sit on the bed to take off my clothes, leaving them on the floor, then slide into bed. With my light off too, the room is black as ink. And quiet. I can't even hear her breathing.

I close my eyes and try to relax. It's impossible not to be aware of Molly, even though I can't see her or hear her.

I replay the day's events. The flight. Molly's nerves. Her warmth and compassion with my family. And with me.

And my nutso family, reminding why I was leery of making this trip. But I needed to be here and needed to see how things were with Grandpa. And honestly, I won't regret spending more time with him while he's still with us.

I hear a rustling noise and a soft sigh from across the room.

Damn. Now I'm thinking of Molly again.

This was a crazy idea, bringing her here, but I have to admit she held her own with my family, and having her with me sort of made things better. Other than when Grandpa accused me of stealing my teammate's fiancée. But I'll forgive him because, Jesus, he's losing his mind.

Heaviness settles in my gut. Life is not fucking fair. But if anything good can come of it, it's that Dad and Uncle Matt are making things up with Grandpa.

"Are you okay?"

The whispered question reached my ears across the room. I turn my head toward it. "Yeah. Why?"

"You made a noise. I thought you were in pain."

I made a noise? Damn. "Sorry. I'm fine."

"Okay. Night."

"G'night." I roll onto my stomach and wrestle my pillow into the right shape beneath me.

Quiet again.

Damn. I'm trying really hard not to think dirty thoughts. Because it's *Molly*. My friend. My teammate's fiancée. Ex-fiancée. But the only times I've shared a hotel room with a woman were for hot, filthy sex. Maybe it's a conditioned response, that being in a dark hotel room make me think about sex. And since Molly's the woman here, I'm thinking about it with her.

I know I shouldn't. Should. Not. Go. There.

But my mind is taking over and I'm imagining Molly slipping into bed with me. Naked. Snuggling up behind me, her arm coming over my side, her hand finding my stomach… sliding lower…fingers curling around my hard-on.

Yeah, my dick is giving her a full salute.

Maybe I can wait till she's asleep and rub one out. Fast and quiet.

My own hand pushes my boxers down and grips my engorged dick. Slowly, I tug. I swallow and grit my teeth as pleasure pours through me and I'm desperate for more.

I listen intently. I hear soft breathing. Is it deep and regular enough that she's asleep? I'm not sure. I don't want to embarrass her, but Christ, I'm hot and hard and I can't stop myself from jerking my cock.

I close my eyes and swallow, jaw tense. My hand moves, sharp sensations prickling over my skin. My muscles tense as I stroke myself, harder, faster. Pressure builds in my balls, which are pulled up torturously tight at the base of my cock. I cup them with my other hand.

The tingling at the base of my spine moves deeper inside. My throat burns with the effort to keep my ragged breath quiet. Sensation builds, fiery and dark. My hand moves faster. Molly's so close…so sweet and sexy and nearly naked…Jesus. I can't stop now, and *please, please let her be asleep, I can't stop…* and ecstasy erupts in my balls, fire racing up my spine and down the backs of my thighs. I shudder through the climax, teeth gritted as I swallow my groan, body tense.

I need to gasp for air, but I can't. I slowly pull air in through my nose and let it out, over and over, my heart hammering.

Eventually my heart and breathing slow. My hand is a sticky mess. Shit.

I rearrange my boxers and wait a few more minutes, hoping like hell Molly's sound asleep. Then I slip out of bed and quietly pad to the bathroom to clean up.

I study my face in the mirror—the high color on my cheekbones, the glitter in my eyes.

Damn. That felt incredible. But my poor, hopeful dick is still half hard, still wishing to be inside a warm, wet woman. An image of Molly naked beneath me flashes in front of my eyes… smooth, creamy skin, bright red-gold hair on the pillow…

Jesus, I'm an animal. Can't I even share a hotel room with a platonic friend without getting all these depraved fantasies about her? What is wrong with me? I'm going to need every bit of self-control I can muster up to get through the next few days until we can move her into a room of her own.

8

MOLLY

I'm not going to make Jax take me with him to visit his grand-parents. I feel bad enough about tagging along to the party yesterday. He needs to do this, and I need time at the pool.

After sleeping late, we have breakfast together in the lobby coffee shop, then Jax goes back up to the room while I visit the hotel gift shop. It's well-stocked and I pick up sunscreen, a tote bag and a paperback romance to read. Sadly, my loaded-up Kindle is still at Steve's place. I toss in a fashion magazine as well.

Back in the room, Jax is ready to go out, wearing jeans and a T-shirt that hugs his broad shoulders and rests loosely on his flat abs. He's just shoving his phone into his pocket and looks up at me.

"Success." I hold up my shopping bag. "I'm all set for a relaxing day."

"You're sure you're okay by yourself?"

I lower my chin and look at him through my eyelashes. "I'm fine, Jax. I'm a grown woman."

"I know," he mutters, dropping his gaze to the carpet.

My body tingles everywhere as tension wraps around me.

I heard him masturbating last night.

My inner girl parts squeeze at the memory of that. Holy mother of hotness.

And…was he thinking about me?

I can't go there. I push that thought aside.

"I just mean you've been through a rough time," he says.

"I'm fine. Maybe some alone time will be good to think things through and gain some perspective."

"Okay, yeah." He hesitates. "I'll see you later. I'll be back before dinner and we can grab something together."

"Perfect." I beam a smile at him and pluck the turquoise bikini I bought at Target yesterday out of a drawer. "Have fun."

He leaves the room, and I drop onto the side of the unmade bed.

Where he masturbated last night.

Oh God.

He was obviously trying to be quiet, but I could hear the bed moving, the rhythm quickening, and soft noises managed to escape his lips. His breathing got harsher and faster, too.

I imagined what his cock looked like in his big hand. It was so hot, I slipped my hand between my own legs where I throbbed. I wanted to do the same as he was, except clearly he thought I was asleep and it would be so embarrassing for both of us if he knew I wasn't, if he knew I was listening, my ears attuned to every shift of the bed covers, every breath.

My body quivered and heated. I was wet.

Then he got up to go to the bathroom. As soon as the door closed behind him, my fingertips found my swollen clit and rubbed wet circles over it. I came so fast, heat spiraling inside me in delicious, blissful pleasure.

My breathing is fast again now, without even touching myself, just remembering.

Get a grip, girl. If you're going to share this room with him, you can't be getting all horned up over him.

And what the hell is up with that? I'm still in love with my ex-fiancé. I mean, I have to be, right? I was ready to marry him two days ago.

Then he let me down in the worst possible way. Showed me who he really is. How could I love a man who would do that?

I shake off these thoughts to change into my swimsuit. I also bought a cover-up, a loose, lightweight caftan. I slide my feet into flip-flops and pack my bag, then make my way down to the pool.

It's a gorgeous day, the sky a clear blue bowl above, the sun bright and hot. I stroll around the pool area and pick out a lounger to station myself at for the day. There are thick towels on a rack, and I pick up a couple of them for when I'm ready to take a dip in that delicious-looking pool.

I make note of the Agave Bar and Grill where I can grab a snack and drinks later as I spray sunscreen all over myself. My skin is pale and freckly and there's no way I can spend even an hour in the sun without SPF 50, so I'm always careful about using protection.

I settle onto the lounger with my magazine, flipping through the glossy pages. An article about how to deal with problems with coworkers distracts me for a while, but then my thoughts drift back to Steve.

It's hard not to feel like a failure. I couldn't even hold a man long enough to get married to him. I can't help but wonder why he turned to someone else. Why wasn't I enough for him?

I remind myself that *he's* the one who cheated. He's the one with the character flaw, not me. But still…it's hard not to feel like maybe it was my fault. That I wasn't good enough.

I've had relationships in the past. A high school boyfriend I stayed with for three years even though near the end I felt like we were friends more than lovers. I can see now that I was comfortable with him and reluctant to break free. I dated a few guys in college, one turned into a year-long relationship that was…well, unhealthy. He had a lot of issues and was afraid of commitment and strung me along for a long time. And I let him. I vowed I'd never let another guy treat me that way. After that, I had lots of guy friends, men I liked, who were fun to spend time with, but they always treated me like a sister or a friend.

I can't deny that troubled me and I wondered if I'd ever find someone who'd love me as more than a friend.

Then I met Steve.

He was like a rock star—rich, famous, talented. I couldn't believe he was interested in me. I fell hard for him, and there was no doubt in my mind when he asked me to marry him.

And look what happened.

So yeah…I'm wondering if something's wrong with me.

I lay my head down and close my eyes. That's a depressing thought. And I don't want to be depressed.

I guess I could have pretended I didn't know about the cheating and gotten married anyway. Or I could have confronted Steve privately and maybe we could have figured things out.

Deep inside, though, I know I couldn't have done that. I may have self-doubts, but I have enough self-esteem that I won't put up with a man who cheats on me. I'm going to be fine.

I spend the day giving myself pep talks, swimming in the pool and drying off in the sun. I luxuriate in the warmth and the beautiful vistas around me of palm trees, bright flowers and tropical plants. I eat at the snack bar, avocado toast enjoyed with a margarita. In the afternoon, I'm joined at the pool by some people my age. They're not wearing swimsuits, but business casual attire, I'd call it—two women, three men. We exchange smiles and strike up a conversation and I learn they're here for the software convention.

One of the guys keeps looking at me, his smile open and friendly…maybe a little flirty? It's been a while since I've been the object of attention like that. It's kind of fun, so I smile back and we get into some teasing banter.

"I'm going to get another margarita," I say, standing. I tug at my bikini bottom discreetly. "Does anyone else want something?"

"I'll come with you," Justin says, rising as well. He takes requests from his friends and we head to the bar. I lean against it, bopping a little to the Latin music playing while we wait for our drink orders.

"So, Chicago," he says. "Have you always lived there?"

"Mostly. I went to college in Charleston. You're so lucky to live in New Orleans. I love that city."

"I love it too. If you ever come visit, look me up. I'll give you one of my cards."

"Sure." I'll never do that, but I play along, smiling at him.

⸻

Jax

Grandpa's not having the greatest day, I learn when I arrive at his place. Chelsea tells me he's probably tired from the family gathering. I sit with him and try to have a conversation, but it's frustrating because he keeps repeating the same things over and over.

I meet Chelsea's eyes at one point and hers are brimming

with sadness.

I follow her into the kitchen when she goes to make coffee. "I gather he's like this a lot now?"

She nods, busying herself with the coffeemaker and not looking at me. "There are good days and bad days, but yes. More and more like this."

"He said he was going to go into the office today."

"Yes. I still take him there because he loves it, but he doesn't do much anymore."

"You drive him."

"Yes. I drive everywhere now. It's safer."

"I saw you encouraging him to eat last night."

"Yes. He forgets if I don't remind him. He's lost a lot of volition. Sometimes I have to remind him to get dressed. I make sure he wears a jacket when it's cold. He misplaces things." A smile touches her lips. "One day I found the TV remote in the fridge."

"Ha. I've done that. Well, not the remote, but I once put the milk in the cupboard."

"We all have our moments. But his are a lot."

I'm silent for a moment, struggling with emotion. "It fucking sucks," I growl out.

"It does." She bows her head as the coffee brews.

What she describes sounds like looking after a child. Not a husband. I feel like a band is wrapped around my chest, squeezing.

She's still here.

She loves him, no matter what.

"What does he do at the office?" I finally ask.

"Not much, anymore. He can't really make decisions. Luckily Théo is there, and I've been helping."

"So I hear."

She gives me a sharp look.

"Everly tells me you've been more involved," I say. "It's good."

"Do you really think that?" She faces me, challenging me in a way she's never done. In fact, I don't think I've ever had a conversation with Chelsea alone before.

Might as well get it out in the open. "I had my doubts," I admit quietly.

"That's why you're here, isn't it?"

"Yes." Honesty is best.

"And?" She arches a brow.

I study her. She's tough, but I see the sadness in her eyes. "I'm sorry."

She tilts her head and peers at me. "Sorry for what?"

"I'm sorry you're going through this. I'm sorry I doubted you. And I'm sorry I've been avoiding Grandpa because I was pissed that he stole Dad's money."

Chelsea sucks on her bottom lip. "Thank you, Jax."

"I guess I'm a little late, but it seems like the rest of the family has already realized all this."

One corner of her mouth lifts. "I think so, yes."

"You've never defended yourself to us."

She slowly moves her head from side to side. "If I'd told you all I didn't marry Bob for his money, would you have believed me? I don't think so. I just wanted to live my life and love my family and I knew that one day you'd all see that. I didn't expect…this." She waves a hand. "But this is our story now."

She turns to pull mugs out of a cupboard. "What do you take in your coffee?"

"Just some milk, please."

She pours the coffee and retrieves the milk from the fridge for me, then adds some to Grandpa's cup as well.

"What about the future?" I ask. "At some point, it's going to be too much for you."

"We can afford help," she says calmly. "Bob doesn't want to be a burden on me or anyone else, so we talked about memory care facilities and we've explored options. We found a nice one not far from here, when the time comes."

"Will you make sure you take care of yourself?"

She picks up the two mugs and smiles. "You sound like Everly." She lifts her chin. "She and the boys have all been great. They'll make sure I'm okay too."

"That's good."

My throat feels scratchy. I take a quick sip of my coffee as I follow her back into the living room where Grandpa is watching a new show.

Back at the resort, I change into board shorts and head down to the pool to find Molly. I find myself out of sorts. Anxious. Guilty. Sad. I really, really want to see her, because her quiet understanding and sunny outlook feel like something I need right now.

I find her at the pool bar talking to a good-looking dude, who's looking at her like she's the most fuckable thing he's ever seen.

Jesus.

"Hey," I say.

Molly turns to me, her face lighting up. "Oh, hey! You're back. Wow, what time is it?"

The dude looks at me, then back at Molly. "Uh…"

"Oh, Justin, this is my friend Jax. Jax, this is Justin from New Orleans. He's here for the convention. The one that has all the rooms full." She rolls her eyes.

I frown, my gaze sliding back and forth between them, then

reach for Justin's hand, eyeing him.

The bartender sets drinks on the counter in front of Molly and Justin, and she pays for hers while Justin charges the rest to his room.

"Do you want to get a drink?" she asks me.

"Yeah."

"Why are you looking like that?" She sips her margarita. "Bad day?"

"Uh." I become aware that I'm still scowling. "Yeah." I order a beer from the bartender.

"I'll wait with you." Molly smiles at Justin, who picks up several drinks and starts off with them.

"Who the fuck is that?" I ask.

She shoots me a startled look. "I told you."

"You just met him here?"

"Yes." She wrinkles her nose at him. "Is there a problem with that?"

I pause. Is there? "You almost got married a few days ago."

Her eyebrows shoot up. "What does that mean?"

"I don't know. I feel like I need to watch out for you. You're Steve's fiancée."

"No. I'm not." She lifts her chin and meets my eyes. "And I can look after myself, thank you. I was just being friendly. I wasn't trying to pick him up."

I rolls my eyes. "Glad to hear it."

"Wait, what? Even if I was, that would be none of your business."

"It is if you're sharing my hotel room." Okay, I'm kind of being a jerk. I feel like I can't help it.

"I wouldn't bring him back to your room, for the love of goats."

"So you'd go to a stranger's room?"

Her mouth fall open. "What is happening here?"

"I don't know." I rub my mouth. The bartender slides my beer across the counter, and I sign the bill to charge it to the room then grab the drink to take a big gulp.

"And furthermore." She straightens. "Sharing a room with you doesn't give you the right to tell me what to do with my sex life."

I cough. "I'm not doing that."

"Yes, you are!"

"No, I'm not!"

She inhales a long breath and lets it out. "Come on, what are we arguing about? We're friends. I'm a grown woman and I can do what I want, and so can you. Although..." She pauses, then sighs. "Never mind."

"What?"

"I was going to say I'd appreciate it if you didn't bring a woman back to the room, but then I realized that you should totally be able to do that because it's your room and I'm just the pesky friend who's crashing your party." She sighs again.

As if I'd want to bring another woman back to the room. "You're not pesky."

"Yes, I am. You've told me that before."

"Okay, you're pesky in a cute way. Look, I'm sorry. I don't know why I reacted that way to seeing you talking to that guy. Like I said, I guess I still think of you as Steve's girl and..." I stop, clear my throat, then continue. "And it didn't seem right. But it's true, you're not his fiancée anymore, and it's none of my business who you talk to."

"Thank you." She eyes me over her margarita.

I nod.

"Come on. Come meet them. They're nice people and we were having fun talking."

She leads me back over to the group. I don't want to meet a bunch of people. I want her to myself. Ah well.

She introduces me to the group.

"Holy shit," Justin says, eyes opening as big as margarita glasses. "You play for the Chicago Aces."

"Yeah." I smile. "You a hockey fan?"

"Big time! The Lightning are my team, but wow, it's great to meet you."

Everyone's in awe, peppering me with questions about hockey and other players, which I try to answer without insulting the refs, the league or other players.

"We need to get going," Sarah says eventually. "We have a dinner tonight."

"Yeah." Justin makes a face. "Duty calls."

"Your boss is here," Sarah reminds him. "You better show up."

They leave to go to their business dinner. Molly and I have finished our drinks.

"We should think about dinner too, I guess." I sets my empty down on the small table.

"Yes, I've had enough pool time for the day."

"No sunburn?"

"I don't think so. How's my back?" She turns.

I cough, admiring the expanse of smooth skin. "Looks good."

"Whew. It's hard to sunscreen your own back." She pushes a book and magazine into her tote bag, folds up her towel and we start back to the room. "So, why was your day so rough? Your grandpa not doing well?"

I blow out an explosive breath. "No. It's just…hard."

She doesn't press me, but I know she will at some point. "What do you feel like for dinner? Something here? Or should we go out?"

"Let's go out. Somewhere fun and noisy."

"Hmm. Okay."

I let her shower first, then take my turn. When I come out, rubbing my hair with a towel, she's dressed in another cute sundress and she's looking at her phone, clearly upset. I stop rubbing my hair, lowering my arms. "What's wrong?"

Her lips tighten. "Steve went on our honeymoon."

"Aw. Fuck." I close my eyes and shake my head. "I'm sorry, Molly."

"It's okay." She pulls in a breath and stands.

"Fuck," I mutter again. "How do you know that?"

She holds up her phone. "Grace sent me a text message. My phone's been off, and I had a bunch of missed calls, voice mails and texts. Most from Steve, but a lot from Grace and Brielle. And one from Mom just checking in." She hesitates. "I didn't listen to Steve's messages, but I did read the others."

"Who's he there with?"

"Grace says she doesn't know." She swallows, a pained expression on her face. "If he's with Claire…"

Goddammit.

"I'll finish getting ready." She darts into the bathroom.

"No rush," I call. "I'll be out on the balcony."

I grab my own phone and go outside where the sun is sinking down to the horizon. The ocean glints silver and turquoise, stretching out to infinity.

Should I text Steve and see who he's with?

I run my thumb over the phone screen. Shit. I hate seeing Molly unhappy. It must feel like a slap in the face that he went without her. Especially if he's with someone else.

It might seem weird if I message him. We weren't best buds or anything. So I don't, but I scroll through Insta while I wait for Molly.

She joins me a few minutes later.

"You okay?" I ask.

"Yeah. I don't care about the honeymoon." She sits too.

"Yes, I was excited to go to Europe, but it was my decision not to go through with the wedding, so I totally gave up the honeymoon too. It makes sense that Steve should go on the trip rather than waste a bunch of money. It just hurts that he may have gone with someone else."

I nod.

"And if he's with Claire, that just reinforces that I made the right decision."

"I guess that's true." That doesn't mean it doesn't still hurt, though.

"This view is incredible."

I set down my phone. "It really is. I get why the rest of my family likes living here."

"Would you want to play here?"

"Christ, no!"

She chokes out a laugh. "Okay, then."

"My family owns both the local teams here. I don't want to work for my family. Holy shit." I shake my head.

"But what if you got traded? Players don't always have a say where they're going."

"True." I grimace. "Let's hope that never happens."

"I found a place for dinner. Mexican. How's that?"

"Sounds good."

We find the restaurant easily. It's a typical cantina with wooden tables and chairs, stucco and brick, and lots of greenery.

We start off sharing cheese chips with guacamole. Molly orders the chicken mole and I go for beef fajitas. While we sip our drinks and wait for our meals, she changes the subject back to my visit with Grandpa.

"So how's your grandpa doing today?"

I purse my lips briefly, then tell her about my conversation with Chelsea, ending with, "She's not bailing on him."

She watches me closely. "Do you feel more comfortable about her now?"

"Yeah. She's looking after him. I tried to talk to Grandpa but I don't think he really understood."

"Oh no."

I sigh. "I left it too late. I thought he was the enemy and now it turns out we know better, and it's too fucking late."

"Maybe he understood more than you realize. At least he wasn't…hostile. Or was he?"

"No."

"So he probably picked up on the fact you want to make amends, even if he didn't understand all the words."

I consider that. I'd like to believe that. I knew Molly would make me feel better. "Last night he seemed so with it." He shakes his head. "Chelsea says his cognitive abilities vary from day to day."

"You'll have more chances to talk to him while you're here. I'm sorry."

I nod, tightening my lips. "Thanks. We have to deal with it. I also heard from Everly." She texted me earlier. "She's getting everyone together tomorrow night."

"Oh good."

"She said to bring you."

Molly shakes her head. "No. That's family stuff."

I shrug. "It's not that big a deal."

"I don't want to intrude. I'm just tagging along to escape Chicago. I'll be fine here."

I tell her a few anecdotes about my afternoon with Grandpa, and she listens so attentively I keep talking.

"Did you ever play hockey with your grandpa?" she asks at one point.

"Yeah." I smile faintly. "When I was little. He'd play with us kids when we got together for Christmas. It was really cool, because he was always so much better than us, but then…Théo started to get better than him. Faster. Softer hands. And then JP, Asher, Harrison and me too. He loved it, though. And Noah and Riley played goal, so we gave them a run for their money every time. There aren't many players in the league today who can say they stopped shots from Bob Wynn."

She smiles. "I guess not."

"Grandpa was so proud of all of us." My lips twist. "Even me. And we loved trying to outskate him."

"What about your dad? And your uncle? Did they play too?"

"Oh yeah, of course. My mom played hockey too."

Her eyes widen as she picks up a chip and dunks it into the guacamole. "Really?"

"Yeah. She just played for fun when she was a teenager."

"That's awesome."

"My mom's pretty cool."

"Where does she live?"

"Toronto, right now. But apparently she may be moving to Los Angeles too." I rolls my eyes. "I hope she doesn't."

"Why?"

I shrug. "My dad's here. He's an asshole. And the rest of the family can be a lot."

"They don't like her?"

"No, no. Actually they do. I just think she's better off not being involved with them."

"Los Angeles is a big city. And…" She grins. "She's a grown woman. I'm sure she can make her own decisions."

My lips pucker up and then I smile. "Yeah. I guess that's true. Women don't like being treated like children, huh?"

"Fuck the patriarchy," she says mildly, and I burst out laughing. Molly and I have always laughed over the same things, and right now it feels good to laugh with her.

9

JAX

Spending more time with Grandpa and Chelsea today was good and bad, which fucked me right up. I want to make up for lost time. But I feel guilty because I want to run away and hide, because it's so fucking sad. I also feel guilty because Chelsea is the one shouldering this burden and she didn't make a single complaint about it. She did say Dad and Uncle Matt are more involved now, and her kids are supportive, so that's good, but… leaving their place, my head was a spinning circle of guilt and grief and pride and love.

Then I arrived at the pool to see Molly flirting with that guy, while standing there nearly naked in a tiny little bikini, displaying lots of smooth skin and curves, and I kind of overreacted. She has every right to flirt with whoever she wants, I guess, but it disturbed me, and then we had an argument which has never happened before and I didn't like it.

Luckily, Molly is a rock star and talked me down and isn't holding a grudge against me for being an idiot.

After a big margarita on the rocks and a few chips and guacamole, not to mention Molly's smiles and easy conversation, I'm a lot more relaxed than I was an hour ago. This place is fun and casual, and so is Molly. I've always liked that about her. Somehow, she always makes me smile.

Except I'm seeing now that she's more than just fun and casual, which sounds shallow. There's a lot more to her than that—caring, compassionate, understanding. And broken-hearted.

I have to keep reminding myself that she just broke up with my teammate. After last night's Lone Rangering, I have to stop thinking about her like that. Seriously.

I can do it. I may like women and sex, but I know enough to keep my hands off a friend who was someone else's fiancée a few days ago.

We continue to chat as we eat. My fajitas arrive sizzling at the table, smelling amazing, and I dive into them. I didn't even realize how hungry I was. Maybe I was hangry earlier. That would also explain my annoyance with Justin at the pool.

"Is Christmas your favorite holiday?" she asks.

"Why do you ask that?"

"The way you were talking about playing hockey with your family at Christmas in the past."

"Oh. Well. Christmas is different now. The whole family doesn't get together anymore, especially the last few years. And I try to make sure I spend time with my mom and my grandma and grandpa on her side."

"And the break at Christmas is short. That must make it hard, too."

"True. But yeah, I like Christmas. Memories, you know?"

"I know."

"How about you? Is Christmas a big family time?"

"Thanksgiving more so, I guess. I don't have much family. My brother's married and has two kids and I love them to bits, but outside of that we don't have much extended family. I love

Christmas though. I love giving presents, and I love snow and twinkling lights."

"I love snow too. Lots of people think that's nuts."

"Well, it can be a pain in the ass, but it can also be beautiful. Actually, it's kind of magical…that nature can form so many incredibly tiny crystals and pile them up and they're perfectly white and sparkly."

I tip my head and smile at her description. She's right. It is kind of magical. "Yeah."

"You'd miss snow if you lived here, Canuck boy."

I laugh. "I definitely would."

It's dusk as we leave the restaurant. Back at the resort, we agree to another walk around the grounds.

"Tomorrow I'll check out the beach," Molly says. "I found the path to get there."

"I'll come with you." I pause. "If that's okay."

She glances sideways at me. "Sure, it's okay. You don't have other plans tomorrow?"

"Not until evening."

She nods. "What about your dad?"

My teeth clench involuntarily. "What about him?"

"You are going to see him again, aren't you?"

"Sure, yeah. At some point."

"How about tomorrow? Give him a call and see if he wants to do lunch."

"Why are you pushing me to see my dad?"

"I'm not!" She pauses. "Okay, I am. I just think it would be good for you."

"Good for me?" Annoyance fizzes in my gut. "What does that mean?"

She doesn't answer right away. Finally she says, "I should stay out of it."

"Good idea."

My words came out harsher than I intended, and I sense her hurt. We walk in silence for a moment, then in a low voice I say, "Sorry. Again."

"Sorry for what?" Her tone is light.

"I was rude."

"No, I was. It's not my business what's between you and your father."

It's true. Molly and I are friends, but not like best buds. It really *isn't* her business. So why do I want to know why she said it would be good for me to see my dad? I really don't care about him that much.

"I came here to fix things with Grandpa," I say stiffly. "Not my dad."

Silence expands between us.

"Jax. You just said it might be too late for you and your grandpa. Why wait to fix things with your dad? What if something happens to him?"

Christ. She's right. As always.

This wasn't part of my plan in coming here. My relationship with Dad is what it is. I had no intention of trying to make things up with him too. But… "I'll call him tomorrow," I say gruffly.

She just nods and we keep walking.

"Do you play golf?" I ask.

"Um. I have. I'm not very good at it."

"We could golf one day. There's a nine-hole course here."

"I guess we could. But Jax, you don't have to entertain me, really."

I'm afraid to open my mouth in case what I say comes out sounding wrong again. I know I don't have to entertain her.

"And don't use me to procrastinate on dealing with your family," she adds.

My head jerks back. "I'm not doing that!"

She purses her lips. "Are you sure?"

Maybe I am. But admitting to that makes it sound like I don't want to be with her. Goddammit, this conversation is full of land mines waiting for me to step on. I rub my face. "Look. I admit hanging out with my family isn't my favorite thing to do. I'd rather hang out with you, and that's not using you. I'll spend time with my family, but I also want to have a little fun on this trip. Okay?"

"Okay. Except I'm not supposed to be here."

"But you are, so let's make the most of it."

We go into the lobby lounge for a drink. A bunch of convention people are in there, and we run into the group we talked to earlier at the pool. They invite us to sit with them. Molly and I exchange a "why not" look, and I pull chairs up to their table.

Once again, I'm the center of attention, but, with amusement, I watch Molly run interference for me. It's like she's protecting my right to privacy. It's kind of sweet. I don't mind talking to fans, as long as it's not all about me, and it seems she knows that. She distracts Justin by talking about trivia.

"No, no," she says to Justin. "It wasn't Mrs. O'Leary's cow who started the fire."

"Yes, it was."

Molly shakes her head. "No, that's a myth. Nobody knows exactly what started the fire."

"*Everyone* knows what started the fire," Justin argues. "The cow that kicked over a lamp."

"I'm from Chicago," she says. "I should know."

I hold up a hand and shake my head at Justin. "Don't argue with her. She's always right."

She shoots me an exasperated but amused glance. "Yes. I am."

The others laugh, because she's so damn cute.

Eventually we call it a night and go back up to the room. And once again, I'm faced with the predicament of sharing a room with Molly.

"Do you want to take the bed tonight?" I ask, because this morning she commented that she was stiff and sore as she stretched and worked kinks out of her back with boner inducing moves. "We can take turns sleeping on the chaise."

"There's no way you can sleep on that. Let's do what you suggested…share the bed. We can make a wall of pillows down the middle."

I swallow a sigh. "Okay."

It doesn't matter. So she'll be a little closer. I still can't touch her. Or think about her. Or think about touching her.

No playing five-on-one tonight though, since she'll be right in the same bed. But that's okay. I don't need that. I'm fine.

We take turns using the bathroom again and I'm trying to disregard the intimacy and closeness of the hotel room. It's hard to ignore the aroma she leaves in the bathroom, though… that fresh and totally addicting grapefruit and flowers scent. It's hard to ignore her dressed in that night shirt, her face freshly washed and dusted with golden freckles. It's hard to ignore the way she bites her lip as she studies her phone.

What's she reading? More about Steve on their honeymoon?

I catch the flick of her eyelashes as she glances my way once, then again. I'm bare-chested as I kneel on the bed and stuff pillows beneath the duvet. Her glance flicks to my thighs.

I'm not the only one trying to pretend indifference at sharing a room.

We settle beneath the duvet. Molly turns out the lamp on her side of the bed, sinking the room into velvety darkness. The fan of the air conditioner is the only sound. My body is alert, my senses hyperactive. I focus on slow breaths. My obstinate dick is half hard again, goddammit. In the dark, I'm picturing Molly down by the pool, that turquoise bikini plumping up her sweet tits and sitting low on her hips, her long legs bare. Christ.

Maybe one more night after this. The convention ends Wednesday and hopefully another room will open up.

But can Molly afford it? This resort is, like, five hundred bucks a night. That's pretty steep for a schoolteacher. But I don't know her financial situation.

Shit.

I close my eyes with resolve. *There is no sweet, soft woman in bed with me. I'm alone. I need to sleep.*

Then Molly lets out a soft little snuffling noise and a sigh, rolls over, tugging the duvet, and I'm back on alert.

The beach sounded like a good idea. Until Molly takes off the shorts and tank top she's wearing to reveal that bathing suit again. There's a little bow between her breasts, and one on each hip. It would be so easy to pluck one of those ties and whisk that bottom off…

I need a quick dip in the Pacific Ocean, which I know is going to be cold. Perfect.

I leave Molly settling onto one of the resort's lounge chairs under a white umbrella. This little cove is nice, with a sandy curve of beach, but I wince as I traverse the rocks lining the edge of the water. Then I'm back onto sand, gentle waves lapping around my ankles in this sheltered area. I wade in deeper, hunching my shoulders against the chill, then dive in. Cold water embraces me as I sweep my arms out and back in a breaststroke and kick my feet. I surface and roll onto my back, turning my face to the sun. Nice.

Okay, that took care of the inconvenient erection. I can't spend all day in the ocean, though.

I turn again and swim in a crawl, staying parallel to the shore, back and forth a few times until I start to feel winded. I swim lazily back to shore and hike back to the umbrella. Molly's wearing big sunglasses, but I feel like she's watching me, so I tighten my abs.

I grab the towel from the lounge chair next to her and towel off a bit, but the sun will dry me fast enough. "We should try out the kayaks," I say, nodding to the kayaks arranged on one side of the cove. "Or paddle boards."

"That would be fun."

I'm glad she's up for that because I'm not good at lying around doing nothing for very long. Right now, though, I'm fine stretching out in the sun, trying not to look at Molly. Trying not to think about looking at Molly.

She's reading her book and we're both quiet for a while. Then she says, "Could you put sunscreen on my back?"

Fuck me. She wants me to *touch* her?

"Sure," I croak.

She hands me her sunscreen bottle and sits facing away from me. It's a spray bottle. Maybe I don't have to touch her?

I spritz away, covering her slender back with the lotion, all the way down to the shallow indents on either side of her spine just above the bikini bottom. She leans forward to give me better access and I swallow. "Okay," I say. "Done."

"Thanks."

I blow out a breath as she adjusts her chair and stretches out on her stomach to read more. The sun gleams on her skin.

"Is your book good?" I ask.

"Yes! It's so good. I love romantic suspense stories. Toni Anderson is one of my favorite authors."

"Is there a murder in it?"

"Several." She grins.

"Bloodthirsty."

"I know." Her grin turns a little evil.

"I wouldn't have thought that of you. You teach little kids."

She laughs. "Yes. And at night I like to read about serial killers. Tell me something about you that would surprise me."

Huh. I think on that. There's probably a lot she doesn't know about me. "I'm a virgin."

After a startled beat, she bursts out laughing. Her head drops down to her book and her shoulders shake. Finally she lifts her head and half-rolls to her side to face me. "Yes, that would surprise me," she says dryly. "If it were true."

I grin. "You don't believe me?"

"Nuh-uh. Come on. Tell me something real."

"I'm afraid of heights."

"Really?"

"Yeah. When we were standing up on the bluff, I didn't want to get too close to the edge."

"Huh."

"What's something else about you?"

Her shiny pink lips purse. With half her face hidden by sunglasses, her mouth becomes the center of my attention. "When I was a kid, I had an imaginary friend."

My eyes widen and I smirk. "No shit. What was her name?"

"You assume it was a girl."

"Was it?"

"Yes," she admits. "Her name was Opal, because that's my birthstone. She lived in the broom closet."

"What? Poor Opal. Did you talk to her?"

"Yes. Until I got old enough to realize how weird it was. Then I just did when I was alone. Or thought I was alone. One of my cousins overheard me talking to her once and made fun of me for years about it."

"Ugh."

"Your turn."

"Well. I don't tell everyone this…" I pause. "But under these shorts, I'm naked."

More laughter spills from her lips. "Good one."

"Okay, how about this. My feet are two different sizes."

"Really?"

"Yeah. I have to buy two different pairs of hockey skates. It was expensive as a kid."

"Do you buy two different pairs of shoes?"

"No. Usually I can get away with just buying the size that fits my bigger foot. But I have to have skates that fit perfectly."

"Let me see."

I stretch my legs out, feet together, for her to inspect them. Luckily my toenails are trimmed. Feet can be gross.

"I really can't tell," she says. "Is it your right foot that's bigger?"

"Yeah."

"No one would ever know."

"Probably not. Just me. And now you."

"Nobody else knows that about you?"

"Well, my mom does."

"Of course. She probably cursed when she had to buy two pairs of skates."

I grin. "Yeah."

My cell phone rings on the small table where I set it. I pick it up and see Paul's number.

"Sorry, I have to take this," I tell Molly.

I answer the call, swinging my legs over the side of the lounge chair and standing. "Hey, Paul. What's up?"

"I have no news for you," he says immediately.

"Shit."

"I know." Paul sighs.

I glance at Molly. Even with her sunglasses on, I can see the concern on her face as she listens.

"July first is coming up," I say, mentioning the start of free agency in the NHL.

"Yep. I've been talking lots to Yarish, but we haven't made any progress. I don't want you to worry, but we do need to be thinking about arbitration." Ian Yarish is the GM of the Aces.

"I don't want to go to arbitration."

"I know, I don't either. I want to sign you to a big fat contract that fairly represents what you're worth. But you know how it is. We've talked about your rights and how it works."

"Yeah." Paul is really good about explaining things and treating me like I'm running a business. It's just me, so it seems weird, but looking at it that way helps.

"We know what your strengths are. I know you're willing to hold out. It takes guts to do that. But I think we're in a good situation."

"Jesus, Paul. You need to push harder. We need to get this *done*."

A few seconds of loaded silence greet my little outburst. "What do you think I'm doing, Jax?" he asks quietly.

I close my eyes. I have to trust Paul. It's just hard leaving everything up to someone else. "Sorry. I know you're on this. Keep me posted."

"Yeah. I'm flying to Chicago after the Fourth of July. We'll talk more then."

"Okay, thanks, Paul." I end the call with a heavy sigh, dropping my arm.

"What's wrong?" Molly asks.

"That was my agent. My contract expired this year and negotiations aren't getting anywhere."

"Oh." She pulls her bottom lip between her teeth. "Do you think…you might end up somewhere else?"

"It's possible. I don't want that, but I want to be paid what I'm worth."

"Of course." She purses her lips. "There's still time, though, right?"

"Yeah. I wanted to get things done before summer, but that didn't happen. Hopefully it will before training camp. Hey, let's go out on those paddle boards."

We venture out onto the ocean, staying in the calm cove, spying a seal on some rocks that gets Molly all excited. I go up to the pool closest to us and return with beers and sandwiches, and after more lounging, we try the kayaks. Molly's never kayaked, but she's up for anything and it's fun helping her learn to paddle the small craft.

The day passes quickly and soon it's time for me to go change and get ready for dinner with my family. I don't want to leave Molly on her own, but she already said she won't come, so I don't push, and she's probably right—this is a family get-together.

I hesitate at the door, dressed in pants and a button-down shirt, fidgeting with the key to the rental car. "You sure you'll be okay by yourself?"

She rolls her eyes. "Of course. I'll have dinner in the bar, take a walk, maybe watch a movie."

I nod. "Okay. See you later."

I don't know why it feels wrong to leave her, but I force myself out into the hall and out of the resort. I found the restaurant where we're meeting on Google Maps on my phone, a seafood place in Manhattan Beach. The drive is about forty minutes, traffic heavy in spots, and Everly, JP and Théo are already there.

"Nice place," I say, taking a chair. "Great view." The big windows look out onto the ocean.

"You didn't bring Molly?" Everly asks.

I act surprised. "Why would I?"

She wrinkles her nose. "You just left her alone at the hotel?"

"She'll be fine." A server approaches and I order a scotch on the rocks.

"What happened with her wedding?" Everly asks, leaning forward. "It was quite the news story."

"Yeah." I rub the back of my neck. "I guess it was. What all has been said about it?"

Everly grimaces. "She apparently read out explicit text messages her fiancé sent to another woman."

"Okay. That about sums it up. He was screwing around on her and she found out."

"Well, she definitely has ovaries," Everly says.

Asher and Harrison join us at that moment.

"Who has ovaries?" Harrison asks. "Jax?"

We all grin.

"Molly. We were talking about Molly and Steve Shevchuk," Everly informs him.

"Ugh." Asher shakes his head as he pulls out a chair. "What a douche."

"Are you close friends with him?" Everly asks me.

"Eh. Not super close." I sit back so the waitress can set my drink in front of me. She takes orders from Asher and Harrison as well.

"Did you know he was cheating on her?" Everly pierces me with her stare.

"No. Definitely not." I shake my head. "I was as surprised as everyone else at the wedding."

"It must have caused quite a scene."

"Oh yeah."

"And you were her knight in shining armor, riding in to swoop her up and rescue her."

"Ha ha. Funny."

Everly grins. "She said that, the other night at the party. Hey, where's Riley? I need another woman here."

I frown. Since when has Everly ever wanted Riley around? Those two have never really gotten along.

As if she summoned her, Riley and Noah walk in together. I rise to give my little sister a hug.

I wait until we all have drinks and have ordered dinner, and then look around at the table. "Okay. Fill me in on what's going on with Grandpa. And Chelsea."

10

MOLLY

I never mind having dinner and drinks alone when I'm in a different city. I have my phone to keep my company, but I like people watching and making new friends. I sit at the bar and the bartender is very helpful in picking out a cocktail to have.

"Are you here for the conference?" he asks me as he slides a drink with gin, honey and lemonade over to me.

"No. Just a little vacation." I smile and take a sip of the drink. "Oh, this is good! Thanks for the suggestion."

"No problem. Would you like a food menu?"

"Yes, please."

The place is filling up and soon every seat the bar is occupied. I exchange a polite smile with the man on the stool next to me. He's probably about forty, wearing a suit but no tie.

"What's that you're drinking?" he asks.

I show him the cocktail on the menu. "It's really good."

"I'll try it." He orders one also. "Here for the convention?"

I repress my smile. "No. Just vacation. How about you?"

"Yeah, I presented today."

"Oh, awesome. What was your presentation about?"

"Domain-driven design for modern architectures."

I blink. "Oh. Cool. I have no idea what that means."

He laughs. "That's okay. What do you do for a living?"

"I teach third grade."

"Fun. Maybe?"

"It is. I love kids, and I love teaching."

"Do you have any of your own?"

"No. I almost got married…a while back." Okay, four days ago. "But it didn't work out."

"Ah. Sorry to hear that."

We chat back and forth about the resort and the weather. I learn his name is Ben and he's a software developer and architect, apparently an expert in domain-driven design, whatever that is. He's being a little flirty, and I'm not looking for anything more than casual conversation, but it's fun.

"Ben."

A woman's voice speaks behind us. We both turn to see her standing there. She's about his age, wearing a suit also, and she's looking at me like I just tried to steal her purse.

"Oh, hi," he says. "Done already?"

"Yes." Her tone is frosty, her eyes ice blue and narrowed at me.

"Let me just settle up for this drink."

I want to tell the woman I'm not interested in her husband or boyfriend or whatever he is to her, that I wasn't the one flirting, but that probably wouldn't be helpful so I just give her a friendly smile and turn away from her to check my phone.

Why are men such douchewaffles? It's not that I was really interested in him, but he sure as hell wasn't acting like he was married.

"Enjoy your vacation," he says, his tone completely different as he slides off the stool.

Asshole. "Thanks."

I sigh as they depart. Another man takes the stool right away, smiling at me. I scrunch my face into a phony smile then focus on my phone.

I order a salad and scroll through social media, keeping my head down as I eat to discourage any chatter. I have one more drink, then I pay the bill and go outside for a walk, which is getting to be a routine while here. Except tonight I'm alone.

I really don't mind being alone, and I totally didn't want to go with Jax to have dinner with his family. They have a lot to talk about. I hope it goes well. Everly was a bit snarky toward him at the party the other night, implying that he wasn't interested in the family issues, but come on! He lives on the other side of the country. And they know what a professional hockey player's schedule is like. He can't just get on a plane and fly to L.A. for a family meeting.

I pause at one of the pools, which is closed, but I sit on a big round lounger and watch the shimmering water. What should I do tomorrow? A different pool? The beach again? Take a hike along the coast? The resort is beautiful but kind of isolated, so without a car I can't get very far. They do have a shuttle service though. I could check out options, like maybe a whale watching tour.

I think about my day at the beach, and how fun and easy it was with Jax. How excellent he looks in a pair of board shorts. How his shoulder muscles bunched and rippled when he paddled the kayak, how his strong legs braced on the stand-up paddle board.

I was glad to see him relaxing and having fun; yesterday was clearly a rough day for him. Confronting the reality of his grandfather's decline would be difficult for anyone to accept, but he also feels guilty about not seeing his grandpa and about doubting Chelsea's commitment to her husband. Having his eyes opened to that was another reality check, and it was obviously hard having those long-held beliefs challenged.

I think about sharing a bed with him last night, which was totally innocent and a bit of a letdown, although I have no idea what I expected. Except the night before that, he'd masturbated and…uuuugh, what did I think was going to happen? Because nothing *can* happen. And I don't *want* anything to happen. I'm still in love with Steve.

I think.

My phone buzzes with a text message and I unlock it to see it. Jax.

Hey where are u

At the pool. I pause and type in another message. *The closest pool.*

On my way.

I smile as a bubble of happiness swells in my chest. He's back. I turn to watch the path and lift a hand to wave at him as he approaches through the dark shrubs and palm trees.

He sits next to me. "Hey."

"Hey. How was dinner?"

"Surprisingly okay."

"Oh, good! I was worried."

"Yeah?" He tips his head, his handsome face in shadows from the palm trees.

Yes, Jax is handsome. Maybe I haven't mentioned that because it just *is*. Not that I'm attracted to him or anything. I mean, he *is* attractive. But not for me. "Um, yeah, a bit. I know you were kind of stressed about it."

"Nah." He pauses. "Okay, maybe a little. They told me how they figured out what was going on with the money. They got a copy of the court documents. They were planning some kind of careful intervention and then Everly lost her shit and confronted her parents and Uncle Matt." He shakes his head.

"Wish I'd been there to see Everly losing her shit. That *never* happens."

I smile.

"But it worked. It got them talking. The fact that we don't know how long Grandpa has left or what kind of quality of life he'll have also made Dad and Uncle Matt realize they needed to do something, and Chelsea…" He shakes his head. "She's figured out a way to repay the loan." He pauses, and I let the silence stretch on as he gathers his thoughts. "She's apparently stepping in for Dad. I mean, Théo's managing the team now." His eyebrows pull together. "I wasn't sure what I thought of that, when Grandpa hired him last summer, but apparently Chelsea trusts him. And it seems everyone else does too. He's doing a great job."

"That's good, then. Right?"

"Yeah. I'm relieved that things seem to be working out, and apparently a lot of it is thanks to Chelsea."

"I knew it!"

He grins, a slow, sexy gleam of white in the darkness. "Yes, you were right."

My gaze lingers on his face, the air around us heating, my heart bumping.

"I haven't done a good job of keeping in touch. It's not that I don't care, but…"

"You try not to care."

He jerks back and stares at me. "What does that mean?"

Oops, have I overstepped? Welp, might as well finish. "I feel like your family is difficult and has had all these dramas and you don't want to be involved but you can't help it because you do care."

He's silent for a moment. "Maybe," he finally says gruffly.

Nailed it. I bite back a smile.

"They all want to get together again tomorrow night," he

says. "But just for fun. Lacey and Taylor will come, too. They said to bring you."

"Oh." I consider that. It sounds fun. "Okay."

"And I'm having lunch with my dad tomorrow." He nudges me with his shoulder. "Happy now?"

I laugh softly. "Why yes, I am."

I don't know why it matters to me, but I hate the idea that he and his dad have that distance between them. His dad seemed so happy to see him when we showed up unexpectedly at the party. And I think Jax does care about his dad, but something hurt him. I suspect it's his parents' divorce, but that's a wild guess. Okay, not so wild. Lots of kids get hurt by their parents divorcing. Maybe he'll talk to me about that at some point.

"Want to walk more?" he asks.

"Sure." I stand. The ocean breeze tugs my hair back off my face and I turn my face to it. "I love it here."

"Yeah, it's nice. Would you ever leave Chicago?"

Steve asked me that once. There was a very real possibility he'd get traded somewhere else eventually, and we'd have to move. "I love Chicago. I don't want to leave. But there's a whole big world out there to explore." I gesture toward the bluff and the ocean. "Like this. It's beautiful."

"True." We walk farther. "You're a pretty smart cookie, Flynn."

"Of course I am. I'm a teacher." I smirk at him and he laughs.

Jax arranges to meet his dad for lunch and it's near a shopping mall, so he drops me off there on his way. It's an outdoor, two-level mall, and I wander in and out of some shops. I spent a bunch of money on things to come on this trip, which was kind of a waste when I had perfectly good clothes and makeup at home, so I probably shouldn't spend more. But I have some savings, which I was going to spend on the honeymoon (sigh). If we're going out with Jax's family tonight, I want to look decent, so I buy a pair of jeans, a black silk and lace camisole and a slouchy gray cardigan. After a salad at the food court, I discover the ice rink. This makes me smile. A skating rink in a California mall! I watch people glide over the ice through the glass on the level above the rink.

Jax texts me when he's done his lunch, and we meet up at one end of the mall.

"How'd it go?" I ask, studying his face.

"Okay." He shrugs.

That's it. That's all I'm getting. Okay. "There's a skating rink in this mall."

He grins. "No shit."

"Really."

"Do you know how to skate?"

"Of course I do."

"Let's go, then." He takes my arm and starts walking.

"Seriously?"

"Yeah."

We find the entrance and pay to rent skates.

"What about your feet?" I whisper to him.

"I'll survive."

We join the people on the ice, lots of kids, some skating independently, others using big plastic animals to hold on to. I do know how to skate, but it's been a while and I'm a little wobbly in my first efforts. Jax, of course, is a superstar, gliding easily around. Sunlight streams in through high windows and it makes me smile.

After a few laps around the ice, I feel steadier and I attempt a little spin, which is pretty much the extent of the moves I learned during my figure skating lessons many years ago.

"Ooooh, show off," Jax says.

"I'm not showing off. You're showing off." He's literally skating circles around me.

He laughs and takes my hands, spinning me around.

I let out a little screech but he's holding on tight.

"How does it feel to be on ice like this?" I ask.

"It feels good." He smoothly switches to skating backward in front of me. "It's fun."

A little boy whizzes between us and crashes into the boards. "Sorry," he says. "I don't know how to stop."

Jax skates over to him. "Want to learn?"

"Yeah."

Jax leads the boy into the middle of the ice and patiently shows him how to stop, and the kid does it a few times to show he's got it.

"Thanks, mister!" he says as Jax skates back to me with a smile on his face.

My heart is warm and soft. "He has no idea he just got a lesson from an NHL star."

Jax rolls his eyes. "Don't know about the 'star' thing."

"Your family is hockey royalty."

"Whatever."

We spend a little more time fooling around on the ice, then head off.

"My shins hurt," I complain. "Who knew there are muscles in the shins?"

"Anterior tibialis."

I purse my lips and look up through my eyelashes as I unlace my skates. "Really? That's good trivia."

"Really. You need to stretch. I'll show you."

With his shoes on, he demonstrates. "Toe drag stretch."

I follow what he does, feeling the stretch. "Thanks."

We walk out. "Where to now?" he asks. "You done shopping?"

"Yeah."

"Let's go for a drive."

We end up at a lighthouse. It's breathtakingly beautiful, sitting atop the cliffs. The lighthouse isn't open, but we wander around and explore the views of the ocean from up here. Then we stop at a Starbucks for coffees and head back to the hotel to get ready for our dinner out.

"Where are we going tonight?" I ask. "Will I be okay if I wear jeans?"

"It doesn't matter what you wear."

"Yes, it does." I roll my eyes and teasingly say, "Men."

He laughs. "Let me check. Everly sent me the name of the place." He pulls out his phone. "It's called Coastal Kitchen." He swipes and taps, then shows me his phone with the website of the restaurant.

"Okay." I nod, satisfied that it's not some swanky place in Hollywood, or something.

"JP and Taylor live in Long Beach, so she was trying to find something in between there and Santa Monica."

In our room, the light is blinking on the phone with a message. I point it out to Jax, who picks up the receiver and listens. He hangs up and looks at me. "The resort has some room openings. We can get you your own room now."

"Oh." As weird as it was at first sharing a room with Jax, we've kind of settled in. Mostly. The last two nights I've been intensely aware of him sleeping only inches away from me in that bed. Yes, it's a big bed, but he's a big man and takes up a lot of space.

There's also the issue of money. I had no idea he was staying a resort this expensive when I impulsively begged to tag along with him. There's no way I can pay five hundred dollars a night for the next…I mentally count…six nights. Holy shit.

"I'll call the desk and see what's available." Jax picks up the phone again.

I sit at the small round table and wait, nibbling my bottom lip, listening to Jax. Eventually, he ends the conversation and hangs up.

I clear my throat. "So?"

"We're going to move tonight."

I blink. "What? We?"

"Yeah." He rises and stretches. "The rooms are expensive here, but they have a suite that has a separate bedroom and a sofa bed in the living room."

I swallow. "I'll pay for half of it."

"Phhhht. No, you won't."

"No, really, Jax. I don't want to cost you more money." I jump up and twist my fingers together. "It's bad enough I made you bring me and we had to share this room the last few nights."

"It's not a big deal, Flynn. Pack your things while I go to the front desk and get the keys."

I sink back down into the chair, my chin dipping. Shit. My chest tightens. I'm sure the suites are a thousand dollars a night, which doesn't save me any money at all if I pay half. And I can't let him spend that much money. I lift my head. "Let's just stay here," I say firmly. "This is working fine."

He cocks his head and scrutinizes me. "Are you sure?"

"Yeah! It's fine, right? And it's a pain packing up and moving."

"Yeah," he says slowly. "It's fine."

11

JAX

I'm only doing it to save Molly money. I know she's not enthusiastic about spending so much. I'd have no problem springing for a suite so we could each have a bed in separate rooms, but I also see she feels guilty about that. So we'll stay put. It's no big deal.

She spends a long time in the bathroom getting ready. I hope she's not upset. When she finally emerges, her eyes are a bit pink and bright, confirming my suspicions. I guess I could say it serves her right for insisting on coming with me, but damn, I don't want her to be sad. She's got enough problems, with a lying, cheating fiancé.

Other than that, she looks amazing—jeans that show off her fantastic ass and long legs, a sexy, lacy cami and a loose cardigan over it. Her bright hair's the usual mess of shoulder-length waves, her lips shiny. "Ready!"

I changed while she was in there, so I'm ready too, also wearing jeans. If I'm wrong and the restaurant is super classy, we'll both be in jeans.

Coastal Kitchen is nice, but we're dressed fine. Everly and

her boyfriend Wyatt are already sitting at a long table. Wyatt plays for Grandpa's team, the Condors. How does it feel to be dating the team owner's daughter? I guess he's okay with it, since he and Everly both look happy.

We all greet each other. Everly and Wyatt are sitting on a long banquette loaded with blue and white cushions on one side of the table, so Molly and I take seats on tall white stools opposite them. We're still looking over the drinks menu when Taylor and JP arrive, followed soon after by Lacey and Théo.

We may have weird relationships, but we're all close in age and we're all united by hockey and our wacky family so hopefully tonight isn't a fiasco.

"It's Trivia Night here!" Molly announces beside me, holding up the table card.

"Really?" I turn to her.

"Yep!"

We lift a hand in the air and high five each other.

"This is a thing?" Taylor asks.

"Yeah, and we kick ass at trivia," I reply. "Let's sign up."

It doesn't start until later, so we'll have time to eat first. I think better on a full stomach.

We order bottles of wine, then appetizers to share. There's lots of noisy chatter and laughter, food being passed around and glasses filled. Molly talks animatedly with Taylor and Lacey, laughing at the story about the fight that broke out at Lacey and Théo's wedding, and telling them about her job teaching third grade.

"I work with kids too," Taylor says. "They're so much fun."

"They can be. One of my kids had been away for a few days because his grandfather passed away. When he came back, he said that he'd been away because his grandpa died and he had to be a polar bear."

They gaze blankly back at her.

"He was a pall bearer," she finishes smiling, cracking everyone up. "It was so cute."

At one point, JP returns from the men's room, shaking his head. "Well, that was awkward."

"What?" Wyatt asks, picking up a potato skin.

"Some dude in the bathroom came and stood at the urinal right beside me. Every other one was empty."

All the guys make appropriate sounds of consternation.

The women exchange looks.

"At least he didn't try to make conversation," I say.

"Oh, he did," JP says.

We all groan even louder.

"That's not allowed?" Molly asks with a grin.

"It's an unwritten guy rule," I reply. "There's nothing than can't wait to be said until you're both finished."

Everyone cracks up.

"Are there other unwritten guy rules?" Everly asks.

"Oh yeah," I say. "We have to kill all the spiders."

"Not me," JP says. "I'm not going near those fuckers."

Taylor grins. "I'm the spider killer."

"Also, when you're in the bathroom in a stall and someone else comes in, you have to cough or make some kind of noise so they know they're not alone," Wyatt puts in.

The rest of us guys nod solemnly in agreement.

"And never leave a bro hanging when he tries to high five you," I add. "That's just wrong."

The women are falling over in laughter.

Molly and I convince the others to sign up for the trivia event. As things get started, she and I do our secret handshake —two fingers, a couple of backhanded slaps and a fist bump.

"What was that?" Théo asks, ginning widely.

"Lucky handshake," I reply. "We do it every trivia contest."

I catch Everly giving me a strange look.

"What?" I ask.

"Nothing." She shakes her head, lips tipped up. "It's cute."

"Cute," I scoff. "Please. This is serious business."

"I'm already regretting participating in this," Wyatt says.

I rub my hands together.

I'm having fun. With my family.

There's a lot less tension than I've ever felt at a family get-together and it's a goddamn relief, to be honest. And it's fun being here with Molly. She fits right in, and everyone loves her.

"How did you get into trivia?" Everly asks me curiously.

I shrug. "I read a lot when we travel…on the plane, on buses. Weird stuff just sticks in my head."

The announcer begins the trivia night, welcoming everyone, outlining the rules and the prizes. "Tonight's theme is 'Carnal Knowledge.' "

"Wait, what?" I turn to Molly at the same moment she looks at me, her eyes big as plates.

"Does that mean what I think it means?" she asks.

"That's right, it's all about the bow-chicka-wow-wow!" the announcer booms. "Driving Miss Daisy! Doing the horizontal greased-weasel tango." The crowd makes a displeased noise. "Putting ranch dressing in Hidden Valley!" Now the crowd boos. "All right, all right, enough of that! Let's get started!"

"I know a lot about this subject," Wyatt says enthusiastically. "I was afraid I was going to look stupid."

Everly cracks up, falling against him.

"First question! Where did the term blow job come from?"

We're given four possible answers. Molly and I confer quietly, our heads close together. Close enough to smell that fresh grapefruit smell. "A musician who said it was like playing a horn?" she whispers incredulously.

"Sounds plausible to me."

"No! That is not the answer."

"Okay, which is it?"

"Number four." A merging of the Victorian slang for prostitute and ejaculation.

Christ. I can't even think about these answers without turning red in the face. How the hell did we end up at sex trivia night?

"Early condoms were made of everything but…a. animal intestines; b. animal horns; c. linen soaked in chemical, dried and tied on with a ribbon; or d. snakeskin."

"Snakeskin condom," Everly muses. "Hmmm."

Molly and I again confer. Again, she seems confident of her answer. "I have no fucking clue," I whisper. "Except an animal horn on my dick sounds pretty damn painful."

She winces. "Um, yeah. It's snakeskin. For real."

"What is the average number of sex partners for women?" the announcer calls. "Three, seven, nine, or twenty?"

I look at Molly. Her lips twist up. "I think it's seven."

I blink at her. Has she been with seven guys? That's…well, that's none of my business. "Okay." Once again I have to go with her answer.

The next question is average number of sex partners for men—four, seven, nine-point-five, or eleven.

"Nine-point-five?" I ask. "How do you have half a sex partner?"

"Maybe blow-up dolls count," Harrison says, cracking us all up again.

"It's an average," Molly says. "What do *you* think? You're a man."

"It has to be eleven."

She bites her lip. "Are you sure?"

"I have no idea."

"Okay, eleven."

"What percentage of woman can orgasm from intercourse alone? A. 25%; b. 50%; c. 85%; d. 100%."

"Twenty-five percent," Molly whispers immediately.

"Uh, wow." I tug at the collar of my shirt. Is it getting hot in here? I think it is.

"How many nerve endings does the clitoris have?" The possible answers are three hundred, one thousand, eight thousand and ten thousand.

"What's the difference between a bar and a clitoris?" Lacey asks.

We all look at her.

"Men have no trouble finding a bar," she answers.

The women laugh, the men groan. "Not you, honey," she says, patting Théo's cheek.

He smirks.

"It's the only organ in the human body whose sole purpose is pleasure," Molly informs us.

I draw back to level a look at her. "Jesus. That wasn't even a question."

She tosses her head with a know-it-all look that's so damn cute.

We run through questions about how many women report having an orgasm during anal sex, where a man's G-spot is, the best position for women to have an orgasm, and if men can fake orgasms.

"Why would you want to?" Wyatt asks with a puzzled frown.

"I have," JP says.

"Wait, what?" Taylor glares at him.

"Not with you, babe." He grimaces. "I just wanted to be done and out of there. Wasn't happening." He pauses. "I *was* hammered."

"Well, we're all getting to know each other so much better," Molly quips.

In the end, Molly and I are triumphant. It's the usual for us, but this time I have to give her all the credit. I like sex, but apparently I'm not as well informed about it as she is. The only question we got wrong was the average number of sex partners for men, which is seven and less than I guessed.

"You're quite the sexpert," I say on the drive back to the resort later.

"Ha ha. Apparently Steve didn't think so."

I can't stop the disgusted grunt that emerges from my throat. "He's an idiot."

"Well, you don't know my sexpertise in bed," she points out. "It's one thing to know trivia, but something else to put it into practice." She almost sounds sad.

Man, Chucky did a number on her.

I don't want to think about her sexpertise in bed. She's beautiful and smells delicious and she's sexy as fuck. I'd be only too happy to…*stop*.

If Chucky didn't appreciate her skills, that's his loss.

"I'm surprised at how many women orgasm from anal sex," I comment.

Why? *Why* am I still talking about sex?

"It's not surprising," she says. "I mean, when you think about it…" Her voice trails off. "Never mind."

Yeah, this is probably not a good topic of conversation. Do I really want to know what she knows about anal sex?

"Well, we're still the champs," I joke.

"Yes, we are! And I had fun tonight. I like your family."

"I had fun, too, surprisingly. Things aren't as tense as I remember."

"That's good."

"They also seemed to like you. So thanks for coming."

Back in the room, we arrange the pillow barrier down the middle of the bed, although I've noticed Molly has shifted it toward herself to give me more room. She's sweet like that.

When the lights are out and we're both under the covers and I'm definitely not thinking about her bare legs and braless tits so close to me, she murmurs, "What's up for tomorrow?"

"I'm gonna go see Grandpa again." I pause. "You can come with me if you want."

She doesn't reply right away. "Are you sure?"

"Yeah, of course."

"I'll think about it."

"You won't be interfering."

I hear a little huff and sense her smile. "Okay. G'night."

"Night, Flynn."

"When are you two getting married?"

I freeze in place and slide my gaze over to Molly, who's wide-eyed, then back to Grandpa. "We're not getting married."

"You have to get married." Grandpa's eyebrows knit together.

I flash Molly an apologetic grimace, but she smiles. "It's okay," she mouths. She sits next to Grandpa on the couch. "We're just friends, Mr. Wynn. I mean, Bob."

"Men and women can't be friends," he says. "You can't be friends with someone you're attracted to, and men are attracted to all woman, so the idea that you can be friends without sex is ridiculous."

I'm honestly speechless at this. My eyes flick over to Molly who also appears dumbstruck.

"And look at you." He gestures to Molly. "Of course Jackson is attracted to you."

"Oh my God," I mutter, dropping my face into my hand. "Grandpa."

"Um, well, thank you," Molly says.

The biggest problem with all this? He's right. I *am* attracted to Molly. The more time I spend with her, the more I see how gorgeous she is, inside and out. She's fun and smart and adventurous, also thoughtful and caring.

I think I already knew those things about her, but when a woman belongs to someone else, you don't let yourself feel the attraction. But now...I feel it.

Damn.

"He never did have much of a filter," Chelsea whispers to me. "But now it's totally gone. Sorry."

"You don't have to apologize."

Grandpa is telling a story, I think it might be about when he met Chelsea...or maybe Grandma? It's not entirely clear, and it doesn't make a lot of sense, but Molly's listening, smiling, and making appropriate comments.

"And then she went outside, and around, and I waited, and that was so much fun," he says.

My heart contracts painfully. There are times he's still with it and times he's not, and it's so fucking sad.

Chelsea returns from the kitchen, setting a plate of cookies on the table. Molly eagerly reaches for one, and offers the plate to Bob, who shakes his head.

"How's your mom doing, Jackson?" Chelsea asks me.

"She's doing great. She has a book coming out later this year."

"Oh, wow! That's amazing!" Chelsea beams.

"Yeah. It's about achieving high performance and staying humble, I think." I add for Molly's benefit, "My mom's a sports psychologist."

She nods. "I think that's so cool."

"Your mom is such a smart woman," Chelsea says. "It was nice to see her at the wedding last year."

"She's talking about moving here," I say. "I think she has a job offer from the L.A. Cougars."

"That would be a big change from Toronto."

Grandpa isn't saying anything, just smiling and nodding. He's totally faking understanding. Which is also heart-rending.

By the time we leave, Molly has Grandpa telling her what a beautiful girl she is and she has to come back. I see the hint of sorrow in her smile, but she nods and agrees, and even though she'll never see him again, I know she's right to say that because he probably won't understand if she says no, and it makes him happy and that's what matters.

"Thank you for being so kind to him," I say once we're in the car.

She gives me a weird look. "You don't have to thank me for that. He's a wonderful man. I wish I'd met him when he could tell more stories. I bet he was fascinating."

"Yeah. He was."

"You still have those memories," she says softly. "You always will."

"Yeah." I blow out a breath. "I wish I had more, though. I wish…"

"What?"

"Dad and Uncle Matt kind of spoiled my relationship with Grandpa. I wish that didn't happen."

"Ah. Yeah. I get it. But…"

Now it's my turn. "What?"

"Well, your relationship with your Grandpa is between you and him."

I huff. "True. But I felt like I needed to be on my dad's side, you know?"

"Even though you and your dad don't get along."

Jesus. This woman. She's always fucking right and it's exasperating, but also…she's right. "Okay, I get what you're saying. My dad's my dad, and I…care about him and also I care about Grandpa."

She smiles.

"And it's hard not to get down about what's happening to him, but he had an amazing life, and we've all been lucky to be part of it. Even though at times he was stubborn and hard to get along with." I pause. "I wonder how much Dad and Uncle Mark regret all the negativity."

"Did you talk to your dad about that when you went out for lunch?"

"No."

"Jax, you should have."

"You're probably right. I'm a coward."

"No, you're not. It's not easy talking about the things that have hurt us. But…"

"What?"

"It's none of my business. Sorry."

"No, tell me."

"It seems like your relationship with your dad is distant."

"Yeah. That's a fair comment."

"Do you want more? Do you want to be closer?"

"Not really."

She blows out a puff of air. "Jax."

"He cheated on my mom."

Her head whips around. I glance sideways at her as I drive. "Oh," she says.

I sigh. "Yeah. I found out by accident. That was why they split up. Mom's never said a bad word about him, but I know she was hurt by it. And I fucking hate it."

She nibbles her bottom lip as Southern California scenery flashes by outside the car. "Do you have questions about that?"

"Questions?" My hands tighten on the steering wheel. "Like, why he cheated?"

"Yeah. I guess. Maybe if you talked to him about it, you'd understand."

"Wait, you want me to understand? Forgive him? You're the one who left your fiancé because he cheated on you. You couldn't get past that." My voice has risen, and I have to take a long breath.

"True," she says quietly. "I'm not saying there's ever any excuse for cheating, but…oh hell. You're right—I probably do need to talk to Steve about it."

Wow, that was a quick spinorama.

"For closure. Understanding. I probably need that to move on. And I think you probably do, too, with your dad."

Well, shit. At least she's not a hypocrite, but she has a point. I did say that about talking to Steve. I better not be a hypocrite either.

"I guess I could talk to Dad again while I'm here," I say gruffly.

12

MOLLY

It serves me right for trying to give Jax advice. As I was telling him he should talk to his dad, I realized he'd told me the exact same thing about Steve. And I had to admit he was right.

I think about this as I lay by the pool. Jax is golfing with Harrison, Asher and JP. Tomorrow he's having lunch with his sister, and the next day he and his dad are taking a helicopter ride to Catalina Island, which sounds amazing. Probably a helicopter isn't a good place to have an intimate discussion, though. But maybe they'll have a chance to talk when they get to the island. Assuming Jax doesn't spend the whole time taking pictures; I know he's looking forward to that.

Likely because he feels guilty, he's going to take me whale watching on Sunday, our second last day here. I'm so excited about that! And I don't mind hanging out by myself for a while as he spends time with his family, which is what he came here for.

Also it gives me a chance to think about a lot of things. Like talking to Steve. Ugh. And how mixed up I felt when Bob Wynn talked about Jax and me getting married and being attracted to each other. My belly got a tight, twisted feeling because I shouldn't be attracted to Jax. He was making it patently clear that we're just friends. But sometimes, I catch him looking at me, especially at the pool or the beach or sometimes in the hotel room…and there was the night we got here and what he was doing in bed…

I flip onto my stomach and kick my feet a couple of times in frustration.

Maybe this was a mistake. I just wanted to get out of Chicago. I can't be thinking about Jax in bed with me…which he has been. But I keep thinking about pushing those pillows out of the way and sliding up next to him and feeling all that hot, bare skin against mine.

Oh God. I let out a little whimper, my face buried in my arms, my belly fluttering with inappropriate lust.

Don't go there. Do. Not. Go. There.

I roll over again, jump up off the lounger and stride to the pool. A quick dip will clear my mind. I jump right into the deep end, letting the cool water close over my head. All sound is muffled briefly as I sink down, then bob back up. I suck in air and shake water off my face as I break the surface, then start a leisurely breaststroke across the pool.

I should think about Steve. The man I loved. Love. The man I was going to marry. It feels like a year ago, which is weird. What do I want to say to him? What do I want to ask him? Why did he cheat on me? Why wasn't I enough?

I inhale a nose full of water and choke. I grab onto the side of the pool and hang there coughing, gasping for air, my sinuses burning. Shit. I can't start feeling sorry for myself again. I thought I was past this. It's not my fault he cheated.

Easy to say. Not so easy to believe, sadly.

When I'm over my near-drowning, I resume swimming,

switching to a crawl and determinedly doing lap after lap. I'm not sure if I'm punishing or distracting myself.

It's not that I'm blaming myself, but it's possible there are things I did in my relationship with Steve that contributed to the problem. I need to keep an open mind about that so I can learn and grow.

I haul myself out of the pool, breathless, and stagger over to my lounge chair where I collapse. I stare up at the blue sky, my chest heaving.

Steve's in Europe, enjoying our honeymoon with someone else. He won't be back in Chicago until early July. That will give me time to get my stuff from his condo. My friends will come help me pack up and move them back to my apartment. Now it feels lucky that I haven't yet been able to sublet it.

Then when he's back, I'll have to face him. All I feel is a sense of calm resignation.

I can do it.

Jax

I'd rather shit in my hands and clap than ask Dad why he cheated on Mom.

So I'm waiting for the right moment on this little excursion to Catalina Island.

We leave from Long Beach. The helicopter ride is sick. I've never been on a chopper before, and I love it. I've got my camera and a few lenses with me to take as many pictures as I can. The view of the ocean beneath us—flat blue, smoothly textured and endless—is stunning. The flight is only about fifteen minutes, so soon we're landing in Avalon on the island.

There aren't a lot of cars on the island, so we walk, checking out the town and the beach. There are tons of things to do—paddle boarding, kayaking, snorkeling, even zip lining. I didn't come prepared for snorkeling, so I let Dad talk me into zip lining. Obviously, that's not the time for a deep conversation.

I've zip lined before and it's really cool—a little adrenaline rush swinging through eucalyptus trees.

As we wander the streets, I keep seeing shops that I think Molly would enjoy. Too bad she's not with us. She's been a trooper about letting me spend time with the family, not realizing that I kind of like having her along. And she fit right in the other night at Coastal Kitchen.

Eventually we stop at a restaurant right on the beach for beers and food. We're seated on the deck next to the railing, overlooking the curving beach.

"This is the life," Dad says, smiling. He sets his sunglasses on the table and gazes around.

A table of four women across the deck are eyeing us. And by us, I mean Dad. Jesus. I guess he's not that old, but those women are closer to my age than his.

Once we have cold beers in hand, my gut tightens. Okay, I have to do this. Molly will be disappointed in me if I don't. I'm not sure why her opinion of me matters, but apparently it does. But it's also for me. She's right; I do need to understand better what happened.

I run my hand through my hair, looking away, then take a big gulp of beer and swallow. I look back at Dad. "Can I ask you something?"

His gaze swivels back to me. He arches an eyebrow. "When you have to ask that question first, that means it's something unpleasant."

I gnaw briefly on my bottom lip. "Yeah, I guess that's so."

"Go ahead." He curves both hands around his glass, watching me.

"Why did you and Mom get a divorce?"

His lips tighten, but he nods. "Your mom and I agreed that we wouldn't talk to you kids about the reasons." Then he sighs. "But that was years ago when you were teenagers. The truth is, I made some mistakes in our marriage and…" He drops his gaze briefly. "I was too focused on my career and not enough on my marriage." One corner of his mouth kicks up in a glum smile. "Don't make that mistake."

"Not a worry, since I'm not getting married."

"You will, one day."

"Nope." I pause, then I say it. "I know you cheated on her."

Dad's jaw drops, and his eyes burst wide open. "What?"

"I overheard Mom talking one day after you left. I think she was talking to Betsy." Her friend. "She said you'd betrayed her."

Dad's head moves side to side and he genuinely appears shocked. "I never cheated on her." Then he grimaces. "I understand why she might have thought that, since I was hardly ever home. But I didn't." Now his eyes narrow. "Were those her exact words?"

"Yeah. I think so. It was a while ago."

"She may have felt betrayed, but it wasn't because of another woman."

I don't know what to do with this. Do I believe him? I've spent my entire adult life thinking he's a cheater.

"If it wasn't that…couldn't you have worked things out?" Christ, I sound like a hurt little boy, still hoping for his parents to reconcile.

"We tried. We went for counseling. It helped us communicate better. Well, somewhat. It helped your mom. Actually, she didn't need help. She's a great communicator."

"It *is* kind of her job."

"Yeah." His smile is wistful. "She's the smartest woman I've ever known."

Jesus. I blink at him. He sounds like he still cares. Is that possible?

"I wasn't great at talking about my feelings. In the end, Mom wanted different things and I wasn't…ready to give those to her."

"What did she want?"

"Only things that she shouldn't have had to ask for." Dad's lips droop and he turns his beer glass in his hands. "It was never her fault. I want you to know that."

I huff out a sigh. "I never thought it was her fault. But I thought…"

"You thought I cheated on her."

"Yeah." My chest feels like I'm being squeezed by giant bear paws. My face heats and I take a fast gulp of lager. My mind is scrambled. I don't know what to think. I don't know how I feel.

"Well. I have to say that explains a lot." Dad's voice is quiet. "And it kinda hurts, Jax."

"I know," I choke out. I can't even meet Dad's eyes. My armpits prickle and sweat trickles down my spine.

"I've never claimed to be perfect," he says. "But I at least hoped that I'd demonstrated honesty and integrity to my kids. But then…" He pauses. "I wasn't around as much as I should have been. Especially after the divorce." For a moment, neither of us speak. Then he says, "I guess I deserve your animosity."

"No." I swipe a hand over my damp brow. "No, you don't deserve it. I'm sorry."

"I wish we'd had this talk years ago. But I'm not blaming you for that. You were a kid. I'm your father. I'm sorry, too."

I swallow thickly, my face tight.

He heaves a sigh and drinks his beer. "What a lot of wasted years. Shit."

I choke out a laugh. "Yeah. Shit." I pause. "Also…what a lot of wasted years for you and Grandpa."

Dad's eyes widen, then narrow. Then he closes them, looking like someone's jabbing the butt end of a stick into his nads. "Yeah. I know. I regret that, too." He opens his eyes and his are a little red as he regards me across the table. "I'm proud of you, Jax."

I hold his gaze and it's the most painful thing I've ever done. But I sit a little taller. "Thanks, Dad."

"And I love you." His voice has turned gravelly. "It always bothered me that we didn't spend much time together. I talked to Tori about it, but she couldn't explain it either. It hurt both of us."

I close my eyes, a wave of shame burning through me. "You still talk to Mom?"

"Not as much anymore. But we have two kids together. We have to talk sometimes."

Does he know Mom may be moving here?

Wait. Is *he* the reason she's moving here?

Whoa.

No. It can't be. Just a coincidence. I'm not going to be that kid, yearning and hoping for his parents to get back together. They have separate lives now, and they're both happy and successful.

"I asked Mom why you split up once," I say. "She said the same thing you did—that you weren't going to talk about it to us kids. I get why, but…"

"We didn't want you to blame either of us. It was actually really admirable of your mom, because she could have trashed me to you kids. She probably wanted to." He chuckles dryly. "But she never did."

"I did it myself." I roll my eyes.

"Well. Let's put that behind us." Dad's jaw is tight, and I appreciate the effort he's making. "What's happening with your contract?"

"Ugh. Nothing. It's making me antsy."

"I get it. But Paul's a great agent."

"I know. We talked the other day."

"What kind of comps are they looking at? Panchyshyn in New York? Gagnon in Boston?"

"Yeah. Those two for sure." I shouldn't be surprised Dad nailed it; after all, he's in the business too. But he's a coach, and the fact that he knows the players in the league who are playing like I am and making the kind of money I want to make surprises me a bit.

We talk more about the contract negotiations. We talk about my photography. We talk about Grandpa, and I can see how hard it is for Dad. We even talk about Chelsea, and he says how good she is for Dad and how she's taking care of him and the business and basically fixing the family.

"We hated Chelsea," I say glumly. "We all thought she married Grandpa for his money."

Dad grimaces. "Yeah. I misjudged her. For years. Christ." He rubs his face. "Like I said, I've made some mistakes in my life."

"You know what Mom says about mistakes."

"No. I don't."

I grin. "If you make a mistake, there are three things you should do about it: admit it, learn from it, and don't repeat it."

Dad laughs. "Like I said, she's a smart woman. Honestly, admitting to mistakes is the hardest part. But I'm getting there."

"Have you told Chelsea that?"

His face changes, his jaw slackening. He shifts on his chair. "No."

I tilt my head.

"Guess I should do that, huh?"

Our eyes meet and we share a smile.

Dad lifts his beer. "Thanks, son."

I clink mine against his in a toast. "To not wasting time and missing out."

Molly

Jax and I board the boat in Huntington Beach Sunday afternoon and find seats at the front. The bow of the ship. Forward. Whatever. I don't know much about boats. Also this isn't a ship, it's a catamaran.

I'm bouncing in my seat, looking all around, taking in the boat and the harbor. "I hope we see whales!"

"No guarantee," Jax says, smiling. "But I hope so too."

The air is fresh and cool, the sun warm. I brought a hoodie in case it's chilly out on the ocean.

The first animals we encounter are sea lions, sunning themselves on rocks in the harbor as we slowly cruise out.

"They're so cute! Look at their faces," I say to Jax. I watch in fascination as we sail by them. He snaps a bunch of pictures.

Out of the harbor, the catamaran picks up speed. My hair is blowing all over the place, in my eyes and my mouth, and I futilely try to keep it back. It's barely long enough for a ponytail, even if I had a hair tie.

Jax disappears inside the catamaran, and returns with a baseball cap with the name of the tour company and a whale embroidered on it. "Here." He gives me the hat and holds my hair back as I pull it down.

"Thank you!" I am now free of hair blowing in my face. That was so thoughtful of him.

The tour guide is speaking over a sound system, telling us what kinds of whales and other marine life we may see on the cruise. I look back to the shore, already distant, then turn my face to the sun. The ocean stretches all around us, shimmering cobalt, the Channel Islands shadowy in the distance, achingly beautiful and awe-inspiring.

"Blue whale season is typically from May through November," the guide tells us. "Blue whales are the largest mammal on earth, weighing up to three hundred thousand pounds and reaching up to one hundred ten feet long as adults. That's approximately the length of three school buses."

I shiver with excitement.

Jax has his camera ready to capture images of whatever we see, with a super long lens. He showed me a bunch of pictures he took on the helicopter trip yesterday and then Catalina Island, and they were amazing.

"Unfortunately, the blue whale species is on the federally endangered species list. We'll talk more about blue whale endangerment and the threats this species faces today."

"Oh no. I hate it that they're endangered." I pout at Jax. "Humans suck."

He snaps a picture of me and I roll my eyes.

"Can I get some of your pictures from today?" I ask. "I want to show my students what I did over the summer. They'd love hearing about whales and dolphins."

"Of course."

We cruise along for a while and then the boat slows.

"Okay, folks, on the port side of the boat—that's the left

side for those who may not know—we have a pod of common dolphins."

Jax and I are seated near the left side, so we jump to the railing to peer over.

I point excitedly. "There!"

Jax has his camera focused, clicking away.

The dolphins are swimming fast, and some are jumping out of the water. I clap with delight at their acrobatics. "There are so many of them!"

A lightness fills my chest and I bounce on my tiptoes. I try to take a few pictures with my phone, but I know they'll suck compared to Jax's. Everyone around is excited, too, lots of kids overjoyed to see the playful creatures.

The dolphins accompany the boat, and I happily watch them until our guide announces we should look out at three o'clock where he's spotted a spout of water, which is likely a whale, and they're heading toward it.

Jax and I stay by the railing. I'm holding my breath in anticipation. It seems to take a long time and I've almost given up, when water erupts near the boat. Everyone shouts and my eyes widen.

The whale comes to the surface and the boat gets closer still. Jax is taking pictures like crazy and I'm breathless and laughing as I see the curve of the back of the huge mammal.

"It's a blue whale," the guide says. "A small one."

"That's *small?*" I smile. "Wow."

The surface of the water bubbles and sparkles as he goes down, but another spout announces him and then his shiny back arcs out of the water again, graceful and majestic. I'm lost in wonderment.

There's another spray of water, a whoosh of air, the whale coming even closer to the stopped boat.

"He's really curious about us," the guide says.

As he surfaces again, everyone on the boat oohs and ahhs.

"Unbelievable," Jax says, a huge grin on his face.

I take my eyes off the whale briefly to watch Jax, who's as delighted and mesmerized as I am. I love his smile, the way it lights up his eyes. My heart skips a beat. I take another picture with my phone, this time of him.

I turn back to the whale, gripping the railing, blinking fiercely. So much beauty.

The next time the whale dives down, his tail comes out of the water resplendently. It's an amazing moment.

"If we don't see anything else, this trip was worth it," I say to Jax a while later when the whale has disappeared deep into the ocean.

"Totally. That was fantastic."

But we also see a humpback whale, and more dolphins, this time bottlenose dolphins that are even cuter than the common dolphins.

"I want one of those!" I tell Jax, making him laugh.

"Sure, you can keep it in your bathtub in Chicago."

"Ha ha. Okay, okay, I can't have one. But I can dream. They're amazing!"

We return to the harbor after about two and half hours out on the ocean. My skin feels tight from the wind and maybe a little sunburnt, even though I used sunscreen, and my hair is tangled beneath the baseball cap, but I feel blissful and contented.

"Thank you so much for bringing me here," I tell Jax as we make our way to the car in the nearby parking lot. "That was one of the best experiences of my life."

He doesn't say anything for a few seconds, then replies gruffly, "Good. I loved it too."

13

JAX

It's our last night here in California.

We're in bed together, with those goddamn pillows between us. Quiet darkness settles over us.

"Jax?"

I turn at Molly's whisper. My eyes have adjusted to the dark, and I can just make out her face on the pillow. She's lying on her side, facing me. "Yeah?"

"Thank you for bringing me here. It's been an amazing trip."

"It has." I didn't think it was a good idea, but I have to admit I've had fun with Molly. I've spent time with my family and time alone with her, and time with her *and* my family. Grandpa loves her, and so does everyone else, apparently, since Molly, Everly, Taylor and Lacey have all connected on social media like best buddies.

"I'm so glad I had this time to process things after the wedding. You've been so kind to me."

I roll to my side, pull my arm from beneath the duvet and

reach over to close my fingers around hers where they rest on her pillow. "I haven't done anything."

"You have, and you know it. I just want you to know I appreciate it. I feel like…" She pauses. "Like we're better friends now. Right?"

Friends.

I really like Molly. I *do* consider her a friend. But over the past week, getting to know her better, spending time in close proximity with her, I have many distinctly unfriendlike ideas about her. Fantasies. Even dreams about her. I want to do dirty things with her, things I definitely wouldn't do with a friend.

Her fingers move under mine, turning so we're holding hands. Heat sweeps through my body, straight to my dick. I push a pillow down so there's nothing between our faces and we're looking at each other in the shadows. There's not much distance between us. I want to taste her mouth. Lick inside. Devour her.

My heart thuds erratically against my ribs, so hard I think she can hear it.

"Yeah," I finally rasp out. "Friends."

She swallows. Moments accumulate, hot and heavy and brimming with emotion. Her lips part. My mouth is ravenous for her. My body vibrates with repressed need.

"Jax…"

"Mmmm."

Her lips curve up at the corners into the sweetest smile. "Thank you again."

My head moves on my pillow in acknowledgement. Words pile up in my brain but I don't know which ones to say. I don't know anything right now. "It was my pleasure, Molly. Really." After another moment of silence, I say, "My dad didn't cheat on my mom."

I hear her suck in a breath. "What? Really?"

"Yeah. I asked him about it."

I'd told her that we had a nice trip to Catalina and a good talk, but not the details. I haven't really figured out how I feel about it or what to do about it, since my entire belief system about love and marriage has been based on this illusion. But now, here in the darkness, in bed, it feels safe to tell her. I *want* to tell her.

"How do you feel about that?" she asks quietly.

"I'm still not sure." I tell her about why I believed that all these years and what Dad said.

"I'm sorry," she whispers, her fingers tightening on mine. "I'm sorry you've missed out on the kind of relationship with your dad that you should have had."

"Yeah." An invisible fist squeezes my throat. "I'm sorry too. It was my fault, though."

"Not entirely. He could have sat down with you and asked you what was going on."

"He wasn't around much."

"Well, that's on him, too. You were a kid."

My heart expands at how she's trying to make me feel better. "I guess we're both responsible."

"The good thing is, you've straightened it out now, and you can build a relationship with him."

"Yeah. He's going to try to come to Chicago or maybe even to the lake while I'm there so we can hang out more."

"That's so great. I'm happy for you."

"Thanks. I probably wouldn't have done that if it weren't for you."

Our eyes meet and hold again. Unspoken words flow between us, a thrumming cord of connection and understanding.

"I don't want to go home tomorrow," she blurts out.

I kind of feel that way, too. "I know. But we have to."

"I'm dreading the rest of the summer, back in my apartment, doing nothing. That wasn't how my summer was supposed to be." Her voice trembles and I feel the emotion radiating off her.

My heart contracts sharply. If I was staying in Chicago, I could make sure she's okay. Maybe go out to the odd trivia night. But I'm leaving again in a couple of days. How can I make it better? "Come with me to Canada."

The air goes very still around us and Molly is motionless too, staring at me.

Did I really just say that?

After a drawn-out moment, she says, "I can't do that."

"Why not?" Why am I pushing this? I tried to discourage her from coming with me to California, now I'm inviting her to come to Canada.

"Because…I already imposed on you and your family once. I can't do it again."

"You're not imposing at all." I smile. "My family freakin' loves you. And I just told you I had fun too. We'll have fun in the boreal forest."

Her forehead furrows. "Forest? For real? I'm kind of a city girl."

I chuckle. "I'm kidding. There's lots of forest if we want to go hiking, but my grandparents' cottage has all the amenities."

She falls silent again, seemingly contemplating this.

"It'll just be me at the cottage, mostly," I continue. "My grandparents and my mom are coming for a few days later in July. Maybe my dad. So you're not imposing." I pause. "You can even have your own bedroom."

"Oh, well then, why didn't you say that?" She laughs softly. "Really, Jax?"

"Yes, really. You don't have to stay the whole summer, like I am. I mean, I'll be back in Chicago mid-August to start skating and working out. But you could come back whenever you want."

"I suppose. School doesn't start again until after Labor Day." She blinks a few times. "I know I have to talk to Steve, but he won't be back until July 5, I think."

"You can fly back to Chicago after that, if you want."

"I know I have to deal with things."

"Yeah."

Her smile deepens. "Okay. I'll come with you." Then her eyes close, her long eyelashes sweeping her cheeks, and her mouth relaxes. I watch her face for a long time in the dark, as her breathing grows deeper, until I fall asleep, too.

Holding her hand.

In the morning, I awaken to find Molly snuggled up against me and my arm over her hip. For a few seconds, I enjoy it, reveling in the feel of a soft, warm woman against me, her silky hair so close to me, her scent in my nose. Then reality bites me in the ass.

Jesus! Did *I* do this?

She wakes up too. Slowly. Then her eyes fly open and she jerks back.

Our eyes meet.

The room is still dark, the curtains drawn over the window and sliding door.

My body goes electric, heat burning over my skin. "God. I'm sorry, Molly." I release her and shift myself away.

"It's okay." She blinks, pushing back too.

The pillows are amassed at the foot of the bed. "I don't know how that happened. I'm so sorry."

"It's okay," she says again. "I don't feel violated."

Her attempt at humor lightens the air in the room. A little. My morning wood is throbbing and it's all I can do to stop myself from reaching for her and rolling her under me.

"Good," I manage to say. "Me either."

She chuckles. "We were asleep. It was just…"

Okay, I don't know if it was me or her who shoved the pillows out of the way. I don't know if she rolled into me, or I pulled her over. What I do know is, I wanted that, and somehow in my sleep it happened and it was probably my fault.

"Yeah." I roll out of bed, keeping my back to her, because the stiffy in my boxers is enormous. "It just happened. I'm gonna jump in the shower."

And whack one out.

It feels so damn good, leaning against the tiled wall, water streaming down on me, my hand gripping my cock and tugging rapidly until the pressure builds and builds, and my groan as I come is lost in the spray of water.

I stay like that in the cloud of steam for a moment, catching my breath, my thighs quivering.

When I played in Philly, one of the players was screwing around with another player's wife for months. Everyone else knew about it but him. Until they day he found out. The two of them got in an actual fight during practice. They both ended up in trouble, and it affected the atmosphere in the room for months. We lost game after game, and I still think that was part of it. Things only got better when they traded Baxter away.

I don't want to cause something like that in Chicago. I *can't* cause something like that. I don't even have a contract signed yet, for Chrissake. There's no way I can even think about touching Molly.

Okay, it's not like anything actually happened. We were just snuggled up together. Two people wanting…connection.

Bullshit. But I'll keep telling myself that.

"You're sure he's away?"

"Yeah." She frowns. "That's what Grace said."

"I don't want to come in there and run into him."

We're at Chucky's place so Molly can pick up some things, including her car and apartment keys. We just flew in, and it's late Tuesday.

"You can wait here if you want," she says. "I'll go up and get stuff."

I'm tempted, but I should at least help her. If I run into Chucky, well, we'll deal with it. "No, that's okay. I'll come up."

We leave my vehicle in the loading zone out front and she uses her code to access the elevator then his condo. I've been here before, many times, but it's weird walking into a team-mate's home with him not there.

Molly's chin is set determinedly as she moves around gathering things up. She finds a big suitcase and fills it with clothes, toiletries from the bathroom, and a few framed pictures of her and her friends sitting on a shelf in the living room. She leaves the pictures of her and Chucky. Then she picks up a trophy and buries it among the clothes.

"What's that?" I ask.

She rolls her eyes. "I was on the Top Team in high school. It's a national trivia game show. In senior year, we won the championship."

"I know what it is. I'm impressed."

She stands in the middle of the living room and looks around. "I guess that's it for now. I can get the rest of my things later."

"What's left in your apartment?"

"Nothing." One corner of her mouth hitches. "I was trying to sublet it. I got rid of anything I didn't take with me here."

"You're coming to my place, then."

Her eyes expand. We haven't discussed this. "I can't do that."

I sigh. "Molly. You begged me to take you there the night of the wedding."

"I know, but…" She swallows.

We both know things are different now. We're both not going to address that.

"Okay." She blows out a breath. "I could go to my parents' place, or maybe Grace's, but…"

"We're flying to Winnipeg on Friday morning. It's no big deal to stay with me a few days."

She nods, not meeting my eyes.

"It's fine, Molly. We're friends, right?"

Her head bobs again. "Right."

I help her carry things down. We put some in her car, some in my SUV, then I drive home. The air feels flat and stale after ten days away. First thing I do is turn down the air conditioning, then slide open the doors onto my balcony to get some fresh air in.

Molly arrives a few minutes later with another suitcase. I carry it into the spare room she stayed in last time we were here. "I don't have much food. We can order something in. Pizza okay?"

"Of course."

"We've been eating mostly restaurant food for a while. I'd like something home-cooked, but since I'm leaving again, it's not worth going grocery shopping. I'll pick up a few things in the morning though."

Molly goes into the bedroom, leaving the door open a crack, while I order a pizza. I hear her moving around in there, but I want to give her privacy. I'm sure it's hard being back in town and back to reality.

It's hard for me, for fuck's sake.

Molly

I've been to my parents' place and talked to them. They were worried sick about me, despite my phone calls and text messages assuring them I was fine. I feel guilty for disappearing like I did, but I don't regret it. It was just what I needed. I apologized for that and for the scene I made at the wedding. Like Jax, they think I should have talked to Steve first, but they understand and are totally supportive of my decision. So that's good. They also were glad that I'd been in contact with Katelyn to deal with wedding cancellation issues.

I get together with Grace and Brielle. My third bridesmaid Allison has gone home to New York.

My bridesmaids were the only ones who knew what I was going to do at the wedding. The fallout from that didn't surprise them. What did surprise them was me disappearing.

"Okay, where did you go?" Grace demands. We're at her house. Her fiancé has gone out, and we're drinking cocktails and eating appies for our girls' night in.

"I went to California."

"Ooh, good choice." She picks up a crab Rangoon. "Why there?"

I bite my lip and look from Grace to Brielle. "Okay, I'll tell you, but you guys have to swear secrecy about this."

Eyes widen. They exchange glances.

"Swear," Grace says, and Brielle nods.

"I was there with Jax."

They both freeze, enormous eyes staring at me.

"Jax?" Grace says carefully. "Jax Wynn?"

"Yes. He came to check on me while you were all beating up on Steve. I asked him to get me out of there. We went to his place. He was leaving the next day to go visit family in California, and I begged him to take me with him. I couldn't face anyone, especially Steve."

"Wow," Brielle breathes.

Grace gulps down her strawberry Moscato cocktail.

"We're friends," I add. "You know that."

"Right."

I grin. "We even did a trivia night there. We won."

"Of course."

"He's a great guy," I say. "But seriously, don't say anything to anyone. If this gets back to any of his teammates—especially Steve—there could be problems. I don't want to cause him any trouble when he was just helping me out."

"Oh yeah, there could be problems, all right." Brielle slides her head from side to side. "Wow.

"Nothing happened between us," I say, ignoring the fact that we woke up snuggled together our last morning there. Ignoring all the times I wanted to kiss him or touch him or… "Nothing."

"Okay. We won't say a word." Grace picks up a paper napkin.

I tell them about what we did, and the time I had to think about things. "I know I need to talk to Steve, and I will. He's not here anyway."

Grace wrinkles her nose. "Yeah…about that."

"What?"

"He's been posting pics on social media. It seems like he's not alone, but there aren't any pictures of him with anyone."

Brielle clears her throat. "I think if he was with a friend, like a teammate, they'd show pictures together."

"Shit." I stare down at my pink drink. "You think he's with Claire?"

"We don't know for sure. But it seems like, yeah." Brielle pushes out her bottom lip. "He's scum."

"Why didn't you tell me that before I agreed to marry him?" I ask.

Their faces all register surprise.

"I'm kidding!" I add hastily. "I'm not blaming you all. I should have known he was scum."

"I didn't think he *was* scum, before the wedding," Grace says glumly. "I feel like I missed a hell of a lot, too."

Brielle flashes me a guilty glance. "I knew he was scum. He hit on me once."

My jaw drops. "Shut up!"

"Yeah." Her mouth twists into a sardonic curve. "I should have told you. But…I thought I was doing the right thing by not telling you. You were so happy."

"When did that happen?"

"Just before you got engaged, when we were all at Orion. I shut him down right away and told him to never say anything like that to me again." She sighs. "I'm so sorry, Mol."

My shoulders slump briefly. "Our whole relationship was a lie."

"I don't know what to say," Grace replies softly. "I'm sorry this happened to you. I'm sorry you got hurt. We're here for you."

"Thank you. I know." I straighten and toss back the rest of my strawberry Moscato. "I'm okay. Really. I'm sure I'll learn something from this." I make a sound of dry amusement. "Actually, I already did. Love isn't real and marriage is stupid."

"Oh no." Grace shakes her head in dismay. "Don't be like that."

"Sorry, I know *your* love is real and your marriage will be perfect. I just mean for me. That's one thing Jax and I have in common. He feels the same."

"Mmmm. Okay." Grace's eyes slide sideways to Brielle, then quickly back to me. "I hate it that you're so cynical. Don't give up on love because of one asshole."

"Eh. We'll see." I pick up a stuffed mushroom. "I'm going to go away again for a while, since Steve isn't here."

"Where to now?" Brielle asks.

"Canada. With Jax." Seeing their expressions, I hold up a hand. "We're just friends! Again, he was planning to go there anyway, and I didn't want to hang out here waiting for Steve to show up—" I pause. "With Claire," I add disdainfully. "So he asked me to come with him."

This is all met with silence and poker faces. I eat my mushroom.

"What? It's fine. This is delicious. I want the recipe."

"Well, good for you," Brielle says. "Have all the fun. Why not?"

"I'm not sure I agree." Grace glances around. "The more time you spend with Jax, the more chance there is that something *will* happen."

"So what?" Brielle asks. "What if it does? They're both single. Neither of them is looking for a relationship. He can be your rebound," she adds, looking at me.

My eyebrows shoot up. "Rebound?"

"Yeah. The first relationship after a breakup is always a rebound."

"Hmm." I consider that. "Well, I'm not even looking for a rebound."

"I suppose that's true," Grace says slowly, apparently unconvinced. "I just wouldn't want you to get hurt again."

I roll my eyes. "I'm not getting hurt, because it's not like that. I'm going to a lake cabin to commune with nature and relax. It's summer, I'm on vacation, and I didn't get to go to Europe. Unlike Steve." I screw up my face.

"That's true." Grace smiles. "You do whatever you want and have fun."

"Thanks."

14

MOLLY

I'm doing what I want, and I'm going to have fun.

I survived another flight and we're in Winnipeg.

All I know about Winnipeg it that it's the home of the Jets. Jax laughed at me when I asked him if I needed warm clothes for this trip. Then he admitted that I would need a sweater or hoodie for at night, as it gets cool up at the lake.

And sure enough, it's a beautiful day as we leave the airport in another rental car, warm and sunny. Jax's first stop is visiting his grandparents.

"I don't need to meet your grandparents," I tell him. "Maybe you can drop me off somewhere. A shopping mall or something."

He eyes me. "You sure?"

"Yes. The fewer people who know about me being here, the better."

"Huh. I guess that's true. Okay, there's a new outlet mall not far from them. I'll leave you there and pick you up in a couple of hours."

"That sounds good."

Not that I need to do more shopping. I've reclaimed my belongings and now have ample clothes, toiletries and my beloved Kindle. But I can hang out there and grab something to eat.

He points out the modern new condo building where his grandparents live as we pass it, then turns into the parking lot of the mall. We make a note of which entrance we're at and he says he'll pick me up at four o'clock. Apparently it's about a three-hour drive to the lake.

I pass a couple of hours easily, with a stop at Starbucks and an impulse purchase of a pair of shoes that are fifty percent off at Saks Off Fifth.

Jax smirks when he sees my shopping bag. I toss it in the back seat and climb in. "What's so funny?"

"You like shopping, don't you? I could tell that day at Target."

I pull my seatbelt down and across my body. "Yes, I admit it. But we're going into the wilderness, and I won't be able to shop, right?"

"Um...not exactly."

"There's a shopping mall at the lake?"

"Not a mall, no. But there are shops."

"Oh. Cool! Now I'm even more excited."

He laughs and pulls out onto a wide street heading west. "I don't know if they'll be your kind of shopping."

We pass the drive chatting and listening to music. I gaze around in fascination as we cross the prairie, flat and open, the sky enormous above us. Farmland stretches out on either side of the highway.

Jax turns off the Trans-Canada Highway to head north on what is called the Yellowhead Highway, and we pass a town called Gladstone. There's the cutest statue with the name "Happy Rock" painted on it.

"Get it?" Jax asks. "Happy Rock? Gladstone?"

"Ha ha. Hilarious." It is funny

Then we arrive at Neepawa.

"Are you hungry?" Jax asks.

"Yeah, I am."

"Good. There's a drive-in here we can stop at."

It's also cute. Jax orders a ton of food including a hamburger, perogies and onion rings. I stick with a burger and a milkshake, but I pilfer one onion ring. We eat at a picnic table on the small patio, then climb back in the car.

"Are we almost there?" I ask plaintively.

Jax laughs. "Yeah. Not much father."

This part of the drive is a change of scenery, with huge rolling hills and valleys, and more trees. Finally we arrive at our destination—Riding Mountain National Park.

"We have to make one stop before we go into the park," Jax says, turning off the highway and into the parking lot of a hardware store. "We need booze."

"Um, at the hardware store?"

He grins. "Yep."

We pick up beer, wine and tequila, then we're back on our journey and entering the park. We actually have to wait in a line of cars at the booth, where Jax purchases a seasonal pass. In a moment, we're cruising through a quaint little town with shops and restaurants and log cabin structures. Not what I expected!

"This is Wasagaming," Jax tells me.

We round a curve and drive along the lake. It's now evening, but still fully daylight with lots of people strolling the beach and walking the sidewalks.

"That lake is amazing!" I gaze at the incredible blue in awe.

"Clear Lake," Jax replies. "The town name, Wasagaming, is a Cree word meaning clear water. We'll see more of it."

We progress a couple of blocks, and Jax turns left into a driveway and rolls to a stop. Made of logs, and with a big fieldstone chimney, the cabin sits nestled among tall pine and aspen trees. On one side, Craftsman-style tapered columns with fieldstone bases support a wide porch. It's old-world picturesque, like nothing I've ever stayed in.

Jax carries our suitcases to the door of the porch and fishes a key out of his pocket. After unlocking the door, he pushes inside with the bags and I follow behind. Through another locked door, we enter a big living room. Here I see the fireplace the chimney is attached to centered on the wall, built of the same fieldstone. A big window on one side and sliding doors on the other side look out onto a deck, and beyond that the lake. The walls, ceiling and floor are all wood, out of date but charming.

"The place is a little old fashioned," Jax says apologetically.

The furniture is clearly well-used—upholstered sofas and chairs, antique tables and a worn rug on the floor. It's clean and cared-for, though. The kitchen is open to the living room, with an antique hutch, a round dining table surrounded with pressback chairs, and cabinets that probably date back to the 1950s.

"It's amazing."

"My grandparents don't get up here much anymore, and neither do my mom or her sister, but they don't want to lose the cottage. These things are passed down for generations here in the park."

"I can see why."

"There are three bedrooms, like I promised." He grins. "You can have the master bedroom."

"No, no, you take it. You're family."

"There's only one bathroom, unfortunately."

"We'll survive."

He wheels my suitcase into a small bedroom with lots more

wood paneling. A pretty quilt covers the bed, and a bookcase holds tons of books. "I love it."

"The sofas in the living room all make out into beds, so this place can hold a lot of people when needed."

I run my hand over the white dresser and admire the framed photograph of a sunset over the lake on the wall. "That must be Clear Lake," I say, nodding.

"Yeah. I took that, years ago."

"Oh, really?" I look closer. "It's beautiful."

"Thanks."

Now I notice there are a lot of nature photos which are all probably Jax's. "I'm sure you want to take a lot of pictures while you're here."

"Yeah, I hope so. If you want to wash up and unpack a bit, go ahead. I'll open things up and meet you out on the deck."

I use the bathroom and change into a pair of cropped leggings and a loose tank top. I eye the bed longingly. After traveling all day, I'd love to stretch out there. But I'll go see if Jax needs any help.

When I walk out onto the deck in my flip flops, he hands me a glass of wine.

I smile with delight. "Thank you!"

Then I spy a lounge chair. Jax has already arranged cushions on the all the furniture, bless him. I head straight to it, adjust the back so it's reclining, and flop down onto it. I let out a gusty sigh. "Okay. I'm in heaven."

I'm looking out over the lake, through some trees and bushes, although there's a path leading to the beach. I think I can see a wooden dock, and I'm eager to explore more at some point. Right now I'm content to lie back with my wine and enjoy the view.

Jax takes a seat, a beer in hand. "Yeah, this is pretty nice."

"Totally different from California. And yet…kind of the

same too. Nature and water and peace. It's beautiful." I breathe in the air, cool and scented with fir trees.

"I loved spending summers here. Riley and I had friends here, and we'd ride our bikes all over and get in trouble."

I smile at that. "What kind of trouble?"

"Nothing illegal. We caught minnows. Once I stuffed one down a friend's shorts."

I laugh.

"Caught crayfish. We'd build little ponds to keep them in along with the minnows. Raced our bikes, tipped each other out of canoes, bought bags of candy at the store."

"That sound so…wholesome."

"Tomorrow I'll chop some wood for the fireplace. And we'll need to pick up food."

"You're going to chop wood?" I lift my head to stare at him.

"Sure."

"Eek."

"What?"

"Don't cut your foot off. That would end your hockey career."

He laughs. "I'll be careful."

He's changed too, into a pair of shorts and a T-shirt. He crosses one ankle over the other knee in a relaxed pose, gazing out over the lake also. His face is peaceful, his mouth curved into a slight smile.

He's a beautiful man. Physically, of course; I've admired his hard-packed abs, strong shoulders and muscular thighs and butt. His face is lean and sculpted, with thick eyebrows, carved lips and cobalt eyes that all the Wynns seem to have. I always knew he was fun and charming, popular with everyone. But now I've had glimpses at what's beneath all that, and I think he doesn't let on how much he feels things because he feels them so deeply. He's caring and thoughtful and intelligent, and that just makes him even more attractive.

I shouldn't be attracted to him.

I'm hyper aware of him sitting near me. The only sounds are the rustling of the aspens, birds chirping, a squirrel squawking crazily in a tree. It's so hard not to reach out and touch him. I grip my wine glass with both hands and stare determinedly forward.

"I hope you won't get bored here," Jax says.

I roll my head toward him. "We just got here."

"I mean, after a while. It's pretty quiet here. We won't be partying or shopping or having spa days."

"Jeez. Is that what you think of me? Parties and spas and shopping sprees?"

"No, no! That's not what I meant. But you said yourself, you're a city girl."

"It's beautiful here. I won't be bored. Don't worry about me. Just do what you want to do. I don't need babysitting."

"You're hardly a baby," he mutters.

I'm not sure what he means by that. He almost sounds angry. Hmm.

I let a few moments pass and then say, "I missed sleeping with you the last few nights."

Jax chokes on his beer. "Jesus, Molly."

I laugh. "You know I mean sleeping as in sleeping, not boinking."

He coughs again. But if I wanted him to say he missed me too, he doesn't. Damn.

What am I doing? I swallow a sigh.

Jax gets up and ambles inside, returning with another beer and the bottle of wine. He refills my glass.

"Thanks."

"So what kinds of things we can do here?"

"Well, we don't have a boat anymore, but we can rent one at the pier. We can fish or water ski."

Now I'm the one choking. "I can't water ski."

He grins. "Okay."

"And I don't think I want to fish either."

"That's okay, I'm not that much into fishing."

I huff. "Tell me things *you* want to do, then."

"We have a canoe. That might be more your speed."

I give him a reproving look, even though he's right.

"There are tennis courts and a golf course. It's a great course. There's the beach, obviously. Different beaches. We can go out to the wishing well. There's a bison enclosure at Lake Audy."

"Bison?" I perk up. "That would be cool."

"Yeah, it is. Maybe we'll see a bear or some moose."

My eyes widen. "Bear?"

"Yeah, they wander around all over the place here."

I glance nervously at the bushes and sit up straighter.

He laughs. "I'm kidding. Well, there are bears, and they *have* been seen in town on occasion, but don't worry."

"Oh my God! Of course I'm worried. Bears!"

"There are also the shops and restaurants and the interpretive center. I think there are still bikes here, but we might have to pump up the tires. Or we could rent bikes. And there are lots of hiking trails. We should definitely do that."

"Will there be bears?"

"Possibly."

I'm a little nervous about this.

"If we make enough noise, they won't come near us," he assures me.

"Mmmm."

"You sound doubtful."

"I don't want to be eaten by a bear."

"I remember when I was a kid, there was a problem with bears in town getting into the garbage. They brought in a bear trap, and one day we walked by and there was one in it."

"Yikes. Was it…" I cringe. "Dead?"

"No, it was a live trap. But he wasn't too happy. We were fascinated."

"What do they do with them when they catch them? They don't kill them, do they?"

"No, no. They take them into the back woods and release them. Anyway, it's why we're careful with the garbage here. Most of the refuse bins are bear proof."

"Good, good." I wipe a damp palm surreptitiously on my leggings.

"There's lots of other wildlife we might see too—fox, moose, deer, elk." He pauses. "Cougars."

"Oh, come on! *Cougars?*"

"There are some, but we won't likely see them."

"I think you're trying to scare me so I'll go home."

He laughs softly. "Not at all, Flynn. But I am amusing myself."

"Jerk." But I slant him a smile.

We sit out on the deck until the sun goes down, which is really late here because we're farther north. It's lovely, the air still warm and soft and freshly scented. But soon after darkness falls, the mosquitoes arrive.

"Jesus!" I slap at my arm. "I'm being attacked."

"Uh oh. Let's go in, then."

"Aren't they biting you?"

"No. They never bother me."

"Well, *that's* totally not fair."

Inside, the windows are open to air out the cottage, but the screens keep the bugs out. I settle onto the couch.

"There's enough wood here for a fire," Jax says. "I'll get one going."

"That would be nice."

"I'll see if there's bug spray around. There are usually a few cans of Deep Woods Off here."

He opens the damper and sets to building a fire, looking impressively competent.

Jesus. I'm getting turned on watching him start a fire.

"Were you a Boy Scout?" I ask.

He laughs. "Nope. Never had time for that. Hockey took all my time."

"Mmmm. I guess. But you know how to chop wood and start a fire and water ski."

"That's just from spending summers here. Grandpa made me chop wood, and I learned to start a fire from him."

"And you learned to play hockey from your other grandpa."

He flashes me a smile as he strikes a match. "Yeah."

Soon the fire is blazing. With the darkness beyond the windows, it's so cozy and charming I could just melt into a puddle of bliss. "I want to stay here forever," I announce.

"Yeah?" He takes a seat on the couch too, at the other end. "Even with mosquitoes?"

"Bastards. I'll douse myself in DEET. It'll be fine."

We exchange a smile, full of contentment, tranquility and…okay, a little tingle between my thighs. And when Jax's eyes darken and his mouth softens as he looks at me, I think he feels something too.

I think about what Brielle said—what would be wrong if something happened? Jax and I are both single. Neither of us is looking for any kind of relationship.

But I know this isn't the right guy to be my "rebound." He's Steve's teammate. That's a huge complication. It wouldn't be fair to put Jax in that position. Except…nobody knows we're here. Other than my girls. And they won't tell anyone.

Heat starts low inside me and spreads through me until I feel like I'm glowing like the fire.

No. We can't do that.

15

JAX

We spend the next few days touring around the park. We wander out onto the pier to gaze at the water, walk the town and explore the shops, which delights Molly, and swim in the lake, which does *not* delight Molly.

"Holy shit, this water is cold!" she squeals on our first venture in.

"Yeah." I grin. "It takes a hardy soul to swim in Clear Lake."

"I'm hardy."

I raise an eyebrow. Luckily it's a hot day, so we'll warm up fast when we come out. She's only in up to her knees. "I'll help you…" I start toward her purposefully.

"Okay, fine." She plunges in.

I laugh and follow her. Oh yeah, the cold water takes my breath away. "You get used to it," I tell her when we both surface, reminding myself too.

"If you say so." She sets out swimming in an attempt to stay warm, I think. "Are all Canadian lakes this cold?"

"No. This one is cold because it's so deep. It's also very rocky, which is why it's so clear."

Of course I have to dive deep and grab her foot to try to drag her down. I already know she's a good swimmer. She fights me, laughing, and I end up with her in my arms, both of us wet and slippery and staring at each other. Suddenly the water doesn't feel cold anymore.

We separate at the same time, forcing laughs, and head back to the beach to lay on our towels and warm up in the sun.

July 1 is Canada Day, so there are all kinds of activities going on to celebrate. We listen to music at the bandstand, dancing in the crowd, bare feet on the grass, then sit on a blanket near the beach to watch the fireworks set off on the end of the pier explode into color and light over the dark lake. I find Molly's enthralled face almost more entertaining than the pyrotechnics, and she leans her shoulder into mine at one particularly breathtaking display. I slide my arm around her, holding her there. I know I shouldn't. But she doesn't move away.

Every nerve ending in my body is on alert with her next to me, her hand on my knee, her smile glowing as bright as the fireworks. I want to lower her to the grass and kiss the breath out of her beneath the sparkling sky.

And when they're done, we gather up our stuff and as we trudge across the lawn in the dark I hold her hand so as not to lose her in the crowd.

Back at the cottage, we go to our separate rooms. It's getting harder and harder to do that.

She told me she missed sleeping with me.

Christ, I miss it too, except I want so much more than just sleeping with her. It's becoming torturous, and I almost regret inviting her to come here with me, except that if I hadn't, she wouldn't be here, and well, it's tough to regret being with

Molly. She's like sunshine and glowing flames and starlight. I love how happy she is about everything I show her, full of questions and appreciation for the history and the beauty of this place that's so special to me. It's not new or fancy, but it's comfortable and familiar.

Tomorrow I have something special planned, if the weather cooperates.

And it does.

"We're going out later," I tell her after dinner the next evening. "So don't fall asleep."

She tilts her head and gives me side-eye. "You told me no late-night parties."

"Ha ha. It's sort of a party. Dress warm and bring the bug spray."

"Hmm. I'm curious."

We're watching TV, thanks to the satellite I installed on the roof a few years ago. I check a sports news channel, because as of yesterday, the free agency period began.

"Holy shit." I stare at the TV and the news that two of my teammates, Olaf Pilkvist and Gabe Gandy, who are unrestricted free agents, have signed big contracts with other teams.

"What?"

Molly understands how it works and we discuss it. "We knew the team couldn't keep all of us because of the cap. But they let Pilker and Gander go." I shake my head.

"That's good news for you, right?"

"Maybe?" I'd like to think so. "That definitely frees up cap space."

Gander is one of my best buddies on the team. This sucks. But it's a business.

I head into the bedroom to grab my phone so I can text my former teammates my congrats. These sound like great deals, especially for Gander, who's a fourth-line winger. He played great for us last year, but I think it had more to do with his line-mates than his own talents. Not being snarky, just realistic. Fans love him, though, because he's gritty, so it's kind of a loss for the team.

As we continue to watch TV, Molly dozes off. I let her sleep because it has to be really dark before we go. And I kind of like watching her sleep, admiring the smooth curve of one cheek, the shape of her lips, her bright silky hair spread on the dark cushion.

When I nudge her awake later, she's a tad grumpy.

"What?" she mumbles. "What are you doing?" She frowns blearily at me. "What's going on?"

"We're going out, remember?"

"Ugh. I don't want to. I just want to sleep." She closes her eyes again.

"Come on. It's the perfect night for it."

She grumbles but hoists herself off the couch, wiping her mouth. "I think I was drooling."

"Maybe a bit." She wasn't.

She trudges into the bathroom, then the bedroom, returning dressed in long pants, socks and a hoodie. I've already changed and have a big duffel bag packed with the things we need.

"Where are we going?" she whines as we climb into the car.

I have to smile. "You'll see."

A few minutes later I pull into the gravel parking lot of the Cove. I haven't brought Molly here yet. It's an open area for boat launching, which of course is not happening at this time of night. We're the only ones here.

I lead her out onto one of the docks. It's a floating dock and it rises and falls gently beneath us.

I drop the bag and pull out a double sleeping bag. I spread it on the wooden surface and pull out two cushions then the thermos of red wine and a plastic container of crackers and cheese.

"A late-night picnic?" She sits beside me on the sleeping bag.

"Sort of." The distinctive odor of Deep Woods Off reaches my nose. Not Molly's usual perfume, but she's still sexy.

"I am kind of hungry." She reaches for a cracker.

I pour wine into a plastic glass and hand it to her.

"Thank you. This is…fun?"

I grin. "Look at the stars."

She tips her head back and gazes upward. Above us, the Milky Way shimmers. Thank God it's a clear night. "Wow," she says slowly. "Look at them…so many…"

"Yeah." I lay down, shoving a cushion under my head. "Amazing, isn't it?"

"You don't see stars like this in the city." Then she swats at her face. "Damn."

"I thought you sprayed yourself."

"I did. They're coming for my face." She pulls up the hood of her sweatshirt and tightens the drawstring around her face so all I can see is her eyes, nose and mouth.

I can't help the snort of laughter that bursts from my lips.

"What?" she glares at me.

"You look cute."

"By cute, you mean stupid. I don't care." She too lies back.

She really is adorable.

"Look over there." I point across the lake. "See that faint glow?"

"Yes."

"That's the Northern Lights."

"That's kind of disappointing."

"Just wait. Hopefully it will get better."

The pale gray haze just above the far shoreline of the lake shimmers and shifts.

"I saw a falling star!" Molly points. "I have to make a wish."

My heart squeezes and I smile. "What did you wish for?"

"I can't tell you that! It has to be a secret."

"Ah." Then a faint green line appears along one edge of the gray haze. "Look now."

"Ohhhh." Molly's wide-eyed.

The green intensifies, moving and changing shape, so slowly and faintly.

"This is amazing!" Molly whispers to the dark sky.

We lie on the dock and watch as the lights grow bigger and deeper green against the indigo sky.

"It's like magic," Molly murmurs.

"Like snow."

She turns her head and our eyes meet, her face shadowy in the dark. "Yes."

My hand finds hers and I curl my fingers around it.

We watch the lights change and glow, then Molly shivers. "I'm getting cold."

"That's why I brought a sleeping bag. Move off for a sec."

I pull back the top layer.

She looks from the sleeping bag up to my face, then back down. Then she crawls inside. I join her, tugging up the zipper on my side.

It's a double sleeping bag but it's not roomy, so her body is right next to mine. She's still shivering. I move closer and slide an arm under her cushion. "You need to warm up."

"Yes," she whispers, turning into me.

That morning in California, we woke up like this. But now we both know exactly what we're doing.

We gaze up at the sky, the entire circumference of the lake ringed with shimmering blues, greens and white.

"Don't you wish you were taking pictures of this?" she asks softly.

"Sort of. But it would take a lot of work. I'd need a tripod. And then…I wouldn't be holding you."

I feel the change in her, the vibration, her body very still. Then she moves her head to look at me. "Jax?"

"Yeah?" I tuck a strand of hair under her goofy-looking hood.

"I like you holding me."

My body explodes with heat, every nerve ending on alert. Fire burns beneath my skin.

"I want to kiss you, Molly." Now I touch my fingertip to her mouth.

Her eyes are big and shiny. I wait, giving her a chance to object. But her lips part and she whispers, "Do it."

A groan rumbles up from my chest. I lean in and brush my mouth over hers. Softly. Once, Twice. The third time I linger, opening my mouth on hers. She responds immediately, a small whimper in her throat. I lick over her bottom lip, then inside as I deepen the kiss. Her tongue slides against mine, tasting of red wine and sweet woman.

God. *God.* We're doing this. Fucking *finally.*

In the back of my brain I know it's a bad idea. I know the problems this could cause. But I can't stop.

Her hand slides to my chest, rests there, then glides up until her fingertips brush my bare neck. My entire body goes electric, humming and tingling, my dick hardening. I cup her cheek so gently,

We move together out of pure instinct, turning into each other so we're pressed together at our mouths, chests, groins, our legs tangling. My hands roam over her. I want to feel her everywhere so goddamn bad, but she's wearing a lot of thick clothing. Still, I skate a hand over the indentation of her waist, the arch of her back, the curve of her ass. My hand lingers there, squeezing, pulling her tighter. She feels so fucking good against my throbbing dick, and yet not good enough.

She whimpers and moans as our mouths suck and lick at each other, hotter, wetter, lust building inside both of us. We're making out and petting over our clothes like teenagers, until I slide my hand up under her hoodie to feel skin, sleek and hot. I stroke up and down her back, tracing the delicate bumps of her spine, over the band of her bra, then I cup her breast.

She reacts with a swift intake of air, but pushes greedily into my palm.

"Damn," I groan, giving her a small squeeze. "You are so fucking perfect."

She makes a small noise in her throat, her hands all over me, grabbing my shoulders, my arms, then my ass. I shift my mouth to her cheek, kiss her jaw, brush my lips over her throat, suck gently on the tender skin just above her collar bone.

"Oh God. Jax." Our hips are bumping together, seeking more.

"I know." I take her mouth again, licking inside to taste her sweetness.

Her hips are rolling against me with need, and I know just what it is she wants. I slip my hand under the elastic band of her leggings and give one firm cheek a squeeze. She's wearing thong underwear and it feels like she's bare. "You want more, sweetheart?"

"Oh yeah." She sighs against my mouth. "I need more."

"This?" My fingers slip daringly between her cheeks, then lower. I brush my fingertips over the softest, plumpest flesh.

"Yes. Oh, yes."

I change our position inside the sleeping bag, easing her onto her back, sliding my arm beneath her shoulders. I slink my hand into the front of her panties and cover her mound.

"Please," she whimpers, clutching my shoulders.

I move my hand, grazing over her pussy, up and down, pressing with the heel of my hand, delving with my fingers. I encounter slick wetness that makes me so hard I hurt. My heart is pounding so hard it's in my throat, and pressure coils in my balls.

"I want to make you come," I whisper, brushing my lips over her cheek.

She slowly closes her eyes, then opens them, staring up at the incredible sky above us. "This is unbelievable."

"I know. It couldn't be more perfect. You feel amazing, sweetheart." I graze her clit and her entire body jolts.

"Oh God…there."

"Yeah? Right here?" I circle wet fingertips over the nub.

"Right…there." She sighs, turns her face into mine and kisses my cheek. "Oh my God."

I fucking love this. I love making her tremble, making her breath hitch. I love having my fingers where she needs them most. I rub faster, her hips lifting against my hand, her breaths coming faster. Then her clit swells against my fingers, her hips lift, and she lets out a low wail.

"Beautiful." I touch my mouth to hers. "So fucking beautiful."

"Yes," she gasps, her body quivering.

I cup her again, feeling her pulse against my palm. Then she rolls into me and I wrap my arms around her to her hold her against me.

She burrows against my chest. "My nose is cold."

I laugh softly and tap her ass. "Yeah?"

"Yeah." I feel her smile. "But I don't really care."

"How often are you going to get an aurora borealis orgasm?"

"Wow." She lifts her head slightly to peer up at the sky. "I don't even know what to say. Except…"

"What?"

"*You* didn't get an aurora borealis orgasm."

"Uh, true. But maybe that should wait until we're back at the cottage."

She bites her lip and her gaze finds mine in the darkness. "With me?"

I sense her uncertainty. "I sure hope so."

Her lips tilt upward. "I can't wait."

We stay a while longer, admiring the ever-changing lights as we drink the rest of the wine. When they start to fade, we pack up our stuff and load it back into the car. Everything is closed and dark as we drive along Wasagaming Drive, past the shops and gas stations and the movie theater. As I pass Columbine Street, I hammer on the brakes as I see a dark shape. I quickly pull over.

"What are you doing?" Molly asks.

"Look." I point up the street. Now under one of the lights, a black bear meanders along the sidewalk.

"Oh my God!" She claps her hands over her mouth and stares. "A bear!"

"Yeah." I grin.

"Now I'm going to be terrified to get out of the car."

"He's a long way from us."

"He could have friends."

I slowly start forward, turn the corner and follow the bear at a distance until he disappears into the bushes on the other side of Tawapit Drive.

"That was pretty cool," Molly admits.

But when we get to the cottage, she hesitates before opening her door, scanning the yard.

"It's clear," I say, amused. I lean over and cup her face in both hands, turning it toward me so I can capture her mouth again. She opens to me and I slide my tongue inside, tasting her. She makes a little noise in her throat and sets a hand on my shoulder, kissing me back. I kiss her again, and again, slow and lush and wet, and then I draw back. She gazes at me with hazy eyes and soft, pouty lips.

Good, good. She's forgotten about the bear.

"Let's go in," I murmur.

MOLLY

Holding my hand, Jax leads me through the dark cottage to his bedroom. He turns on the lamp, then sits me down on the end of the bed, sitting beside me. We both shift so we're facing each other.

Not saying a word, we study each other in the warm light. I love his face…the strong nose and jaw, thick eyebrows and sculpted lips. He lifts a hand and touches my face, then leans in to kiss me. Our mouths cling together, lift apart, then join again in slow, sexy kisses. I set one hand on his shoulder, the other on the side of his neck, and he catches my bottom lip in his teeth in a naughty bite. Then he smooths the pad of his thumb over my lip.

One languid sensation melts into another, dissolving my spine, gathering low in my core.

His hands slide down and around to cup my ass as we kiss over and over. I caress his neck and slide my hand into his thick hair. Then he draws away from my mouth, not far, our foreheads touching as he drops his gaze to the zipper of my hoodie.

Slowly, he draws it down, lifting his eyes to meet mine again. Nose to nose, I give a tiny nod.

He pushes it off my shoulders, leaving me in a T-shirt. He meets my eyes again as he cups one of my breasts.

"Oh yeah," he groans. "So perfect."

I'm aware that my breasts are small. Painfully aware of it after seeing pictures of Claire. But I love having them touched, especially my nipples, so I'm just going to go with it and let myself enjoy this.

He tugs the shirt over my head and off, and I reach behind my back to unfasten my bra. Then I'm sitting next to him topless, the air in the room brushing over my nipples and tightening them even more.

He smiles, meets my eyes and covers both breasts with his hands, gently squeezing and shaping them. I smile back at him, sensation sliding through me, flames licking over me. Then he grabs the back of my neck and brings me closer for another kiss, this one hotter, rougher.

My hands are all over him, squeezing his big biceps, smoothing over his chest, curling around his shoulders. Still kissing me, he eases me down, my back to the mattress. I bend my legs to bring my feet up onto the bed.

His mouth moves on mine, his hand beneath my head, his tongue sliding in and out of my mouth erotically. I'm going up in flames, my breasts full, my nipples straining and aching to be touched again, and I whimper.

He lowers his head and kisses one nipple.

"Oh God!" Pleasure zings through me, my body electrified.

Opening his mouth, his tongue swirls over the stiff peak, then his lips close over it and he draws it into his mouth. Sensation swells inside me, enormous, my pussy aching and needy, every nerve ending alight.

He slides his hand down over my belly and into my leggings

like he did on the dock. He cups me there as he sucks on my nipples and I'm drifting, lost in it, lost in the bone-melting, mind-obliterating decadence. He plays there, kisses me again, then lifts me up to sitting and goes back onto his knees.

I reach for the button and zipper of his jeans and work on those while he pulls his T-shirt off over his head and tosses it to the floor. I already know how his chest and abs look, but now I get to touch and oh my God, I am going to touch them.

I look up from his zipper. His eyes are hot and greedy. I slowly lower the zipper and he pushes his jeans and underwear down his thick thighs. His cock juts out and I lose my breath momentarily. Then I suck in air between my teeth and reach for him. Closing my hands around his hot girth, I gently tug.

A groan rumbles up from his chest. "Jesus," he mumbles.

But then he tumbles me back onto the bed. He shoves off his clothes and stretches out beside me, naked. His hand slips behind my neck again, and he kisses me, hungry and ferocious. He starts pushing at my leggings, and I use one hand to help him. Together, we get them down my thighs, and he moves to tug them over my feet along with my socks. On his knees in front of me, he slowly drags my panties down too, and I bend my knees to help. His eyes are focused on mine as if making sure that I'm with him on this. I'm *so* with him.

He gently eases my thighs apart, still watching my face. My lips part. Heat flushes through me and up into my face when his gaze drops to my pussy.

"You have a beautiful pussy."

I shiver, my insides jumping.

His thumbs stroke over my outer lips then part them. He licks me, dragging the flat of his tongue over my flesh, kisses me, gently sucks, nibbles. My body is undulating, and I slip a hand over his head, through the silky strands of hair.

He takes his time. My body is glowing, a heated core of sensation, my toes and fingertips tingling.

He rises up, his fingers still inside me and leans over me to kiss me. Cupping his face, I taste myself on his lips and his tongue. His fingers move inside me, rubbing over super sensitive tissue, heat coiling.

"I'm so close," I moan.

He slips his fingers out of me to support himself on both arms as he kisses me. His cock nudges at my entrance and I want him inside me.

My hands gliding over his hot skin, I whisper, "Condom?"

It's already occurred to me that Steve and I hadn't used protection for a long time, but he was sleeping with someone else. It pisses me off that he could have passed something on to me and I'm going to have to get tested when I'm back in Chicago. Right now I have to protect Jax.

"Yeah. I have one."

He moves off me and I tease, "Just one?"

He walks to the dresser against the wall and digs around in a toiletry bag. I get to admire the back view for a moment. Dear God—his glutes are a work of art. I'm melting into the bed, taking in his wide shoulders, muscular back and massive thighs.

He turns and walks back, rolling on the condom, smirking. "I may have more."

I smile.

He climbs back on the bed and moves over me again, capturing my mouth with his. I can't get enough of touching him, running my hands up and down his sides, over his shoulders and arms, back up to his hair.

He shifts his knees closer to me, his cock sliding through my slickness, rubbing over my clit. Oh God, yessss... As our mouths move together, as our tongues slide against each other, his clock glides over my pussy, tempting me, making me ache. Then he pauses, the blunt head of his cock at my entrance. He lifts his head a fraction of an inch to meet my eyes.

I hold his gaze, encouraging him to go on, and I bend my knees, tipping my pelvis to give him the access he needs to push inside.

"Oh yeah…so damn tight…and hot. Fuck, you feel amazing."

My eyes close and my head goes back as I'm filled with heaviness, a sweet, piercing pressure. I squeeze around him and that sensation alone almost makes me come. Fire twists inside me in a spiraling blaze.

Jax's nose rests alongside mine as he moves on me, inside me…gliding in and out in slow strokes, setting me on fire. He catches my bottom lip between his lips and pulls gently, then slides his mouth to the side of my neck where his open mouth kisses me and sucks. My breath comes faster, or maybe I stop breathing, I don't even know because sensations tumble through me, building, twisting, tightening, burning, and I'm flying, surrounded by sparks. I'm vaguely aware of the cries that I'm shouting as I clench hard around him.

His breath is hot against my neck, the noises he makes increasingly guttural and desperate as he drives into me, harder, deeper, then he shouts my name as he tenses. "Molly, fuck, Molly…" I feel him pulsing inside me and I tighten around him, milking him and also the last spasms of my own orgasm in delicious, shivering bliss.

"I know we shouldn't have done this."

My tone sounds more matter-of-fact than regretful.

I'm draped over Jax's chest in the king bed in his room the

next morning. We're both naked, and his skin is hot and smooth, but also hairy in places, which is good because it feels very masculine and I love it. I rub my foot up and down his rough calf to explore that.

"Probably not," he agrees in a brusque tone. "But we did." His hand curves over my butt and squeezes and wow, I'm ready again.

Did we ever. After the aurora borealis orgasm, we had sex three times and I came every time. Jax made sure of that. It makes me want to kiss him. Everywhere. Again. "I don't think I can stop."

After a brief pause, he says, "Me either."

"Can we agree, though, about what this is?"

He closes his eyes, the corners of his mouth tightening. Then he opens them and nods. "There's no such thing as a long-term relationship."

"I know. And I'm not looking for that either, anymore."

"So we're on the same page."

"Can we agree that this will end when we go back to Chicago?"

He swallows. "Yeah. That would be best."

My heart feels like a lump in my chest, but this is what I want. "Okay. While we're here, we're good, but this will end when we go home. And you have my word that Steve will never know about this."

Jax's jaw tightens. "But *I* will."

I suck on my bottom lip. "Is that a problem? You know Steve and I aren't together and we never will be now. And if he took Claire with him on our honeymoon, then obviously he wouldn't care about us."

Jax draws in a long breath through his nose and his chest rises then falls beneath me. "You're right."

"I'm sorry." I hold his gaze. "I really, really didn't want to cause problems for you."

"Oh, you caused a problem for me. A big, hard problem." His hips lift, and I feel his erection. His eyes gleam.

"Oh, *that* kind of problem I can take care of."

He gives a low laugh as I press my lips to his chest, then slowly kiss my way down over those sculpted abs.

I didn't do this last night. Not that I didn't want to. But I'm a little self-conscious about my oral skills after that text message Steve sent Claire. Ratfucker.

What if it's not good for Jax? His oral skills are amazing. His fingers are as talented as his tongue. And his cock...oh my God...

I press my lips to the tender skin of his lower belly, just above the dark curls at his groin. They're trim and tidy and that's freakin' hot. I shift lower on the bed between his legs and he parts them obligingly. Then I kiss the neat hair, pausing to breathe in his musky male scent. It's so good...

He groans and his hand slides into my hair. "Molly..."

"Is this okay?" I peer up at him, my mouth a breath away from his straining cock.

"Fuck, yeah. I'm dying."

Oh good. I'm still wounded from Steve's comments about my BJ skills, and anxious about doing it wrong. Even though I really, really want to do it... I lick my lips, still hesitating, and Jax's fingers tighten in my hair. Not in a gross "do this" way, but in a way that tells me he's desperate and eager. He wants this. It encourages me.

I throw my worries out the window and go to town. I want this to be good for Jax, but I want to enjoy it too. I take my time, because I'm savoring it, although it might be torturous to Jax. But maybe that will make it better. I lick him all over, up and down and around, letting my tongue learn his unique shape and taste and texture. I look up at his face from time to time as I leisurely explore, reveling in his taut expression, his beautiful lips parted, his cheekbones flushed. I kiss and lick the place where his thigh joins his hip, one side, then the other, even nipping at the corded tendon of his thigh.

"Christ, Molly." Now both hands are threaded into my hair, gentle on my head but compelling.

I smile. He wants this.

I want this too. So much. I want to show my appreciation for how good he makes me feel. I want to make him feel just as good. Better than good. I want to blow his mind. Ha.

I open my mouth and close my lips around the head of his cock while I curl my fingers around the base. He's wet and slippery and my lips slide over firm flesh. He tastes delicious and feels incredible—thick, ridged, pulsing with desire. I take him deeper into my mouth, relaxing my throat. He's big, so I'm not going to be able to take all of him, but I use my hand in concert with my lips. I swirl my tongue, I hum, I swallow when he hits the back of my throat.

"Jesus!" he gasps hoarsely.

Pleasure pours through me because I'm giving him pleasure. It's so hot, so erotic. His hips are lifting like he wants to fuck my mouth and that makes my pussy wet, my inner muscles squeezing.

Teasing him, I lift my mouth off him and smile up at him, kissing the tip of his cock.

"Molly." He groans, his fingers tightening in my hair. "Jesus, I'm close."

"Good." I go back down, bobbing my head, my lips a tight, wet ring around him.

His hips elevate again, following my rhythm, guttural noises failing from his mouth. I'm buzzing with arousal, heat rushing through my veins, my pussy hot and wet. It's such a turn-on that I'm making him feel these things. Then he shouts, his fingers on my scalp, his abs and thighs tightening. "Molly…"

He's warning me, I know he is, which is thoughtful and considerate, but I want all of him, so I keep sucking, taking him deep, and he comes, hot liquid sliding down my throat.

"Holy fucking shit," he gasps.

I slow the pace of my mouth until his body relaxes, then let him slide out. My hand still grips him, though and I hold him in place to gently lick him and sweep up every last drop. "Mmmm."

"Fuck yeah." He lets go of my head and reaches for me, doing an impressive ab crunch then lifting me right off the bed to pull me up on top of him. He wraps his arms around me and squeezes, finding my mouth with his, and I love that he's not afraid to kiss me even though he just came there.

We kiss on and on, hot and eager and appreciative.

"That was fucking incredible," Jax murmurs long moments later.

"Was it?" The words sound vulnerable and I immediately regret them.

"Yeah." He strokes my hair, his other hand resting on my low back. "Oh hell yeah. I'm still seeing stars."

"You're not just saying that?" Oh my God, could I sound any more inadequate?

He goes very still. I don't look at him. Then he rolls me under him. Propped on his elbows above me, he frames my face with his hands and stare into my eyes. "I'm not just saying that," he growls. "Molly. You know I'm always honest. Right?"

Holding his gaze, I nod slowly. "I do."

"I said it was incredible, and it was."

I give another tiny nod, warmth spreading though my chest, a smile tugging at the corners of my mouth. "I really liked it."

He groans again and buries his face in the side of my neck. "That's so fucking hot."

"O-okay."

"I love blow jobs," he mumbles. "You can do that any time."

A little laugh escapes me. "*Any* time?"

"You know what I mean. Like, maybe not in public."

"Why not? You made me come in public."

He lifts his head and meets my eyes again and his are warm and bright. "There was nobody else around. But you have a fair point."

A smile slowly overtakes my face, and he returns it. A hot glow fills my body. I think it's happiness.

MOLLY

"This is the best cinnamon bun in the world." I pull off another piece and pop it in my mouth.

"I agree. Never had one better."

Out of the corner of my eye, I see the family at the table next to us in the small restaurant looking at us and whispering. Then the mom nods and the two boys slide off their chairs to approach us.

"Hi, are you Jackson Wynn?" one ginger-haired boy asks.

Jax smiles at him. "I am."

I catch the excitement on the mom's face.

"Could we get your autograph?" the boy asks

"And a picture?" the other adds.

"Sure."

Jax complies, bringing one boy around to the other side of his chair so Mom can take a picture of them all. By this point everyone in the restaurant is watching us, and I hear "Jackson Wynn!" a few times.

People are apparently thrilled by this, and Jax signs a few more autographs and poses for more pictures. Some players are awkward around their fans, Steve being one of them. He was never good at the small talk, but Jax has a way about him that's so effortless and charming. He comments on a boy's Batman shirt and on a little girl's Frozen dress, and he chats easily with the adults.

"Well, that was interesting," I say as we walk down the sidewalk leaving the restaurant. "You're pretty popular around here."

"Yeah, I guess."

I elbow him. "You guess."

"I grew up here. Or not far from here."

We walked here for brunch, so we leisurely retrace our steps along Tawapit Drive. It's super hot and muggy today, the air close and heavy, the sky overcast.

"Feels like a thunderstorm coming," Jax says. "Maybe this is a good night to go to a movie."

"That would be fun." We've walked past the log cabin theater a few times but I'm curious to see inside.

It starts raining just as we arrive back at the cottage, but the drops feel cool and fresh so I don't mind. I laugh and turn my face to the sky, my arms extended. "Oh my God, the rain smells so good!"

It's a great day to sit on the screened in porch, rain pattering gently down onto the trees and grass. I'm reading when Jax gets a call from his agent. He goes inside to talk, and I can hear his voice but not exactly what's being said.

When Jax returns to the porch, the expression on his face tells me it wasn't a good conversation.

"Still no contract?" I ask hesitantly.

"No." He sits next to me and rubs the back of his neck.

"I don't totally understand what's so difficult about it. Are you way far apart in what you want compared to what the team is offering?"

"Yeah. It's complicated as hell. They have to worry about the salary cap and signing the players they for sure want to keep. Duper and Army's contracts are up this year, and those guys are looking for huge dollars. The team is gonna want to sign them for sure, so then guys like me end up waiting. And we don't know if they'll be able to afford to sign me too, for what I want."

"Hmmm."

"Paul says not to panic. There are a lot of players in the league in this situation. It seems like nobody wants to do deals and be the first to sign someone and then set the market for everyone else."

"Okay, I get that."

"Yeah." He makes a face.

"There's nothing wrong with trying to get the most money you can," I add. "It's a business, right?"

"Exactly. We need to make as much as we can while we can, because our careers are short."

I nod. Jax is young, but he has a point.

"It'll work out," I say confidently, rubbing a hand over his chest. "You're a good player."

"Thanks." He smiles and pulls me closer for a kiss. Within minutes, his hands are under my shirt and in my shorts, and we make out for a while in the damp air then move into the bedroom for slow, sweet afternoon nooky.

There's something so lovely about having endless time, rain falling outside, and silvery daylight that provides enough illumination to see Jax in all his wonder. He kisses me everywhere, lifting and shifting me as he wants with his powerful muscles, caressing me and licking me and fucking me until I'm weak and boneless and blissed out.

———

"I found this old game of Trivial Pursuit." Jax sets the box on the dining room table.

It's an original edition, the teal blue box worn on the corners. It appears to have been well-used.

"Ooooh!" I clap with excitement. "We can play that tonight."

"After our ice cream."

We walk to the little ice cream place downtown. I love how everyone calls it "downtown," but I guess it is, now that I've seen the extent of two different cottage areas and the campground. Wasagaming is a sweet little town. Even the fire station is cute.

Back at the cottage, Jax lights a fire and sets the Trivial Pursuit box on the coffee table. "Prepare to go down, Flynn."

"In your dreams, Wynn."

"Pretty confident, huh?"

"I am."

"Let's make it more interesting."

"Okay." I arch an eyebrow.

"If we don't get the answer, we have to remove an article of clothing."

I blink, then laugh. "Strip Trivia? I love it!"

He shoots me an evil grin as he sets up the board.

My first question is from the entertainment category.

"What is the name of Warner Brothers' romantic pet skunk?" Jax reads.

"Phhhht. Pepe le Pew."

His mouth twists up as I roll the die again. This time it's Science and Nature.

Jax frowns. "Shit. What Russian physiologist went to the dogs to write *Conditioned Reflexes*."

I laugh. "Pavlov."

"Yeah, but what's his first name?"

"Oh, come on!"

He arches an eyebrow, waiting.

I squeeze my eyes shut, thinking. "Ivan. Ivan Pavlov."

"Crap."

"I'm still fully clothed."

"I know."

"I can't fucking believe this," Jax says as he reads the next card. "I'm taking another card."

"No!" I sit forward, grinning. "You can't do that. We have to play by the rules."

"Babe. When it comes to getting you naked, I'm not gonna play fair."

"Yes, you are. What's the question?"

He sighs. "Who declared 'As long as I am mayor, there will be law and order in Chicago?'"

I laugh delightedly. "I see why you're annoyed. Richard Daley."

"Yes." He tosses the card down with disgust.

My luck runs out, however, with the next question. "What two cities usually mark the extremes of English Channel swims?"

"Dover and…um…" I rack my brain for a French coastal city. Damn. "Uh…" I'm coming up blank, but finally say, "Bordeaux."

"Wrong. Calais."

"Shit! I knew that!"

He gestures at me, reminding me to take something off. I look down at myself. I'm not wearing a lot of clothes. I stand up and step out of my shorts.

Jax's smile turns carnal and he nods approvingly.

Now it's his turn. "You're going down," I say, pulling a card from the box.

He lands on Arts & Literature, which I happen to know is not his strongest category.

"Who's the clown in Shakespeare's *Henry IV* and *The Merry Wives of Windsor?*"

"Fuck." His lips curve down in disgust. "I have no clue." He peels his shirt off.

My mouth drops open. "You didn't even try." Then I smirk. "You just want to get naked."

He smirks back at me. "True. But remember, I'm very competitive."

"You could have at least guessed."

"I couldn't even come up with a guess."

"Hmmm."

"Why are you complaining?" He sticks out his chest.

"Solid point. I like your abs. Okay. My turn."

"What metal makes up to ten percent of yellow gold?" he reads.

"Copper."

He nods. "Yes."

Then it's, "What's the only U.S. state that borders a Canadian territory?"

"Maine."

"Wrong."

"What?"

"Territory." He taps the card on my nose. "It's Alaska. It borders the Yukon, which is a territory."

"Ohhhh." I'm annoyed at my careless mistake. "Shit, I answered too fast. If it was a province, it would be a lot of states." I sigh and pull off my T-shirt. I am now sitting on the couch in my pink lace demi bra and matching thong.

"This is getting good." Jax rubs his hands together.

"Sports and Leisure. Okay. What makes a Black Russian black?" I pause. "Wait, this is a sports question?"

"I guess booze is leisure. Too easy. Kahlua."

"Yes."

He keeps getting questions right, and I'm tempted to cheat and make up something I know he can't answer. But that would be unsportsmanlike. Finally, I get him with, "What's a California long white?"

He gazes blankly at me. Finally, he says, "A coffee."

"Ha! It's a potato. Finally, those jeans are coming off."

"Nope." He toes off one sandal.

"What!" I stare at him. "That's not fair! I was barefoot."

He smiles. "You should have thought of that."

I narrow my eyes at him and pick up the die. I keep my underwear on a little longer, then have to decide whether it's the bra or thong that goes. I decide on the bra.

"Good choice." Jax leers at my boobs.

My nipples have tightened, not only due to being exposed to the air but responding to Jax's lascivious stare. I've never been an exhibitionist, but this is turning me on. And Jax too, judging from the bulge in his jeans. I squeeze my thighs together.

"Are we going to finish this game?" I ask breathlessly.

"Hell yeah. I have to beat you."

I suck briefly on my bottom lip, and his eyes darken. "Okay." I pluck a card from the box. "What is the rain's name in 'They Call the Wind Mariah'?"

"Whut?"

I smile. "It's a song."

"The rain's name," he repeats.

"Right."

"Rain…Rachel."

"Wrong. The rain's name is Tess."

"Did you know that?" he demands.

"Nope." I beam at him. "Wasn't my question though." I gesture at him, and he takes off his other sandal.

I'm losing badly at the strip aspect of this game, although I do have more game pies than him. "I have to keep my panties on."

"That's what she said."

I laugh.

"Why?" he challenges. "Can't you think when you're naked?"

"I can think, but it's about…sex."

"Is there a sex edition of Trivial Pursuit?"

"I have no idea."

"There should be. You were a star that night at the bar in California for Carnal Knowledge."

Well, I have to lose my panties for the game to continue far enough for him to get naked, and soon he's sitting there in his boxer briefs, me naked, and I ask, "Who won the 1942 Nobel Peace Price?"

His forehead creases up and his eyes narrow. "Hmm. 1942…I'd say…Albert Schweitzer."

"Wrong. Nobody won it that year."

"Huh?"

"It was during World War II. I think they didn't give any peace prizes during the war."

"Shit."

I wave my hand for him to stand up and strip.

With a grin, he does so, although looking at him wearing nothing but boxer briefs is not a hardship.

I actually lick my lips at seeing him nearly naked now. He's hard and it's beautiful. His whole body is beautiful—all those sleek muscles now lying under tanned skin after our two trips. I've seen him naked and I've seen him in board shorts, so this isn't a surprise, but it's unexpectedly erotic, sitting in the living room in front of the fire, both of us unclothed.

"Are you sure we're going to finish this game?" I ask, my voice husky.

"Forget the game." He drops to his knees in front of me and hauls my ass forward.

18

JAX

Molly lets out a little squeal as I yank her closer to me. But her thighs fall apart, revealing that sweet, sweet pussy to me. The fire flickers behind me, illuminating her, and I study her for a few seconds, enjoying the view. She's pink and plump and wet.

I set my palms on her inner thighs and lean in to taste her with a long slow lick.

She moans, her hands going flat on the couch cushions.

I lick her again and again, gliding my tongue over slick lips, up and down, probing deeper, then pressing gentle kisses all over her pussy, sucking her soft flesh into my mouth. Her body quivers in response to my touch, and she makes needy whimpery noises. When I touch my tongue to her clit, she jolts, a soft cry escaping her.

"Yes," she says on a soft moan. "Oh yes…"

I take my time, but give more attention to the sensitive, swollen bud, touching my fingertips to her wet entrance, massaging lightly there, then sliding a finger inside. She clenches around me, and I add another finger as my tongue flicks faster. God, I love this. She's so responsive, so sweet.

I reach one hand up to cup her breast, her softness filling my palm perfectly, her nipple a hard little nub. Her hips rock up and her abs tighten and I keep lashing at her clit with my tongue, faster, until she's undulating and crying out, her clit swelling against my tongue.

Jesus, that's perfect. Beautiful. So fucking hot. I'm so hard I'm hurting, my dick a throbbing spike, but I ignore it as I suck on her clit until she's drained and limp. I lift my head, my mouth wet with her essence, to study her pulsing pussy, gently rubbing all around it with my fingertips. I'm so turned on I can't stand it, and I rise to my knees.

Shit. I don't have a condom.

I lean down to kiss the patch of hair on her mound. "Be right back," I whisper.

I bolt to the bedroom and roll the rubber on as I walk back. She's right where I left her, spread open to me, still breathing hard. I kneel again in front of her and slide inside her. She's so wet it's easy, and as her heat envelops me, I suck in a sharp breath of relief and bliss.

"Christ, Molly." I wipe a hand over my mouth, then lean over her to kiss her. Her lips respond, opening to me, clinging to mine as I glide in and out of her. I support myself on one outstretched arm as I fuck her. "You feel amazing. You taste so sweet. I need to fuck this sweet pussy into another orgasm."

Her body flutters around my dick. "Oh my God."

"Yeah." I rock my hips, in, out, again and again, each stroke twisting the hot sensation in my balls higher and higher. "Find it…what do you need, baby?"

She slips her hand down to her clit and comes again after only a few rubs, wailing the most satisfying sound, clenching around me, and I let my orgasm roar over me, exploding at my center, flashing up my spine. My balls squeeze and my cock swells and pulses.

I go still, my hands on her legs, every muscle in my body tense. I'm panting, blind, a mass of jangling nerves. Finally, when my vision clears and the noise in my ears lessens, I move, giving another slow glide in…and out. Gripping my cock, I remove the condom and wrap it in tissues from the box on the table, then I scoop Molly up in my arms and sit on the couch with her on my lap.

She's naked. Warm. Soft. Curling into me like a kitten, her hand sliding around the nape of my neck as she tucks her head beneath my chin. We sit like that for a while, who knows how long, and then she says, "That was the best trivia game I've ever played."

I blow out a soft laugh. "Yeah. Same."

Molly

The third weekend we're there, I'm sitting on the deck with coffee in the morning when a man walks around the corner of the cottage. I nearly spill my coffee I'm so startled.

"Hi!" he says. "How are you?"

"I'm, uh, good." I stand, only a little embarrassed that I'm wearing a huge pair of Jax's plaid flannel pants and a hoodie.

"I'm Oliver MacDonald." He jerks his head. "We have the cottage next door."

"Oh! Nice to meet you. I'm Molly."

"Are you…I mean, I heard Jax is here."

"Yes! He just walked to the store for milk. He should be back any minute."

"Oh, cool. We kind of grew up together here, when he used to come and spend summers with Mr. and Mrs. Thompson."

"I've heard a lot about those summers." I smile, my chest warming. "Jax loves it here."

"It's great that he still comes back. My wife and I live in Toronto now, but we try to come back every summer too, and usually we meet up with Jax."

I hear the door of the porch open and close and footsteps in the cottage. "Jax," I call through the screen door. "There's someone here to see you."

Jax appears, and a broad grin breaks out over his face. "Big Mac!" He slides open the door, steps out and they do a bro handshake-hug combo. "How the hell are you?"

"Great, man. You?"

"Good! You here for the week?"

"Yeah. The whole family's here this weekend, but Sophia and I are staying next week, too."

"Oh hey, this is Molly," Jax says.

"We met," Oliver says with a smile. "I didn't know you had a girlfriend."

"I…" Jax's voice trails off.

There's a brief awkward silence as our eyes meet.

"You're from Chicago?" Oliver asks me.

"Yes!" I nod vigorously.

"Your first time here, then?" Oliver asks. "How do you like it?"

"I love it. Jax has been touring me around and sharing all his memories with me. Was it you whose bathing suit he shoved a minnow into?"

Oliver barks out a laugh. "Yeah, that was me! Asshole. Anyway, come over tonight for a drink and say hi to Mom and Dad. Abby's here too. My sister," he adds for my benefit.

"We just may do that." Jax follows Oliver around the cottage, and I can hear their voices before Oliver hikes through the bushes separating the two cottages.

Jax reappears, still smiling.

"Well, that was awkward," I say.

He grimaces. "Whatever. Just go along with it. It's easier than explaining everything."

"I guess so." Unless Oliver keeps up on hockey gossip and knows that I'm the one who jilted Steve Shevchuk at the altar.

We do go next door later, carrying our drinks with us. Jax pauses outside our cottage door. "Um…Oliver's sister Abby is going to be there."

I blink. "And…?"

"She always had a little crush on me. Maybe you could stick close?"

I purse my lips. "Oh, come on. That was how many years ago? You think you're such a stud she's still going to be after you?"

He shrugs. "It could happen."

I laugh. "Sure, big guy." I pat his back as he starts through the bushes toward the next door cottage.

Everyone is out on the deck, and Jax is greeted like a long-lost son by Mr. and Mrs. MacDonald. I watch Oliver's sister Abby greet Jax with a clinging hug that's not at all sisterly, and she regards me with chilly eyes as Jax introduces us.

Dammit, he was right.

Okay, I can do this. I slide my arm into his and press my body against him, eliciting raised eyebrows from Abby. Ha. I'll sit in Jax's lap all night if I have to.

Abby ignores me and asks questions about Riley and how she's doing, and Jax is happy to brag about his little sister. Oliver's wife Sophia is pregnant, six months I learn as we chat. I hear a lot of reminiscences, including a hilarious story about Jax and Oliver capturing crayfish in the lake and putting them on the counter under a plate for Mrs. MacDonald to find.

"I damn near peed myself," she says, laughing. "They looked like giant bugs. I ran out of the kitchen screaming and the boys were howling."

"I nearly died too," Abby says. "I came in asking what the heck is going on, and I saw those things crawling across the counter. Oh my God!"

I laugh and smile lovingly up into Jax's eyes. "Troublemaker."

He smiles back down at me. "Good times."

"Are you still a prankster in the dressing room?" Oliver asks.

"I like a good practical joke on occasion," Jax says.

"Like the time you hit Marc Dupuis with a faceful of shaving cream while he was being interviewed on TV?" I ask.

Oliver laughs. "I saw that!"

"Captain Codger?" Mrs. MacDonald asks with amusement. "How did he take it?"

"He's not as serious as he used to be," Jax says.

"Jax always did like to have fun," Mrs. MacDonald tells me. "And the girls followed him everywhere."

"I don't doubt it," I say with a smirk.

I love how easily Jax fits in with these people and the fact that he's kept in touch with a friend from his childhood. I'm not loving Abby's aloof attitude toward me, but whatever.

We go out for dinner with Oliver and Sophia one night the next week, which is fun. They're a nice couple. They're excited about their first child, and Jax seems super happy for them, too, asking questions about how Sophia is feeling and how much time she'll have off work. Apparently, she and Oliver are both accountants. When she says she'll have a year off, I nearly fall off my chair.

"That's amazing," I say. I haven't looked into maternity leave in detail, but I have friends and coworkers who have babies and they sure didn't get a year off. We discuss mat leave in Canada compared to the United States.

That morphs into a discussion about politics, which could be a field of landmines, but luckily Jax and I have similar views to Oliver and Sophia, so it's an amicable discussion. It's fun talking about these things with likeminded people and also getting to know Jax's opinions. We've never talked about this stuff, and my admiration for him grows.

I've always liked him. But now...I *really* like him.

Jax

Molly's preparing dinner tonight. I can hear her moving around in the kitchen. My ears perk up at a muttered "fuck" and then "goddammit." I consider going in there to see what's happening, but hold off. I'm sure she's got this. I grilled chicken breasts earlier that she's going to use in some kind of salad.

I'm reading an advance copy of my mom's new book she sent me. It's fantastic, but I grew up with a lot of her ideas about how to stay humble as an elite athlete.

"Oh, for fuck's sake!"

My eyebrows fly up at another expletive from the kitchen. Then I hear a loud thunk and a crash.

I jump up. Okay, now I need to check in.

I stride into the kitchen and find a disaster—an avocado has been thrown against the wall and a salad bowl sits upside down on the floor with greens scattered all around it. And Molly's in tears.

"What's going on?" I approach her. "What happened?"

"I had three avocadoes," she sobs. "They were *rotten* when I cut them open. *All* of them."

"Ah…" She's crying about overripe avocadoes? "That's okay. We'll have the salad without them."

"You can't have a Cobb salad without avocado!" She sweeps a hand out. "And then I was so frustrated I threw an avocado and I knocked the salad bowl on the floor." Another sob bursts from her lips and she swipes at the tears on her cheeks. "Now we have no dinner and a big mess to clean up and dinner is ruined." She cries harder.

I take her in my arms and press her head to my shoulder, rocking her slightly, a little mystified. "Shhhh. It's okay. It's not that bad."

"It is," she moans against my shirt. "It's a disaster. I just wanted to make a nice dinner."

"We have other food." I pat her back. "Or we can go out."

"I can't go out! I'm a mess."

"I can go get us something."

She nods and sniffles, not lifting her head. Okay, good. Maybe that calmed her down. What the hell?

"What would you like?" I ask.

After a short pause, she mumbles, "I could really go for a bacon double cheeseburger and fries. Large fries. And ice cream."

"Okay. We can do that. I'll pour you a glass of wine and you go sit on the deck and I'll clean this up."

"You're so good," she sobs, stepping back. Her face is red and blotchy, her nose pink, eyes swollen. She's still gorgeous. "I'm sorry."

"It's okay." I hand her the glass of wine. When she's outside, I survey the mess. Wow.

There's bacon, which looks delicious. That salad would have been epic. Oh well. I put some things in the fridge, throw out the greens, and clean the floor. Then I grab my keys and step out onto the deck. "I'll go get the food now. How are you doing?"

"I'm fine." She heaves a sigh. "Thank you, Jax."

"Sure."

I drive to the Wigwam and place my to-go order. While I'm waiting, I order a beer in the lounge and watch the baseball game on the big TV. Some guys there recognize me and start talking to me, which is cool. They even pay for my beer.

Then I carry the big bag of food out to the car and head back to the cottage. Molly's still on the deck. Her tears have dried and her face looks less red. She gives me a wan smile as she joins me in the kitchen to unpack the food. I slide the ice cream into the freezer for later.

"I'm really sorry about my meltdown," she says when we're sitting at the table. "I, uh, have PMS."

I blink. "Ah." That explains it. I remember when Riley had her period—nobody could even look at her, never mind talk to her. Luckily, Mom explained it to me. "Do you need anything else? Midol? Tampons?"

She smiles. "I'm good. Actually, what I need is someone to rub my back and play with my hair while I watch *The Notebook* and eat ice cream."

"I can do that. We even have a DVD of *The Notebook*."

"It's probably not your favorite movie."

I grin. "No. But we watched my favorite the other night, so it's fair."

"You're the best." She sighs. "I'm sorry. I just feel so yuck. I'm bloated and crampy and my boobs hurt."

I nod. This is a lot of info. But I can handle it.

"On the upside," she adds with a grin, "at least I'm not pregnant."

Holy shit. *That* would be a huge complication. "Good

point." I give my head a shake. "Have you always had bad PMS?"

"Yes. When I was in ninth grade, I got frustrated because we were having a discussion about something, I can't even remember what, it was a history class, and people were asking such stupid questions, I put up my hand and asked if I could murder someone."

I laugh.

After she devours her entire burger and fries, we move into the living room. I start the movie and when she's done her ice cream, she lies on the couch with her head in my lap and it's no trouble at all to stroke her hair and back while we watch. And yeah, she cries.

After the movie, she rolls onto her back and looks up at me. "That's such a great love story. But so sad."

"Yeah."

"I'm so horny," she adds.

My eyes widen.

"But I'm so gross."

I smile and stroke her hair again. "You're not gross."

"It's shark week. You're probably not into that."

"We can do other things."

"Oh yeah?" She bites her lip adorably.

My hand moves down to her lower abdomen. I gently press and rub here there.

"That feels good," she says with a sigh.

I move lower, over her shorts, to cup her pussy. Slowly I move my hand back and forth.

"Ohhhh." Her eyes close.

"Is this okay?"

"Yessss…"

I slip my fingers into her shorts and panties. She's wet, and I slick up the lubrication and circle my fingertip over her clit.

She adjusts my hand at one point, sighs with delight, and I fucking love watching her come on my fingers, her body trembling, her hand gripping my wrist.

A smile curves her lips and her eyes flutter open. "Thank you."

"You're welcome." I cup her pussy gently, then withdraw my hand.

She lays her hand on her lower belly. "My cramps feel better. I think orgasms are supposed to be good for cramps."

"You should have told me sooner." I lean down to smooch her mouth. "We could have dealt with that before you threw an avocado across the kitchen."

Luckily she smiles at that, then shimmies off the couch. "Okay, your turn."

I smile too, letting her unzip my shorts and pull my stiff cock out. She looks so eager and enthralled; it's a huge turn-on. And her mouth is amazing—soft and wet, her tongue agile and slick. My entire body buzzes with arousal.

She takes me deep and sucks on me. Pressure gathers in my full balls, my lower back aching, my thighs tensing. I slide my fingers into her hair, holding it off her face so I can watch, because, fuck, it's sexy as hell seeing her lips on my cock, her eyes peering up at me. "You really are fantastic at this," I mutter.

She lifts up and off. My dick pulses in protest. "Really?"

"Really. Please…don't stop."

She smiles and resumes her amazing blow job, her tongue smooth and supple, licking over the head of my cock, around me, all the way down to the base and back up, then her tight lips sliding up and down in tandem with her fist. My consciousness narrows to that tiny slice of reality, her on her knees in front of me, her mouth on my cock. My skin prickles, tension building inside me, then torquing as sensation explodes through my nerves in a blinding surge of ecstasy.

My chest heaves as I try to gather air into my lungs. I cup her face with both hands when she lifts off me. I can't breathe, can barely see, but my gaze focuses on the sexy satisfied smile on her lips, and it's all I need in this world because hell yeah, I love blow jobs, but I also love that she loves it and that she knows she blew my fucking mind.

19

MOLLY

"We've been here four weeks," I say to Jax as we finish the hamburgers that Jax grilled on the barbecue.

"Yeah." He eyes me.

"I should probably go back to Chicago." I sigh because I really don't want to. I've been keeping in touch with my friends and family. And I know that after he got back from Europe, Steve went home to visit his parents in upstate New York, so there was no need to rush back to see him. There's no reason I need to be there, but I feel like I shouldn't spend the whole summer hiding out with Jax. I guess I need to face reality.

"I can drive you back to Winnipeg if you want, so you can fly home."

"That's a three-hour drive. And you'd have to turn around and come back."

He shrugs. "It's not that big a deal. But Mom and my grandparents are coming next weekend. You could drive back to Winnipeg with them Sunday if you want to fly home."

"Oh." I consider that. "That makes sense, I guess. But are

you sure you're okay with me being here when they come? They're going to ask questions."

His jaw tightens. "We'll tell them the truth. We're friends."

Friends who fuck. Friends how know how each other taste. Who know how it feels when he's inside me.

One more week. Well, ten days.

I watch Jax lean back in the chair on the deck. He stares out at the lake, his expression impassive. My Spidey senses tingle, and I feel like he's not happy about me leaving either.

But we agreed. We agreed this would end when we're back in Chicago. I can't hide out here forever.

I'm freaking out. I admit I'm freaking out.

The sound of a car door closing outside makes me jump.

They're here.

Jax's mom and grandparents are coming today and I've had a ball of anxiety knotted in my stomach all day. I don't know why. I guess I'm worried what they're going to think of me being here.

I swallow and press a hand to my belly as Jax strides out, across the porch and throws open the door. "Hey! You're here!"

"We're here! We made it!" a light, feminine voice calls. "Come give me a hug!"

I follow along behind Jax and stand at the door as he jogs down the steps and hugs his mom.

She's tall, but compared to him she's not. She squeezes him then steps back, beaming, studying him. "You look great. All tanned and relaxed. You must be enjoying your summer."

"It's been awesome."

An older man emerges from the back seat of the Chevrolet

Malibu, and Jax hugs him too, then his grandma who was in the front passenger seat.

Victoria Wynn catches sight of me and pauses, cocking her head. Then she smiles faintly.

She's so pretty—high cheekbones and a slightly pointy chin, her short, layered hair in tousled waves, a warm brown with gold highlights. A pair of rectangular dark brown glasses sit on her small nose.

"Let me introduce you to Molly," Jax says, leading his grandma toward the door. "Molly, this is my grandma, Pat Thompson."

"Hello." Mrs. Thompson wears an expression identical to her daughter's, and I see a definite family resemblance. "Nice to meet you, Molly."

"Hi!" I step forward to shake hands.

"This is my grandpa, Gary."

I shake hands with him too as he eyes me appraisingly.

"And my mom, Tori."

I shake her hand also.

"Everyone, this is Molly Flynn, a friend of mine from Chicago."

"So nice to meet you all," I say, hoping they didn't notice how sweaty my hand is.

Jax helps bring in their bags. We've sorted out sleeping arrangements. I've been sleeping with Jax every night since that first night we had sex, many of my things gradually migrating into the master bedroom. I've moved all those back to my own room.

Jax carries his grandparents' bag into the master bedroom, which he'll vacate temporarily. His mom is taking the other bedroom and Jax is going to sleep on one of the pull-out couches in the living room for a few nights.

It's just after noon and we picked up some things for an easy lunch, so I busy myself in the kitchen setting out deli meats, crusty rolls from the amazing bakery, and a big salad. Mrs. Thompson enters the kitchen.

"I know this is your kitchen, I hope it's okay that I've made myself at home here."

"Of course!" Her smile is warm, but her eyes still gleam with curiosity. "Have you been here the whole summer, or are you just visiting for the weekend?"

"I came with Jax back at the end of June."

"Oh, lovely."

"I'm just putting out some lunch. I don't know if you've eaten?"

"No, we haven't. That speed demon Tori wouldn't even stop for ice cream in Neepawa, she was so excited to get here and see Jax." Mrs. Thompson opens the fridge and pulls out a bottle of mustard. "Oh, I see you have some fancy mustards."

"Yes, we picked those up at one of the stores. They're apparently made in Winnipeg. I really like the honey horse-radish one."

"Hmm." She picks them up as well and carries them over to the dining table.

I don't know what that means. Does she disapprove of fancy mustard? Or maybe it's me she disapproves of?

I bring everything else to the table as Jax chats with his grandpa and mom. They cross the big open living room as Jax updates them about the small plumbing leak he fixed and how he cleaned up the area going down to the dock.

We sit down at the table, very informally as everyone makes their own sandwich and helps themselves to salad as well as some pickles and olives I put in small serving dishes. Jax and his family are all talking at once, and I just try to take it all in.

Then Mrs. Wynn says to me, "Did I hear you say you came here with Jax?"

"That's right."

"So you've been here a few weeks then."

"Yes, almost a month, actually."

"What do you do for a living?" Mrs. Wynn asks.

"I'm a teacher. I teach third grade in Chicago."

"Ah. So you have the whole summer off."

"Yes." I smile. "And it's been so nice. I really appreciate the opportunity to stay here. It's a beautiful place."

"It's nice that you haven't been alone this whole time." Mrs. Wynn slants Jax a glance.

"Don't get any ideas, Mom. Molly and I are just friends."

I feel a little pinch in my chest.

She feigns indignance. "I don't have any ideas."

"Uh huh." Jax's mouth twists up against a smile.

Despite this warning, Mrs. Wynn is very interested in me and my life, asking lots of questions. She has such a warm and attentive manner that it doesn't feel like I'm being grilled. I want to tell her my life story from birth up to leaving Steve at the altar. Okay, maybe not that part. Then I remember she's a psychologist. Is she analyzing me? She absolutely knows how nervous I am. That I'm a bit crazy. And that I might be a bit crazy for her son.

What?

I force that thought away so I can focus on the conversation. I'll take it out and examine it later. Or maybe never. I should never think of that again.

After lunch, we all walk down to the dock. Jax carries chairs down from the deck for his grandma and mom to sit in. It's another hot, sunny day, and I sit on the dock and swish my feet through the cool water, taking in the vista of the bright blue lake, the shoreline opposite rough with jagged evergreen trees.

A swelling sadness fills my chest at the thought that I only have a couple more days here. I'll be leaving Sunday afternoon with Jax's family. They're going to drop me at a hotel near the airport, and I'll take an early flight Monday morning to Chicago. Jax's mom is staying another week in Winnipeg with her parents.

There are things I'm looking forward to—I *am* a city girl, after all, and I love my hometown. I miss my friends and my parents. I miss night clubs and restaurants and Nordstrom Rack. But I know without a doubt I'm going to miss this place when I'm gone. Especially knowing I'll never come back here. And also knowing it'll never be the same with Jax again.

I might go to hockey games and see him play. We might run into each other, although Chicago's a big city. Will we ever compete in trivia night again? Would that be weird?

My eyes sting and I bow my head, staring at the water, so clear you can see each smooth rock on the sandy bottom of the lake. The conversation goes on around me.

How could everything change so fast?

Mrs. Thompson wants to see the wishing well, so Jax drives them out there. I elect to stay at the cottage to get a few things ready for dinner and read the book I'm enjoying. I prepare some potatoes and vegetables. I'll rub the steaks with the spice mix later, and there's a salad.

I find my favorite place on the deck for catching the afternoon sun. I'm having a hard time focusing on my book, though. I keep thinking about Jax.

Dammit.

I can't be sad about this. It's been wonderful, and I'll treasure every memory of every moment. Every kiss and touch. Every toe-curling, heart-exploding orgasm. The feel of his body and the taste of his mouth on mine. Every small thoughtful gesture, like bringing chairs for his mom and grandma, like taking me to see the Northern Lights, to bringing me another glass of wine when mine is empty. His patience with my PMS.

I wish it didn't have to end.

It's only been weeks since I was going to marry another man. There's obviously something wrong with me if I can forget about Steve that fast and fall for Jax.

Rebound.

I close my eyes, remembering Brielle's words. The first guy you're with after a breakup is your rebound. That's what this is. Once I'm away from Jax, I'll forget about him too. Probably.

Am I that shallow? I kind of hate myself for being so fickle. I learned that lesson, though, when I found out Steve was cheating on me. I thought my heart was broken, and now…I guess it really wasn't. Because it kind of seems like maybe I never really loved Steve all that much.

After Jax barbecues the steaks and we eat dinner, we gather around the fireplace to play another game of Trivial Pursuit. It turns out Jax's whole family is into trivia.

This time we keep our clothes on.

We're drinking wine and beer, laughing uproariously at jokes about Mr. Thompson's balding head following a question about phalacrosis, which means hair falls out, when there's a knock at the door.

We all turn toward the porch door and Jax rises. "I'll get it." As he opens the door, we hear him say, "Holy shit. Dad."

Tori immediately goes on alert, and Mr. and Mrs. Thompson exchange a wide-eyed look.

"Seriously?" Tori mutters. "Mark is here?"

"Uh, he did say he might come up for a visit while Jax is here," I say.

Three pairs of eyes fix on me intently.

I swallow. "I, uh, went to California with Jax at the end of June," I say. "We saw him there."

Their eyes widen.

I want to spew a bunch of stuff to Tori to tell her that Jax and his dad had a talk, and Jax found out that his dad never cheated on Tori, and they're working things out, but that's not my place, especially with Mark now walking into the living room with Jax.

"Oh." Mark stops. "I didn't realize…"

"We didn't know you were coming, Dad," Jax says.

Mark sighs. "I thought I'd surprise you. I should have let you know." He pauses. "Hi, Tori. Hi, Pat. Gary."

"Mark." Mrs. Thompson rises with a polite smile. "Long time no see."

"Yeah, it has been a while."

Mr. Thompson rises too, but he's frowning. The atmosphere that moments ago had been full of laughter and is now charged and heavy.

"Molly." Mark smiles at me. "I didn't expect to see you here."

I stand and walk over to him. "It was a last-minute decision. Nice to see you again, Mr. Wynn."

"Mark. Please." He claps a hand on Jax's shoulder. "Sorry to interrupt. I'll go see if I can get a room at one of the hotels."

Everyone glances at each other. It's acutely uncomfortable for a few seconds. Then Tori says, "You don't have to do that. There's lots of room here."

"Yeah, Dad." Jax appears relieved. "I'm sleeping on one of the couches. You can have one of the others."

Mark hesitates. His gaze lands on Tori, and for a moment they share a long, indecipherable look. "You sure?" he finally says quietly.

"Of course." She smiles. "You can join our Trivial Pursuit game. I have to warn you, though, Molly is a whiz."

Mark meets my eyes and grins. "I suck at trivia."

"I guess Jax gets it from his mom's side of the family."

"I had no idea Jax was into trivia."

"He's a champ," I tell his dad, feeling a twinge of sadness that Mark doesn't know that.

"Dad, can I get you a drink?"

"Sure. I'd love a beer." Mark pulls an armchair closer to the coffee table.

I follow Jax to the kitchen to get a bottle of wine. "You okay with this?" I ask quietly.

He grimaces and closes the fridge door, a beer in his hand. "Don't have much choice, I guess." We pause, face to face, so close we're almost touching. He smiles down at me. "Family, huh?"

"You definitely have a lot of it." I smile back at him, my insides melting at the affection in his eyes. "They're all great, though."

One corner of his mouth lifts. "They're okay. As long as Mom and Dad get along. And as long as Grandpa doesn't go after Dad with the axe."

"Eek. Hard feelings?"

"You could say that."

We carry drinks back to the living room. The fire has burned low, so Jax takes a minute to poke at it and put another log on, and then we resume our game.

Tori gives Jax and me a run for our money. She knows who lives at 39 Stone Canyon Way (the Flintstones). But Mark knows what an eagle is in golf and that Blackjack is the better-known name of the card game Twenty-One.

"What was Little Miss Muffet eating when she sat on her tuffet?" I ask Jax.

He lifts an eyebrow. "What the fuck is a tuffet?"

"I don't know, but that's not the question. And keep it clean."

His family guffaws. I'm fitting right in here.

"A tuffet is like a footstool," Mr. Thompson says.

"Ah. Okay. I think she was eating…a buffet." He pronounces it to rhyme with tuffet.

I fall over laughing.

"Oh, come on!" Mrs. Thompson says. "You don't know that?"

Jax grimaces. "Nope."

"Eating her curds and whey," say Mr. and Mrs. Thompson, Mark and Tori all at the same time.

"Kids these days," Mark says, shaking his head, eyes twinkling.

"Right?" Tori agrees.

"Okay, Boomer," Jax says with a grin, drawing groans from his parents.

"We're not even Boomers," Tori protests. "We're not *that* old."

"I'm kidding, Mom," Jax says.

We continue the game.

"What mosquito's bite draws blood, male or female?"

I frown. "Whichever it is, they've been drawing a lot of *my* blood."

That gets a sympathetic laugh.

"I don't know for sure, but I'll guess female," I say with a touch of bitterness.

"That's right!"

"Okay." Mrs. Thompson reads the next question for Mark. "Who stood at the top with 'Stand By Your Man'?"

"Too easy. Tammy Wynette."

"Stupid song," Tori mutters. Her eyes meet Mark's, and they have a little stare-down. "Story of our marriage."

"What the…" Mark stops himself, his jaw tense. "How the hell can that be, when you didn't stand by me?"

"I did so!"

My eyes go wide, and I slide my glance over to Jax. His face has reddened. The atmosphere in the room has become loaded.

"Sorry," Tori says with a big fake smile. She waves her hands. "Got sidetracked there. Keep going."

Finally, Jax ends up with the last question for the win. I read the card and roll my eyes. "Oh my God. How do you get so lucky with your questions?"

"It's not luck," he says with a fake modest smile. "I'm smart."

"Ha ha. Okay. What hockey player was *Sports Illustrated*'s Sportsman of the Year for 1970?"

He smirks. Then he wrinkles his nose, thinking.

I cock my head. "Not sure, smarty-pants?"

"Bobby Orr."

I sigh. "Right. You win."

"Attaboy." Tori pats his shoulder. "No wonder you two are so good at those trivia nights you go to."

"It's good to have some purpose for all the useless information in my head," I say, smiling.

Things still haven't gone back to the fun atmosphere we were all enjoying before that little exchange between Mark and Tori. They keep looking at each other.

I gather up the tokens and Jax folds up the board.

"I'm going for a walk," Tori announces. "I need some air."

"It's dark out," Mark says.

"Really?" she says sarcastically. "Who would have thought it gets dark at night?" She heads to the door.

Mark rolls his eyes.

I bite my lip, packing up the game into its box. "Well. Who needs more wine?"

"I do," Mrs. Thompson says eagerly.

"I need another beer." Mark stands and picks up our glasses. "I'll get you more wine, ladies."

Mrs. Thompson gives him a small smile that suggests to me she doesn't really hate him.

Mr. Thompson, on the other, glares balefully at Mark's back as he walks to the kitchen.

I meet Jax's eyes and he makes a face.

"We saw the Northern Lights," I tell Mr. and Mrs. Thompson. "One of the first nights we were here. It was amazing."

My change of subject works, and things feel somewhat easier when Mark returns and hands me and Mrs. Thompson a glass of wine. Mark keeps glancing at the door, though, as if watching for Tori.

Eventually he stands and says, "I'll just go make sure Tori's okay."

"It's pretty safe here, Dad," Jax says quietly.

"Except for the bears," I add. Then I clap my hand to my mouth and widen my eyes.

"Jesus," Mark growls, striding out.

"We saw a bear one night," I tell Jax's grandparents.

"Yes, they do come into town occasionally," Mrs. Thompson agrees calmly.

Mark and Tori still haven't come back by the time I finish my wine. "Well, I think it's bedtime for me," I announce.

"Should I go look for Mom and Dad?" Jax asks.

Mrs. Thompson rises. "I'm sure they're fine. I think I'll head to bed, too."

I help her gather up the glasses and set them in the dishwasher in the kitchen.

We hear voices outside and I peer out a window. Tori and Mark are sitting on the deck in the dark. "They're outside," I tell Jax, jerking my head.

"Ah. Okay."

"Good night, everyone, "I say. "This was so fun."

"It *was* fun. Good night, Molly." Mrs. Thompson smiles at me, a warm, genuine smile that makes me feel at ease.

I use the bathroom and then shut myself in my bedroom. Sitting on the side of the bed, I pout. Jax and I have been sleeping together every might for a couple of weeks now. I don't want to sleep alone. But with his family here, and us telling them we're "just friends," I guess we don't have much choice.

I change into my nightshirt, keeping my socks on because it does get cool here at night and my feet are always cold, and crawl into bed. I turn on my Kindle to read for a while.

But I can't focus on the story I'm reading. I keep thinking about Jax. I keep thinking about how kind he is, how he's been my rock and my knight in shining armor. I could have saved myself. I mean, I *did* save myself. But he helped. I'll always be grateful to him for that.

I like him so much. Oh God. This feeling…this swelling, warm feeling in my chest when I think about him. Not to mention the fact that I want to jump him every time I see him. This feels like more than liking him…it feels like love.

I've been in love before. And not that long ago. I was crazy about Steve. And yet…there's something about this that's different. I feel like Jax and I fit together.

There were ways Steve and I didn't fit together. He didn't like dancing. Cooking. Reading. Nothing wrong with people who don't like those things, and I don't think you have to like all the same things to be well-suited, but Jax and I always seem to be in sync—when it's time to sit together quietly and read, when it's time to get up and go for a hike. We do some alone things, like he goes for a long solo run every morning, heads to the gym in Onanole to work out while I sit on the dock and gaze at the lake or do some yoga, but he good-naturedly tagged along as I explored the cute little gift shops and I had no problem following him while he hiked around taking photographs at Deep Bay.

The bedroom door opens quietly, and Jax slips in.

My heart bumps and I smile.

He closes the door quietly, takes a couple of steps and stretches out on the bed next to me.

I toss my Kindle aside. My entire body reaches out to him, every cell full of longing for him. "Hi," I whisper.

"Hi." He lifts a hand to smooth my hair back.

"You can't sleep here."

"I know. Fuck. But I want to kiss you goodnight."

He rolls toward me, sets hand on my stomach over the quilt and leans in for a kiss. Our mouths meet in a long, heated kiss. We kiss again, and again, and I'm getting dizzy and hot.

God. I'm brimming. Overflowing with emotion and things I want to say to him. Does he feel the same?

When he draws back our eyes meet, and I search his face for any sign that he wants to say something, too. My pulse accelerates, my breath coming in tiny puffs. The air pulses around us and I wait, moments piling on moments as he cups my face, his thumb rubbing over my bottom lip.

"You're beautiful, Molly."

My face heats and my heart beats faster. "I wish you could stay."

"Me too," he groans. He kisses my forehead and rolls off the bed. "Good night, little trivia whiz." He slips noiselessly from the room.

I close my eyes, my throat tightening and my lungs constricting.

I guess he *doesn't* feel the same.

I mean, in fairness I didn't say anything to him about how I feel. Oh my God. My feelings are getting way too caught up in all this. It's a good thing I'm leaving Sunday.

I turn off the light and roll so my face is pressed into the pillow.

20

JAX

Mom, Grandma and Grandpa are planning to leave around four o'clock. I'm acutely aware of every passing hour on Sunday and the fact that Molly is leaving with them.

This makes me unaccountably angry. Not at her. I'm not sure what I'm angry at, to be honest.

I know I have to get her alone before she leaves. The last couple of days have been fun with the family but torture not sleeping with Molly. In a short time, I've gotten accustomed to having her in my bed. To having her. Every night. Every morning. Sometimes afternoons.

So after lunch on Sunday, I announce that Molly and I are going for a walk. I ignore the looks exchanged between my parents and grandparents.

We walk to the main beach and out onto the pier. At the end, we sit on the bench and look out over the lake. The sky is overcast and the lake is more gray than blue today with white-caps. The air is heavy and sultry with the promise of a thunder-storm. I want to say something, but I don't have a fucking clue what to say.

"Jax."

"Yeah?"

"You've given me so much this summer." She sighs.

"Like what?"

"Experiences. Seeing dolphins and whales in the ocean. Bison. A moose." Driving back from Lake Audy where the bison enclosure is, we saw a huge moose standing near a creek. "Seeing the Northern Lights."

"An orgasm under the Northern Lights."

She laughs. "Yes. That was spectacular. So much beauty and fun."

"You were supposed to go to Europe." Fuck. Why did I bring up the honeymoon?

"Yeah." She pauses. "Steve didn't even want to go to Europe."

"Why not?"

"Because people don't speak English there."

My eyebrows shoot up. "Um. Well, I think some do, but yeah, isn't that part of the experience?"

"Exactly!"

"No offense but the more you tell me, the more it seems like you and Steve weren't all that compatible."

She wrinkles her nose. "Yeah. He doesn't even like trivia."

"See?"

She appears to sink into thought.

I clear my throat. "Anyway. You've given me a lot, too."

She turns to me. "No, I haven't."

"Yeah, you have. The impetus to fix things with my dad. You listened to me go on and on about my contract." I pause. "I can't really talk to many people about that."

She nods. "Blow jobs."

I burst out laughing. "Yeah. *Fantastic* blow jobs. And lots of fun. I had a great summer."

"I'm glad. I did too."

Our eyes meet. I feel my heartbeat through my whole body. My breath quickens and my hands tingle with the need to touch her. Hold her. Keep her.

We agreed this is when it would end. She's going back to Chicago.

I don't believe in long-term relationships. I have this crazy fear that if I was ever in a relationship, I'd repeat my father's mistake. So I avoid relationships and commitment.

And even if I did, if I thought I could take the chance that I could actually be faithful to one woman…she's my teammate's ex. The bro code that says that's something you just can't do.

I think about Baxter, who I played with in Philly, who had an affair with another guy's wife. I think about the turmoil that caused for the whole team. If it gets out that Molly and I had an affair, I'm fucking doomed. I can kiss that contract goodbye.

It *was* a great summer, though. The best.

I almost laugh remembering how I tried to talk Molly out of coming to California with me. And then how much fun it was having her there. And how much better she made me feel about my family.

I see my own feelings reflected in Molly's eyes. The same gratitude. Happiness, yet sorrow. The same longing.

We share a smile, a slow sorrowful smile. I lean in and she turns up her face so I can cover her mouth with mine. My lips cling to hers in an achingly tender kiss and my heart nearly beats out of my chest.

"It has to be this way," she whispers. "Right?"

It takes me a few seconds to get the word out. "Right."

We plod back to the cottage, holding hands, not saying anything.

When we get there, Grandma and Grandpa are sitting on the deck.

"Where's Mom and Dad?" I ask.

"They went for a walk too," Grandma says.

Grandpa frowns.

"Oh. Okay." I'm not sure what's going on with them, but I'm sure as hell not going to be crazy enough to think they could get back together.

"I'll just go finish packing," Molly says. "I'm almost ready to go."

She disappears into the cottage, and I sit with my grandparents.

"She's a lovely girl," Grandma says.

"Yeah."

I feel the unspoken questions weighing heavy in the air. How can I answer them? She's a friend. A sweet, funny, smart, caring friend who gives unbelievable blow jobs and fucks like a dream. But she's off-limits. She's a teammate's ex.

The crunch of footsteps on the gravel driveway has our heads turning and we see Mom and Dad rounding the corner of the cottage. They both wear an expression on their face that I can't read, but it's…something. I wouldn't say anger, but there's a definite tension.

Mom smiles. "Well. Just about time to go, I guess. Jax, come help me with my suitcase."

I'm pretty sure Mom doesn't need help with her suitcase, but I follow her into the cottage just as Molly pulls her bag out of the bedroom. "I'm all set!" she says with phony cheeriness.

"Okay, we'll head out in a few minutes," Mom says.

In her bedroom, she waits until she hears the sliding doors onto the deck close, meaning we're alone in the cottage.

"Your dad says you two had a good talk in California."

"Oh. Uh. Yeah."

She holds my gaze steadily. "You thought Dad cheated on me?"

"Yeah."

"Why did you think that?"

"I overheard you talking to Betsy once. You said you felt betrayed."

She closes her eyes, nodding slowly. "I did feel betrayed. But not because he cheated on me with another woman. I felt betrayed that our marriage didn't turn out like I expected. I felt betrayed by the fact that he was always working. Traveling. Never around to deal with family stuff. His career took precedence and mine got put on hold. That was why I felt that way."

I swallow.

"Why didn't you ever say anything, Jax?"

"You didn't talk about what happened. And I didn't want to bring up something that would upset you."

"All these years, you believed that, though." She closes her eyes, the corners of her mouth turning down. "I'm so sorry, Jackson. We didn't want to burden you and Riley with our problems. But maybe we should have said more." She sighs and opens her eyes. "I'm glad that you two talked."

"Molly made me do it," I say jokingly.

Mom has the best poker face. Her expression doesn't change, but her gaze fastens on my face in that penetrating way she has. "Oh, did she?" She pauses. "Is everything okay? With you and Molly?"

"Oh yeah. Of course." I'm lying. I should end it there, but stupidly I ask, "Why?"

"You both seem sad. Are you sure she wants to come back with us?"

"Yeah." I clear my throat. "She needs to get back to Chicago. She, uh…well, she was engaged to one of my teammates."

Mom's not surprised. "I heard."

I gnaw briefly on my bottom lip. "That's why she's here.

She found out he was cheating on her. She needed to get out of town."

"That poor girl. That's terrible."

"Yeah. It was pretty hard on her. I, uh, think this summer away's been good for her though."

Now Mom's eyebrows lift. "Jax." She stops.

"What?"

"I know she was just engaged to someone else, but…I think she has feelings for you."

My lips push out and my forehead tightens. "What?"

Mom touches her fingertips to her lips. "She's crazy about you, Jax."

"No." I give my head a violent shake. "No, she's not."

"Oh, dear." Mom sighs. "And what about you?"

"What about me?"

"Do you have feelings for her?"

I scoff. "No. Of course not. I mean, I like her, obviously, but that's it. I don't get involved with women."

"I know that." She waits, but I don't say anything more. She shakes her head. "I wish you'd talk to me more."

"I talk!"

"I mean talk about real things. About how you're feeling. You mentioned your contract and I get the feeling you're worried about that, but you just brush it off. And now clearly you're unhappy about Molly leaving, but you won't admit it."

I roll my eyes. "I'm fine, Mom."

Sometimes it sucks having a mother who's a psychologist.

"Look at all the years wasted between you and your father because you kept everything locked up inside you."

I'm not sure what to say to that.

"Is the reason you don't get seriously involved with women because of what happened with Dad and me?"

I don't want to blame her for it, so I just shrug. "Maybe. Whatever. I see lots of guys getting married, getting divorced. Cheating." I'm thinking of Steve. "It's better not to go there."

"It's not as if men are programmed to cheat," she says. "There *are* men who are faithful."

"Yeah, I guess."

She sucks in a breath. "Clearly I shouldn't have waited until we're leaving to have this conversation." She pauses. "But you probably wouldn't say much more anyway. Come here." She pulls me in for a hug. "I love you. Maybe you should talk to someone else about what's going on with you."

"Like a shrink? Jeez, Mom."

"It can't hurt. I'll get some names for you."

"Oh my God."

"It's not a weakness, Jax. You should know that."

"I'm *fine*, Mom." I give her a reassuring squeeze.

"Okay, if you say so."

We return to the living room, and we all head outside to exchange hugs and goodbyes next to the car. Their bags are already loaded into the trunk. Molly's wearing the brightest smile, laughing at everything, so animated I know it's totally fake.

It has to be this way.

When it's my turn to hug her, I try to keep it casual, but man, it's impossible. I want to kiss her again and again. Feeling her curves against me, I want to squeeze her tight and never let her go.

But I can't do that.

***

Dad's staying a couple more days after everyone else leaves.

"It's been a long time since I was here," he says over barbecued hamburgers that night. "This place hasn't changed at all."

"I know. I don't think Grandma and Grandpa get up here much anymore. Actually, I'm thinking of buying it from them."

"What? Really?"

"Yeah. They been talking about selling for a few years, but they don't want to give it up. Cottages are hard to come by here."

"True. It would be a shame to lose it."

"I've been coming here every summer the last few years. I like how quiet it is. I can hike and take pictures and sometimes some of my buddies come for a week or two. So I'd hate to lose it. I think I can afford it, but I'm kind of waiting on my contract. Probably not a good idea to spend a few hundred grand on something until that's settled."

"Yeah, that's smart."

"Then I could put a bit of money into updating things. Maybe new furniture. I bought the barbecue last summer." I nod at the stainless steel beauty I picked up in Brandon and put together up here. "And the year before that, new appliances. They never had a dishwasher."

"It would be a good investment. Properties here keep going up in value. Even if you get married and have kids and settle somewhere else, you'd easily be able to sell it."

"I'm not getting married and having kids," I remind him wryly.

"What about Molly?"

I grit my teeth and drop my gaze to my plate. "We're friends. That's it."

After a beat, Dad says, "You're so full of shit, the toilet's jealous."

My mouth drops open. I laugh, then frown.

He grins.

"You and Mom apparently had a good talk about me."

"Yeah, actually, we did. Parents do that. What's going on with you and Molly?"

"Why is everyone all up in my business?" I set down my burger and reach for my beer. "Jesus, this entire family keeps asking me 'what about Molly.' I keep telling everyone, we're just friends. So just drop it, okay?" I take a big swig of lager.

Dad blinks in surprise, then gives a terse nod. "Sure. Okay."

We eat in heavy silence for a few minutes, and I take a few deep breaths. Then I change the subject and ask Dad about his coaching plans for the coming season.

After dinner, I wander down to the dock on my own. I sit and dip my feet into the water. My chest feels hollow and my body weary.

I can't believe how bummed I am that Molly's gone. It's ridiculous. We agreed that this was going to end. We both know why. I don't even believe in love. So I don't get why I feel like my right arm has been hacked off?

I close my eyes. Whatever these feelings are, this is all for the best. Even if it is love, I know it's only temporary. Marriage is for suckers. Long-term relationships don't really exist.

I've seen it with my own parents, not to mention friends and teammates. Relationships are hard enough, never mind in the hockey world where you're on the road half the season and women are always hanging around and your career has to come first.

With Molly, I kept having weird visions, though. Glimpses of being with her in the future, years down the road, being faithful to her and worshiping her and cherishing her like she deserves. Her trusting me. I can't believe how much those images made me want that…with a deep, almost painful hunger.

Except I don't believe I'm capable of those things.

Molly

I held it together during the drive from the lake to Winnipeg. I kept the smile in place as I hugged Mr. and Mrs. Thompson and Tori goodbye and thanked them for letting me stay at the cottage and waved to them as they pulled away from the hotel. I booked a room here because it's close to the airport and they have a shuttle that will take me there for my flight in the morning.

I trudge through the lobby, my smile gone, my energy dissipated. Wow, that was exhausting. I just want to check in and hole up in my room alone.

Soon I am doing just that. I change into a pair of shorts and a T-shirt. I lie back on the bed with the room service menu to peruse options. Not that I'm hungry.

I end up ordering a sandwich. While I wait, I turn on the TV and flick through various channels. Nothing catches my interest. I end up leaving it on a food channel and let myself slide into a crater of depression.

I already miss Jax.

My heart aches, the throb echoing in my head.

I can't be like this. It'll be fine. After being with him basically twenty-four seven for the past six weeks, of course I miss him. But when I get back to Chicago and back to my normal life, I'll forget him.

Whatever my normal life is now. I still have things to do. I have to get the rest of my belongings from Steve's condo and move them back to my apartment. Soon it will be time to get back into the classroom and prepare for the new school year. I always look forward to that, especially going shopping for supplies and cute things to decorate the classroom with.

I'll be fine once I'm home.

21

MOLLY

I've moved back into my apartment. My parents helped out with the move and also bought me a new couch because my old one was atrocious and I trashed it when I moved in with Steve. I've picked up more stuff from Steve's place and made a few trips to IKEA for things, and I'm happy with how it all looks.

I messaged Steve and told him we can talk when he gets back to town. I haven't heard from him since the trip to Europe, so I guess he's accepted that we're done, after the flurry of frantic and pissed-off messages and voice mails. I've come across a few Instagram posts from his trip home, but he's not on social media much.

Now he's back and we're going to meet for lunch.

I was so angry at him when I found out he was cheating. I was heartbroken. I was also dreading talking to him because I knew it was going to hurt. Now…eh. We have to do it, but I'm so far past it at this point, I barely care.

I do question how much I really loved him, if I got over him that quickly. Maybe it was for the best that I found out he was cheating. Especially that I found out *before* the wedding. I found a meme on Instagram that says not all storms come to disrupt your life; some come to clear your path. So I'm staying positive and considering this event to be a good thing in my life.

I don't know what my future will be, but I know I'll be okay. Even if I am really sad that spending so much time with an amazing man and coming to care for him all happened with the wrong guy at the wrong time. If only Jax didn't play hockey with Steve. If only I hadn't just jilted my fiancé. Because I've come to realize that Jax was my rebound. Brielle was right—the first guy I care about after my engagement ended is *not* going to be my next long-term relationship. It just doesn't work like that.

I walk into the Good Egg, a little diner not too far from my apartment in Andersonville. They serve breakfast and lunch.

Steve is already there, seated in a booth along the wall.

Regret settles in my stomach like a lump. This is all so sad.

I make my way over. It's awkward. He stands. Neither of us know whether to shake hands or hug or punch each other. So I slide into the booth opposite him without doing any of those.

"You look great," Steve says, taking his seat again. "All tanned and relaxed."

"You sound surprised. Did you think I was pining away for you?"

His face flushes. "No."

I sigh. "I don't know where to start."

"Neither do I." He picks up his mug of coffee. "This is fucking weird."

"I know."

A waitress arrives with a pot of coffee. I nod and she fills my cup then asks if we're ready to order. I glance quickly at the menu. I've been here before, and I love their eggs bennie—the one with smoked salmon and avocado. So I order that. Steve gets a chicken Santa Fe wrap.

I pull the small box out of my purse and push it across the

table to him. "Here's your ring back."

He stares at it. "I don't want it back."

"Take it. You paid for it."

He shakes his head and the box sits untouched between us.

"I don't want it, Steve," I say quietly. "I don't even want the money I could get if I sold it. I know there are some wedding things you can't get your money back on and I can't afford to pay you back for all of them, but you can use that to pay for some."

He sighs and pockets it.

"Katelyn says all the wedding gifts were returned."

"I guess."

He doesn't even care.

I curl my hands around my coffee cup and meet his eyes. "Why? Why did you do that?"

"I don't know." He shoves a hand into his blond hair and looks away. "I really don't know."

"The things you said about me…to that woman…that really hurt."

"I'm sorry." He meets my eyes, and I see genuine remorse there.

I swallow. "Well, thanks for that." I pause. "Was she the only woman you cheated on me with?" I watch his response.

"Yes."

"Really? Because Brielle said you came onto her once."

His eyes widen. "What? I did not."

I tilt my head. Hold his gaze. Say nothing.

"I might have flirted a little," he says. "But it didn't mean anything."

I nod sadly. "And Claire? Who is she? Are you still together?"

His lips tighten and his throat works. "Yeah."

I nod again. I guess I'm not surprised. It hurts. But not as much as I might have thought. "What were you thinking?" I shake my head. "We were getting married. What were you *thinking?*"

"I *wasn't* thinking, okay?" He rolls his eyes. "I don't know. I guess I was freaking out about getting married or something."

"Oh my God." I pull in a long breath through my nose. "Do you love her?"

He lifts one shoulder. "I don't know."

Poor Claire.

"Did you take her to Europe?"

"Wait. Where the hell were *you* all summer? Where did you disappear to?"

"That's not an answer." Damn deflection. Nice try, though.

"Fine, yeah, I did. Why not? You were gone and clearly didn't want to go. I paid for the trip."

It makes me so, so sad that I wanted to marry this man. He's not a bad man…okay, cheating isn't exactly honorable, but he's not mean or abusive. But he's not…

He's not Jax.

I bow my head briefly.

"Was it her who sent me those screen shots?" I ask. "I've been wondering."

He shifts in his chair. "I asked her and she said it wasn't."

"Who else could it have been?"

"I don't know." He looks away. "I changed the password on my phone."

I narrow my eyes at him. "If she did that…" I stop. "Whatever. It's your problem."

"So where were you hiding out?" he asks, changing the subject. "I know you weren't with Grace or your other friends."

"No. It doesn't matter who I was with or where I was. I just wanted to get away from Chicago for a while."

Our lunches arrive and we stop talking for a few minutes.

Waiting for the waitress to refill our cups and leave, I pick up my knife and fork. When she's gone, I ask, "Why wasn't I enough for you?"

I hate asking this. It's the question I asked myself over and over again since the day I found out he cheated on me. I hate sounding so pathetic, but I still want to know.

He shakes his head. "Molly."

"No, really. I want to know."

"It's not that. Look, I haven't been in that many relationships. I didn't think it was that big a deal."

I blink. I still haven't cut into my eggs bennie. "What? Not that big a deal? Cheating?"

"You went out with other guys all the time."

My eyes fly open and my fork clatters to the table. "What? I did not!"

"Well, you went out with Jax. All those trivia nights. You're saying nothing ever happened between you two? Or other guys you met?"

My jaw hangs loosely. "Are you kidding me?"

He waits.

"Nothing ever happened! I never cheated on you. That's crazy. Why would you think that?"

"I don't know." He shrugs and doesn't meet my eyes. "Like I said, I kind of thought maybe fidelity was…flexible."

"Oh my God." I didn't think it was a problem going out with a friend; I certainly didn't believe that fidelity was flexible. I'm trying to understand, but it's hard for me. Cheating is a hard limit for me. Isn't it for most people? Maybe not. "You should have told me," I whisper. "If only you'd told me."

"Yeah. I guess I should have. I don't think I'm, uh, mature enough for marriage."

Clearly not.

"I've been thinking about it a lot. I still don't understand why I did it. I wanted something…" He pauses. "I don't even know what I wanted. But it wasn't about you, Molly." His tone is softer. "I don't want you to think that. It was never about you. It was me, going through some stuff, looking for something."

Huh. I appreciate him saying it. But the thing is…I already know that. I figured it out for myself, maybe sometime while I was lying around the pool in California, or while I was pretending that everything was fine while I raged inside. Or while Jax was looking at me like I was precious, laughing at my jokes, and taking care of me like I mattered. This whole experience may have kicked my confidence in the teeth, but in the end…I'm okay. I'm really okay.

"I wish you'd talked to me." I try to eat some of my lunch, but once again I've lost my appetite.

"I'm sorry."

"You were pissed about the wedding."

He frowns. "Yeah. Jesus, Molly. That was humiliating."

"You deserved it," I say calmly.

He makes a rough noise and I don't know if he's disgusted or agreeing with me. Or both.

I ask how his parents are doing. We talk about what he did at home, and how he's been skating with some of the guys who are back in town.

"Who's here?" I ask casually.

"Well, Duper and Army, of course. Jax, Bomber, Benny."

I nod. I feel a piercing little pain in my heart. Jax is in town. I haven't heard from him since I left the lake. Even though I texted him when I was back in Chicago to let him know I made it safe and sound.

Steve insists on paying for lunch. Maybe he has a guilty conscience. Even though he thought fidelity was "flexible." Jesus.

We part outside the diner on the sidewalk. It's a sultry mid-

August day, overcast, hot and windy. I eye Steve uncertainly. "Well. Thanks for lunch."

"You're welcome. Molly." He opens his arms for a hug.

I move into them. It feels…okay. Like hugging a friend. I don't get that close, and then I step back. "Bye."

His mouth tips down at the corners. "I really blew it with you."

"I don't think it was meant to be. For us."

"No?" He eyes me, then nods. "Maybe so."

Well, it would have been gratifying if he'd been all broken up and fell down on his knees and groveled for me to take him back. But I guess it's good that we're on the same page and again, another sign that things worked out for the best.

I watch him walk away, that big frame and long-legged stride so familiar to me. My bottom lip pushes out as emotion engulfs me. But it's not because I want him back. It's just because it's sad that we were once so happy together, and now we're not.

But I wouldn't be happier *with* him.

I walk along the sidewalk and around the corner onto West Argyle where I parked my car.

Weirdly, now I miss Jax more than ever. I've been trying so hard not to think about him. But that's impossible. It's only been a few weeks, though. I keep telling myself that I'll get over him, that he was just my rebound. I just have to keep going.

The girls and I are going out for dinner and drinks tonight. I spent the day at school, setting up my classroom. Now I'm home, getting ready to go out. I'm happy to see my friends, but unexcited about going out.

I twirl a few waves into my hair and mess it up, and decide

to go all out on the makeup—smoky eyeshadow, lots of mascara, and bright lip gloss. I dress in a new jumpsuit I just bought—black, off-the-shoulder, fitted bodice and loose pants. Then I take the train to Michigan Avenue. We're meeting at Aster, a rooftop bar near the Riverwalk. As I walk from the train station to the restaurant, I'm acutely aware that I'm only a few blocks from Jax's place. I have the crazy thought of skipping dinner and dropping in on him.

Ha.

I imagine arriving there and finding him entertaining another woman.

Bleh. A small sharp knife twists in my heart.

I know Jax. I know he likes to date lots of women. I have to accept that.

I take the elevator up to the roof of the building to get to Aster. I'm the first one there, so I let the hostess seat me outside at the table for four. I've never been here, and it's gorgeous—I'm at a table with a couch and two chairs loaded with cushions. A huge lamp sits next to us for when it gets dark. Chicago architecture towers all around us, the views unobstructed by glass walls. Big tubs hold plenty of colorful flowers.

I study the cocktail menu while I wait for my friends. They have drinks that come as a single glass or in a decanter, so I go crazy and order a decanter of a wild concoction of tequila and things I've never heard of. And grapefruit. I hope it's good.

Grace arrives and I jump up to greet her with hugs, then repeat the process when Brielle shows up. The waiter brings us the pitcher of cocktails and the girls are all impressed as immediately drinks are poured for them.

"So, how did it go?" Grace give me big curious eyes.

"With Steve?"

"No, with the mailman." She rolls her eyes.

I laugh. "It went okay. He's calmed down."

"Pffft. Like he had a right to be angry." Grace tosses her mass of spirally black hair.

"I suppose. I feel a little guilty for handling it the way I did."

"You should not," Brielle says firmly. "You were betrayed. You can handle it however you want."

"Well, I'm glad you didn't take a baseball bat to his Jag," Grace says.

"Ha ha! You could've sold his Jag on eBay!" Brielle says. "That would have been hilarious!"

"Or replace his shampoo with Nair," Grace adds.

"These are amazing ideas," I say calmly, taking a sip of my drink. "Is it too late for them?"

"No!"

"I'm kidding." I smile. "I don't even care anymore."

"Really?" Grace studies my face. "You're okay?"

"I really am." One corner of my mouth kicks up. "About Steve, anyway."

"Oh no." Grace pouts. "Are you still missing Jax?"

I sigh. "Yeah. Seeing Steve weirdly just made me miss him even more."

Sympathetic silence falls over us for a few minutes. Then Brielle says, "Have you talked to him?"

"Jax? No."

"Maybe you should."

I shake my head. "We agreed things would end when we came back to Chicago. He doesn't do relationships." I smile glumly. "And neither do I, anymore."

"Well, I think you should start dating," Brielle says. "Get yourself back out there."

"Ugh."

"Download those dating apps again," Brielle says.

"I thought I was done with those," I say with a sigh.

"Come on. Let's get Tinder on your phone. Hand it over."

"I can do it."

"Do it now."

I laugh at Brielle's pushiness. "Fine." I pull my phone out and download the app.

"Okay, let's look at some options. Start swiping, girl," Brielle says.

They peer over my shoulder as I scroll through profiles, half-heartedly swiping right on a few of them. Probably nothing will come of it; I'm not exactly the type of sexy babe men go crazy over.

But maybe this is the answer. Meet new men. Have some fun. That will get Jax out of my system.

"Why are you so sure it's a rebound relationship?" Brielle asks about Jax.

"You said it would be! The first relationship after a breakup is a rebound."

"I said that? Huh." She frowns. "Well, I mean, chances are good it's a rebound, but it doesn't have to be. I was just reading about this the other day."

"Rebound relationships?" I lift my eyebrows.

"It was an advice column. The guy was asking if he's a 'rebound.' The advice columnist told him…wait, let me pull it up." She swipes her own phone to find the column. "It's a rebound if she's still bitter about her ex. If she wants to make him jealous. If she's fixated on her ex in general. If she's totally in love with you for no reason. If you have lots of sex."

I grin. "Well, that's the only one that applies."

"I'm jealous," Brielle says. "Jax is so freakin' hot."

"Okay, I'm definitely not fixated on Steve. I don't even care anymore. And I don't care about Jax for no reason. I always liked him, and I got to know him better and he's such a great guy. Just a little…repressed."

"Sexually?" Grace frowns.

"No! God, no. Emotionally."

"That's not a good thing," she replies, lifting her hands.

"I know. If he would just open up a bit more about his feelings, he'd be better off. His family's a bit overwhelming though, and I know he was hurt by his parents' divorce, so I can kind of see why he's like that."

"Maybe it's not a rebound," Grace points out. "Maybe you have real feelings for him."

"It doesn't matter." I shrug. "He obviously doesn't feel the same. It was just a fling for him, which is all he ever does with women."

"The advice also says that when someone gets dumped unexpectedly, they don't have as much time to heal as someone who knows a relationship is over for a while before it actually ends."

"Well, that's true," I say slowly. "I don't know how much time someone needs to heal, but it's probably more than a day."

They all laugh, even though I'm not really joking.

"I think that's different for everyone," Grace says. "Although I do believe time to heal is important before committing to someone else."

I nod slowly. Maybe I do need more time. Maybe my feelings for Jax *weren't* real.

"One thing I can say in Jax's favor is that he never made a pass at me," Brielle says. "Sadly, for me."

I laugh. "Steve denied doing that. But then he said it didn't mean anything. Bastard."

"Hell yeah. You're better off without him. Lying cheating motherfucker."

We all lift our glasses in a toast.

22

JAX

It's nearly the end of August. And I still don't have a contract.

Fuck.

I started skating with some of the guys when I got back to town. It feels great to be back on the ice again. I've been working out harder too, training at the gym.

I have to admit, the first time I stepped onto the ice with Chucky, I kind of wanted to drive him hard into the boards and then punch him in the face. I did none of that. I greeted him casually and pretended nothing had changed.

I fucking hate it.

I feel like I'm lying, even though I haven't said a word to him about Molly. I don't know what's happened between them because I haven't heard from Molly since the day she arrived back in Chicago. It's killing me, but it is what it is.

For all I know they could be back together.

That only makes me want to punch him even more.

I don't have to worry about that anymore though, because everyone else is now skating every day at the Aces' practice facility, and I can't.

Because I don't have a contract.

It's less than three weeks until training camp starts, and I'm still at the community rink, basically on my own.

It's really bugging me, even though Paul keeps assuring me it's fine. I'm trying not to get snarky with him, not to blame him for the delays. This happens every year to a few players. And even if I have to miss training camp, it's not the end of the world.

I'm not so sure about that. I'm working hard, but it's great to have other elite-level players around to push you to work harder and do better. It would be tough coming in without having that kind of preparation and time with the team.

And I want to be with the team, not practicing all by myself. This sucks ass.

I've had calls from the media, and I know Paul has too, not to mention Ian Yarish, the team GM. I keep telling them what Paul told me to say, that I'm not worried, I know it will get done, blah blah blah.

"Obviously you'd prefer that a deal get done before training camp?" the reporter asked.

"Well, yeah, that's the plan. We never want to miss training camp, so that's our goal, yeah. But nothing to panic about yet, these things just take some time."

But I am worried. I trust Paul. I know he's working on it. But still...

"Are you or the team waiting for someone like Charbonneau to make a deal?" the reporter asked, referring to another free agent in New York who still hasn't signed.

I refused to comment on that and so did Paul, but it's definitely a factor.

The dude on TSN announced the other night that the team and I aren't even close on contract negotiations, apparently confirmed by Paul. Another sports reporter announced that other teams have reached out to the Aces about a possible trade.

I don't want a fucking trade. I want a long-term deal here in Chicago. That's what we've been pushing for. I want six years. Would I take five? Probably. Four? I don't know. So far they've only offered three and not enough money.

I already knew about this from Paul, so it wasn't a shock, but I hate that this shit is making the news.

I feel like I have no one to talk to about this. The guys with contracts are practicing together. I still see them, but I'm leery of saying anything that could get out when Paul has drilled into me how important it is to keep our negotiations private. Mom and Dad have both called, so I've told them what's happening, but I kept up the positive façade I present to the media so they don't know how much I'm freaking out.

Tonight I'm going out for dinner with Paul to get an update on their meeting today. I'm not optimistic that the news will be good.

We're meeting at a steak house near my place, so I walk there and meet him at the restaurant. This place is upscale and expensive, but not stuffy, and the food is great.

We're at a table for two in the dimly lit restaurant when for some reason I lift my head as the hostess shows a couple to a table across the room.

It's Molly.

And who the fuck is that she's with?

I frown. I don't know the guy. His suit looks expensive. I'd say he's about ten years older than Molly and me. Jesus.

"Jax?"

I look blankly back at Paul.

"Did you hear me?"

"No. Sorry."

Paul repeats his questions about what it would take to get me to sign a four-year deal.

"I don't know."

Paul rolls his eyes, then follows my gaze across the room. "What's going on? See someone you know?"

"Yeah. Sort of."

"Ex-girlfriend?"

I huff an unamused laugh. "Sort of."

Molly, apparently sensing my attention, turns and looks straight at me.

I don't react. Just hold her gaze.

Her eyes widen and she visibly flinches back. Then she lifts a hand in a tiny wave.

I lift my hand too, smiling wryly.

She turns her attention back to the toolbox she's with. Is she on a fucking date?

"Jax."

I give my head a shake and try to focus on my conversation with Paul and my delicious twenty-eight-day dry-aged bone-in rib eye.

I'm hyper aware of Molly just across the room, though.

After she left the lake, I was a sad panda. I kept a happy face on until Dad left and I was alone. And then I was really alone. I've been at the lake by myself before, and I don't mind it. But this year it was a definite downer. I ended up coming home sooner than I planned, which didn't actually help because then I knew I was in the same city as Molly and still couldn't see her.

And now she's here. A few feet away from me. Looking beautiful and sexy, her hair its usual mess of waves brushing her shoulders. Smiling at another man.

Fuck.

I order another whiskey, since I'm walking home and also

since I don't have a fucking contract. Getting hammered suddenly seems like a great idea.

Paul and I are done our dinners and are finishing off our drinks when Molly gets up and walks toward what I assume are the restrooms. My heart leaps in my chest.

I watch her companion. He pulls out his phone and starts looking at it, but he's not making a move to leave the table. I give it a few minutes, then right in the middle of one of Paul's sentences, I stand. "Excuse me," I say abruptly. "I'll be right back."

I set my napkin on the seat of my chair and walk the same way Molly did. The hallway to the restrooms is narrow with low lighting, the walls painted black with gold sconces and gold framed pictures on the walls.

But I don't enter the men's room. Nope, I hang out in the hall hoping nobody comes along and thinks I'm some kind of creeper.

My timing is perfect, though. Molly emerges from the bathroom with shiny lips and a small purse in her hand. She stops dead at seeing me, her lips parting.

"Hi."

"Hi." She gives me a tremulous smile. "How are you?"

She's beautiful. She has on more makeup than I'm used to seeing, with her eyes all smoky and her skin gleaming. She's gorgeous either way, though. "Shitty. Thanks for asking. You?"

"I'm...okay."

"Are you on a date?"

"Y-yes." She blinks.

I close my eyes at the churning feeling in my stomach. Then I open them and nod. "So you and Steve didn't get back together?"

Her eyebrows pull down. "No! Of course not. How could you think that?"

"I don't know. How would I know?"

"Haven't you talked to him? He mentioned you were skating together."

"Not anymore." I rub the back of my neck. "I still don't have a contract so I can't skate with the team."

"Oh. Oh no." Her eyes shadow and she takes a step closer. "What's going on with that?"

"Nothing. We're miles apart. Still waiting."

"I'm sorry."

"Yeah, it's frustrating as hell." It feels good to admit that out loud to someone.

She studies my face. "Is that your agent you're with?"

"Yeah. He had a meeting with Ian today so he wanted to update me and talk about some other scenarios he can take to them. Who's your date?"

"Um. His name is Nicholas. We met…online."

I mutter a curse under my breath.

"What?" Her eyebrows lift. "Is that a problem?"

Hell yeah, it's a problem. It's a big fucking problem. I don't want her to be with any other man but me. I'm not interested in dating and goddammit, it hurts that she is.

How can I say that, though?

She seems to be waiting for me to say *something*. The noises of the restaurant—clinking cutlery and glasses, voices, music—fade away and we're standing alone in this dark, narrow space in a bubble of our own personal space.

"Molly."

She nods.

"I miss you."

Her bottom lip quivers. "I miss you, too," she whispers, her fingers tightening on the little purse.

"Shit."

Neither of us move. My body aches for her, though. My hands want to reach out for her. My mouth wants to taste her.

"Does Nicholas like trivia?" I ask roughly.

"I don't know. This is our first date."

I nod tersely.

"I better get back," she says softly. She walks forward to pass me in the hall. I step back even though I want to block her way. She pauses near me, near enough for me to smell her sweet citrusy scent. "Good luck with your contract."

"Thanks." Right now, that seems meaningless. I just want her. More than anything.

How did things get so fucked up?

She brushes past me. I watch her walk away. She's wearing a black halter dress fitted to her curves, baring her shoulders. It ends just above her knees and her legs look killer in black heels.

Emotion swirls inside me, filling my chest. Anger. Frustration. Regret.

Without using the men's room, I go back to the table where Paul is waiting for me, not looking at Molly and Nicholas. Paul's already taken care of the check. "Thanks, man," I say as I sit again. I pick up my whiskey and down the remainder.

"I have to fly to Toronto tomorrow," he says. "But I'll keep you in the loop about any more talks with Yarish."

"It's not going to get done before training camp, is it?"

"Not looking like it right now. But before the season starts, sure."

I nod. "Okay."

I can't resist another look at Molly as we walk out, and she turns her head and flashes a tiny sad smile that fucking breaks my heart.

I stroll along the Esplanade on my way home. It's dark now, but there are still lots of other people around. The river reflects city lights on its inky surface, and I pause at the low wall to gaze out over it.

I have to get my shit together. But right now feels like a low point in my life. I finally found a woman I actually want a relationship with, and I can't have her. And I found a team I want to stay with, and they don't want me.

Okay, I'm being pathetic. It's not that they don't want me. I know it's a business. It's all about the numbers. But it's hard not to take things personally. I know I'm not in a good frame of mind, and both these deficiencies in my life seem worse because of that.

Maybe. Or maybe they really are shitty.

I need to do what Molly's doing—move on with my life. Find some other woman to bang. Maybe prepare myself to play elsewhere this year.

Or maybe I'll just go home and finish getting drunk.

Molly

"I can't believe I saw Jax the first time I went on a date."

"I know. That's a hell of a coincidence." Grace and I are sitting on her big sectional in her living room. Her fiancé is out tonight.

"Nicholas was a nice guy, but it felt like so much work being with him. I get that we don't know each other at all and it takes time, so I was going to agree to a second date. But after seeing Jax that night, it only reinforced how bored and uninterested I was in Nicholas. So I turned him down. Which pissed him off."

"Ugh. Men."

"I know! I'm getting all kinds of action on Tinder, and not

all of it's good. Holy shit, there are a lot of assholes out there. One guy asked me if that was my real hair or a wig."

"Oh my God."

"Right? Another guy sent five cringe-y pickup lines in a row, not getting the hint after I didn't respond to the first one that I wasn't interested. Then there was the dude who asked how my head game is."

"What did you tell him?"

"I told him he'll never know."

Grace laughs.

"And the guy who told me how beautiful I am and begged me to have sex with him."

"Ugh."

"Right?" I shake my head. "I really just want to give up on this dating game."

"What about Andrew?"

Yeesh.

There was another guy on Tinder who seemed okay. Grace and Brielle were supportive and encouraging. I didn't think it was going to work, but dammit, I was determined to give it a shot.

"His mouth was gross."

"What?" She stares at me.

"I looked at his mouth and tried to imagine kissing him. I couldn't."

I met Andrew for drinks after work one day. Once again, he seemed like a nice guy. He had a good job, he dressed well, he was well spoken. He didn't get some of my jokes, but maybe that's something that takes time. I gave it an honest shot and went out with him again. Still turned off.

"What is wrong with me?" I ask Grace. "Why am I not interested in anyone?"

"Nothing is wrong with you." She sighs. "Maybe we were

wrong to push you into dating again. Maybe you need time by yourself to heal."

"Honestly? I'm healed. I don't care about Steve."

"I mean, maybe you need to time to heal from *Jax*."

My head jerks around. My mouth falls open. Shit.

For some reason, my throat constricts and my eyes sting.

Jax is…everything. Smart. Funny. Kind and generous. Yes, he's a little bottled-up, but I think he just needs to feel safe with making himself vulnerable. Also, he's incredibly attractive.

I think what's upsetting me is the thought that I need to get over him. That we can't be together. I drop my head forward, my chin hitting my chest. "Fuck."

"Yeah."

After a moment I lift my head. "There *is* something wrong with me. Steve didn't care enough to be faithful or honest. Jax just wanted a sexy fling. I fell for him, but he didn't fall for me. It's me. I'm not good enough."

"Molly, that is not true. You're amazing. Smart, kind, wonderful with kids. With all people, really. Fun to be with."

"Thank you." I try for a wan smile. It's great to have the support of friends, but deep inside I still feel inadequate. "Maybe you're right. Maybe I do need time by myself. Not just to heal. But to come to terms with who I am."

Grace tilts her head. "I know you've had a couple of disappointments. But you've always been someone who's comfortable in your own skin. You should take some time, though, and sort out what you really want."

I feel like I've already taken time. It's been over a month since I left Jax at Clear Lake. I've had a lot of time to reflect and evaluate what happened. To consider my feelings for Steve and for Jax. A month isn't very long, out of a whole lifetime, but I'm confident that my feelings for Steve are over, and my feelings for Jax…aren't.

After seeing him the other night, my stomach was in knots worrying about his contract. He seemed so glum about it. I *hate* that he's unhappy. There's nothing I can do to help, except…I could be there for him. Listen to him. Tell him it's going to be okay. I wish so much I could do that.

Should I try?

23

JAX

I frown as my doorman tells me there's someone here to see me. "Who is it?"

I'm not expecting anyone. Is it one of my teammates here to commiserate with me? Jesus. I rub my face.

"It's Molly Flynn, Mr. Wynn."

My heart stops. Then it slams into a rapid rhythm against my chest. For a few seconds I can't get words out. "Okay," I finally croak. "Send her up."

I drop my phone and stare across the room. What the fuck?

It takes a few minutes for the elevator to deliver her to my floor, but my door is open and I'm waiting for her, leaning against the doorframe trying to look casual and curious.

She walks down the hall toward me, wearing a pair of ripped jeans and a black T-shirt that says *I'm a teacher. To save time let's just assume I am never wrong.*

My lips twitch.

Her mouth is tight, her eyes flickering. "Hi, Jax."

"Hey. What's up, Flynn?"

She plays with the strap of the small red purse she's carrying. "I was wondering if we could talk."

I keep my face expressionless.

For some reason, the first thing I think of is that she's pregnant. It's been a while since we were together. What if...

I can't stop the big grin that breaks across my face.

She frowns.

I don't know why I love this possibility. I must be fucking nuts.

"Sure, come on in."

Giving me a strange look, she walks past me and into my condo. She stands in the foyer and I gesture to the living room.

"Something to drink?" It's seven o'clock on a Wednesday evening. "Glass of wine? Or a beer? Water?"

"Tequila?"

I laugh, but quickly sober. That means she's not pregnant. Damn.

I stride to my kitchen, shaking my head at my own ridiculousness. Things are weird enough already, and adding a pregnancy in sure as hell wouldn't help.

I bring the tequila bottle and two glasses and set them on my coffee table. She's taken a seat on the couch, the same place she sat that night I brought her here after the aborted wedding.

"So what's up?" I pour Gran Patrón into a glass and hand it to her.

"Not much with me. Getting ready for school to start next week."

"How's Nicholas?"

Her head jerks back. "What? Oh. I don't know. I only went out with him once."

"Ah. Seeing someone else now?"

"No." She shakes her head. "I've decided I need to be alone for a while."

I'm good with that. Because it really fucked me up seeing her with that dipstick that night. I don't know why. She deserves to be happy after what happened. On the other hand, I don't want her to be lonely.

I gulp my own tequila. "So what brings you here?"

"I wanted to see how things are going with you. With the contract."

I sigh. "Nothing. The team hasn't even wanted to talk."

"Oh no." Her mouth turns down at the corners. "Are you okay?"

"Of course I'm okay." She's studying me, head cocked, and I drop my gaze. "Sort of," I mutter.

She fidgets on the couch and takes a mouthful of tequila. "I thought maybe you'd want to talk about it."

"There's nothing to talk about."

I look up and catch a flash of hurt in her eyes before she drops her gaze. Shit.

"My agent is handling it," I add. "He's doing what he can."

"Are you worried about being traded?"

"More worried about an offer sheet. But nobody's put one in."

"A what?"

"Offer sheet. It's basically a contract offer from another team. If they put in an offer sheet, the Aces have seven days to decide if they want to match it."

"I see."

"It doesn't happen very often, but there's been a lot of talk of it this year because of the salary cap crunch some teams are feeling. Including the Aces."

"So…no other offers, no contract. You just sit in limbo and wait for a contract or to get traded."

"Basically, yeah. We could go to arbitration. But we have to sign a contract by December first or I can't play for the rest of the season."

"That would suck."

"Fuck, yeah."

We're both silent for a few minutes.

"Have you talked to your parents?"

"Oh yeah. They've called. But I don't have much to tell them either."

I don't tell her that every time I talk to them, they ask about her. Not only that, every text message and email I get from Riley, Everly, and Grandpa and Chelsea asks about her. What the hell happened? She tagged along on a couple of trips with me and my whole goddamn family fell in love with her, apparently.

"Jax. It's not just talking about news. It's talking about how you're feeling about all this. How you're dealing with it."

"I'm dealing with it fine. I'm skating and working out."

She lets out a short sigh. We sit silently for a moment. I want to ask her a million questions about her classroom and how she's doing and if she's played trivia and…

She finishes her tequila and sets the glass down. "Well. I'll go." She stands.

Shit. I don't want her to leave. I like having her here, even if we're not saying anything.

My mouth goes dry and I jump to my feet. "Wait."

She pauses.

I don't know what to say. I don't want to tell her that I feel lost. Weak. Scared. I don't know what my future holds, and I fucking hate that. I've kept up the carefree, lighthearted front for the media and for my family. I can keep it up for her.

After a moment, she turns and walks out.

I follow her to the door, a bitter taste in my mouth. "Don't worry about me," I say lightly. "It'll all be fine."

She turns to face me, her pretty eyes shadowed, her mouth soft. "I know that," she says quietly. "But I'm not so sure you do."

Then she leaves.

I let the door fall closed with a click, staring at it.

I return to the couch and the bottle of tequila. Sure, I'll have another.

Fuck. I'm an asshole.

Molly came here to talk to me and listen to me, and I shut her down because I don't want to look weak. Or be vulnerable. I've always thought it was a strength that I could hide my emotions. When my parents split up, I didn't want to let on to either of them, or to anyone, how busted up inside I was. And that has always served me well. I've had bad games, made stupid mistakes and had disappointments in my career. I get through it by shrugging it all off. I've had all kinds of family shit going on that I stayed apart from.

Ever since Molly walked out of her wedding, I've been dragged into a whole bunch of emotional shit. Telling her all the crap about my family. Taking her to meet them. Her making me talk to my dad when I would rather have a hockey stick poked in my eye. Then…the sex.

I keep thinking about lying in that sleeping bag with her under the Northern Lights. Fingering her pussy to the most incredible orgasm. Her mouth on my cock and the look of delight in her eyes as she sucked me. I think about playing Trivial Pursuit with her, and yeah, the naked part was fun, but I love how she challenges me and makes me laugh. I remember sitting in front of the fire with her and just talking about anything and everything, including my hopes for my career. And hers. I remember how passionate and excited she was about the new school year and the kids she'd be teaching.

I've mastered the art of the one-night stand, even a few

nights of no-strings sex with a woman. But with Molly…I felt stuff I've never felt before. Stuff I don't want to feel.

And right now…I'm goddamn miserable.

I blow out a long breath and slouch down into the couch, tequila glass in hand.

Once this contract shit is settled, I'll be fine. *That's* what's messing with my head. Not Molly.

Molly

I ride the elevator down, cruise through the lobby of Jax's building and then walk the sidewalk to where I parked my car. It's getting dark and a chilly wind is blowing off the nearby lake.

In my car, I start the engine and lock the doors, then I sit there for a few minutes. My heart is shrinking in my chest. I close my eyes on a wave of pain.

I knew I was taking a chance going to see him. I knew there was a possibility he wouldn't want to see me. I don't know why I feel so hurt. Maybe I had a tiny pinch of hope that we could still have something?

That wasn't my intent in coming here. I really did want to help him, if I could. Because I care.

I suck in a shaky breath and let it out slowly.

This wasn't supposed to happen. I don't just care about Jax. I love him. Is it a rebound? I don't think so. I *know* it's not. I'm in love with him.

I was running away from Chicago because I was hurt and humiliated, and didn't believe in love anymore. And I fell in love…for real.

Sadness washes through me, heaviness weighing down my arms and legs, my throat burning.

I could see Jax wasn't being honest. Maybe that "whatever" attitude works with some people, but I know Jax pretty well now, and I can see past it. He's not happy. He just doesn't want to admit it.

I hate that he feels that way. I hate that things aren't working out for him.

But they will. I *know* it. It may not be exactly what he wants, but he's a talented player and some team will snap him up if things don't get done soon. The idea of him leaving Chicago, though, feels like a fist ripping out my internal organs.

I lean my forehead on the steering wheel. What does it matter to me where he is? We can't be together regardless. I do know he wants to stay here, though.

Finally I get my shit together and put my car in drive to head home.

I still feel like a lump of fractured ice has replace my heart.

<hr>

Jax

Having just showered at the rink, I'm getting dressed when my phone rings. It's an actual phone call, which usually means it's Mom or Paul. I reach for it and see it's Paul.

Fuck, I can't take more disappointment right now. I ignore the call and toss my phone back into the locker as I finish dressing.

Training camp started yesterday. I'm not there. Obviously.

Whatever he wants to tell me, I'll find out later.

My legs have the strength of garden hoses right now. I pushed myself hard out there on the ice. Whatever happens,

I'm going to be in shape to deal with it. Unless I have a heart attack first. Ha.

I zip up my bag of gear and hoist it to leave the arena. I have a massage booked with the trainer I've been working with, which is going to feel fucking amazing.

I turn off my phone while I'm getting worked over by Viktor. Stretched out on the table, my face planted down into the opening, I let him dig into tight muscles from my feet up to my neck and shoulders for an hour and a half. I damn near fall asleep. I haven't been sleeping that great the last few weeks.

Molly's hurt face floats in front of my closed eyes and as usual when I think of her, my gut clenches.

I try to push that aside though. I heard from Everly yesterday, and Grandpa's doing okay. His Alzheimer's hasn't progressed very much in the last few months, but Chelsea is still doing a lot. The money stuff has been taken care of, and Dad and Uncle Matt are involved in Grandpa's life again, helping Chelsea more. Now the hockey season's started, they're probably busy too, but I hope they can find the time to be there more.

After my massage, I go for lunch. Eating healthy is a big part of staying in shape, and I haven't been very diligent about that. But I stop at a Freshii for an Oaxaca bowl that's full of healthy things like brown rice, black beans and avocado. I sit down to eat it there.

I pull out my phone to scroll through sports news while I eat, and when I turn it on I discover a bunch of voice mails and about a hundred texts from Paul, the last one in all caps shouting at me to ANSWER YOUR GODDAMN PHONE.

Jesus. Shaking my head, I tap to call him. I hold the phone to my ear as I fork up some rice, beans and corn, waiting for Paul to pick up.

"Jesus Christ!" he bellows in my ear.

I hold the phone out and frown.

"What's up, man?"

"I've been trying to get hold of you all morning!"

"Yeah, I was busy. At the rink skating, then I had a massage."

"For Chrissake. Listen. I have news."

I pull in a breath, preparing myself. "Okay, lay it on me."

"They're offering five years."

I straighten. "Yeah?"

"AAV 3.8 million."

I drop my fork. I close my eyes. We were hoping for four million. That's pretty close. "What's the breakdown?"

"First year, three point five, second year, four mil." He continues to outline the rest of the contract.

My heart is hammering. All the tension in my muscles releases and I nearly fall off the stool. "Okay."

"Let's get together and go over all the details. Can you meet now?"

"Sure. I'm just eating lunch."

"Where are you?"

I tell him.

"Okay, not what I had in mind. Meet me at Maxime's."

I guess a place like that has a little more privacy for business discussions. I haven't even eaten my bowl, but I can bring it with me.

I'm a freakin' millionaire, but I don't want to waste my ten-dollar lunch. I laugh out loud as I pack it up and exit the restaurant. I jump into my SUV and drive to the place Paul suggested.

He's already there with a bunch of papers in front of him. He stands and shakes my hand, giving me a big grin. "Congratulations."

"Fuck." I grip his hand. "Not signed yet, right?"

"I think it's a good offer."

The money and the length of the contract are important, but there are a lot of other things that go into it—whether it's a one-way or two-way contract, bonuses, buyouts, movement clauses, restricted activity clauses, the payment schedule, ticket/travel/housing/vehicle allowances and obligations like media, autograph and promotional appearances.

It takes us a good while to go through everything. Paul knew what I wanted, so there isn't anything I have an issue with. I have questions on a few things, which he explains.

In the end, I'm satisfied.

"Okay." I sit back in my chair. I managed to eat a steak salad while we reviewed things. "Let's do it."

"Great." He smiles. "If we can get this signed, you can join training camp. Provided you pass the physical."

"I'll pass," I vow. "I've been working my ass off, waiting for this day."

When I leave the restaurant, I'm surprisingly calm. This is fantastic news and I should be jumping up and clicking my heels. It's fair money. I'd like to make ten million dollars a year, but that's not realistic for me. But I knew I was worth more than three.

I want to tell Molly.

I'm driving home and I want to slam on the brakes, turn around and find her.

I don't even know how to find her. I know she lives in Andersonville, but I don't know her address. I've never been there. It's late afternoon and she's probably done teaching.

I should tell my parents first. That's what I should do.

I stop at a store and pick up beer, because nothing says celebration more than a good Shock Top. When I'm home, I sit down on my couch with my phone. I want to tell my teammates, but I should wait until everything is signed and the team can announce it.

But I have to tell Molly.

I send her a quick text message. *Good news. We worked out a deal. Going to sign the contract tomorrow.*

Her response comes right away. *Oh, that's so good! I'm so happy for you. Congratulations!*

Thanks.

I stare at my phone and the message thread for a few minutes, smiling. Then I sigh.

I call Dad first, then Mom. I swear them both to secrecy until it's made public. They're both happy and relieved, full of congratulations.

Then I sit in my living room with my beer, all by myself.

I look around the room. I take in the spectacular view out the floor-to-ceiling windows. The place is dead quiet. I'm celebrating but…why do I feel so empty?

This is what I've wanted all year. We got it done before the start of the regular season. Why am I not happier?

24

MOLLY

The last place I want to go is the Chicago Aces Fan Festival. I'd rather go to the running of the bulls in Pamplona. Okay, maybe not.

But how can I say no to my two little nephews who I adore? I'm looking after them this weekend because my brother Travis and his wife Erin have gone to New York. It's a business trip for Travis, and Erin tagged along so they could spend the weekend there, and they won't be back until Sunday night. So I have two little ankle-biters who loooove hockey begging me to take them to the Fan Fest. They know I know some of the players, but they don't get that I might not want to see Steve.

Or Jax.

Maybe we won't see them. The players will be signing autographs, but not all at the same time, so if we're lucky, we can avoid them.

The event is held outside the Aces practice facility. It's a warm September day, bright and sunny, and the place is crowded with people. I refused to wear my Aces jersey with

Steve's name and number on it, but I am wearing an Aces T-shirt, black with silver and white logo.

Cam and Josh are both wearing their little jerseys, and they're practically spinning they're so excited to see some of their favorite players.

The scent of hot dogs fills the air as we make our way through crowds. Of course I buy the guys hot dogs and lemonades. They get to play ball hockey with the team mascot Blade, who's a giant basset hound wearing a brown leather bomber jacket, a scarf and goggles on his head.

I watch, smiling and laughing, but I'm on edge, constantly glancing around so if I see Steve or Jax I can duck into a hiding spot. And abandon my nephews, sure.

After the ball hockey, Blade obligingly poses for photos with Cam and Josh. As I turn to move on to another event, Cam spots Steve.

"Steve!" he calls.

Steve's head turns and he spots us. His eyes widen at seeing me, then narrow.

He looks…pissed.

What the hell? Is he angry that I'm here? I have a right to be here. I'm still an Aces fan.

Steve forces a smile at seeing the kids. He's met them many times, of course. They don't know what happened at the wedding since they weren't there, luckily, and they're happy to see him.

"Hi guys," he says, pausing. "How are you?"

"Good! We just played ball hockey with Blade."

"Cool." Steve raises his eyes to me and says curtly, "Hi, Molly. I can't believe you're here."

"Why not?" I frown. "I'm a fan too."

"I mean, I just saw a picture of you…"

"What?" I'm confused.

"We need to talk."

I shake my head, trying to figure out what's going on. "Obviously this isn't a good time."

"Oh hell yeah, it is."

"Hey, language," I mutter.

"Blade!" Steve calls to the mascot. Blade turns and lumbers toward us, a big dog smile on his enormous face. "Can you take these two guys and get them T-shirts?"

Blade claps his hands and holds them out to the boys.

"No…" I start to protest.

"They'll be fine, right, Blade?"

Blade nods his big head.

"Bring them over to the autograph table after," Steve says.

"What are you doing?" I demand under my breath.

"Come this way. I need to sign autographs in a few minutes." He pauses. "With Jax."

My heart bumps.

Steve takes hold of my upper arm and pulls me along with him. We go behind the table where a couple of players are signing autographs for a line of fans.

Jax is there.

Great. Perfect.

"Wynn," Steve snaps at him, jerking his head. "Come here."

Jax's head swivels, and he takes in me and Steve together. His jaw tightens and his shoulders tense, but his face stays remarkably expressionless. "What's up?" he asks, ambling forward.

Steve moves us behind a tent set up beside the autograph table. He pulls out his phone.

"Just tell me…" He unlocks it and swipes a few times, then holds it up for us to see. "What the hell is this?"

I peer at his phone and see a photograph of Jax and me at

Clear Lake. We're standing on the beach, arms around each other, smiling up at each other.

I freeze. I feel like darkness descends over the festival and only Jax, Steve and I are standing here, in a quiet bubble. I look at Jax. He looks at me.

What the hell do we do now?

My throat has gone dry, and I swallow.

I turn my gaze back to Steve. "Uh…"

"This is who you were with all summer?" he demands.

Welp, there's no point in lying about it. I don't like lying anyway, but he's holding proof in his hands.

I look at Jax, trying to convey my regret. He gives a tiny, resigned nod.

"Yes," I say to Steve.

I don't offer any other explanation or info. What more does he need to know?

His face reddening, Steve shakes his head and turns to Jax. "What the fuck, man?"

Jax holds up his hands. "You two weren't together anymore."

"I know, but Jesus Christ! We were engaged! She dumped me at the altar. What did you do, go after her?"

"No," Jax says quietly, lifting his chin. "She asked me to help. She wanted to get away from the wedding and she wanted to get out of town."

"He tried to talk me out of it," I put in. I know this is bad for Jax. Steve can go jump in Lake Michigan, for all I care. "He encouraged me to stay and talk to you and maybe go for counseling. Really."

"Counseling?" Steve's eyebrows fly up and his face gets even redder. "What the fuck?"

"I was trying to help."

"You call this *help?*" Steve shoves the phone in Jax's face. "I can't fucking believe this!"

"Where did you get that picture?" I ask, as if that even matters.

"Rico showed it to me. He just stumbled across it on Instagram. Somebody tagged the Aces because of the festival today."

"I saw it yesterday," Jax says quietly.

"Shit," I say, dropping my head forward.

"You were just going to keep this secret?" Steve says. "Forever?"

"It's over," I say, but unexpectedly my throat closes up. I try to say more, but I can't get any words out. To my horror, tears prickle the corners of my eyes.

Jax watches me with concern, and jumps in. "It's over, Chucky. It was just a summer fling."

If possible, Steve appears more outraged at this. "You fucked her and it was just a *fling?*" he yells.

"Shhhh." I cast a nervous glance around. We sure don't need anyone else hearing this.

"She's better than that, goddammit!" Steve roars. "You're nothing but a manwhore, fucking everything in sight! But *Molly?* Jesus!"

Jax's expression becomes alarmed. He's been doing so well at staying calm. He holds up his hands, palms out. "We both knew what it was going in," he says quietly. "Calm down, Chucky."

I shove at Steve's shoulder. "I can have a summer fling if I want to!" I speak up, now able to talk again.

He stares at me in disbelief. "That's what it was?"

No. That's not what it was. My chest fills with emotion and I want to burst into tears. I'm scared and wretched and...and

I'm in love with Jax and I can't admit it. But I can't deny it, either.

Steve gets it.

His jaw drops. A vein in his temple pulses. "You fell in love with him?"

I swallow painfully and give a tiny nod.

Steve's lip curls as he turns back to Jax, who's staring at me open-mouthed. "You motherfucker! You broke her heart!"

Jax shakes his head quickly, but his gaze is fastened on me, not Steve, who's lifting his fists.

"Don't hit him!" I cry, grabbing Steve's arm.

"I'm gonna break his fucking nose!"

"No! No, stop. It's not his fault, Steve. We agreed it would just be a summer thing."

"You fell in love with me?" Jax asks quietly, putting out a hand to shove Steve away. Apparently Steve's fists don't concern him.

"I—I'm sorry." A tear tracks down my cheek. "I didn't mean to. I thought it was a fling. I thought it was a rebound fling. But I—I can't get over you."

"Jesus." Now Jax is cursing.

Steve's coming at him again.

Jax turns to him. "Fine," he says with resignation. "Get your shots in. I deserve it."

"No!" I step between them. "This is ridiculous!"

My heart is racing, my hands shaking. Every coherent thought has spun out of my head. All I know is I can't let Steve hit Jax.

"Stop this," I order Steve. "This is ridiculous. This is none of your business, Steve."

He goes still, slowly lowering his arms. He scowls at Jax. "You need to apologize to her."

Jax scowls back at him. "Are you fucking kidding me? You

screwed around on her. *You* broke her heart. You two were done. It was crystal clear. I know I probably shouldn't have fallen for the ex-girlfriend of a teammate, but I did, and I'm not sorry."

My eyes fly open so wide I'm amazed my eyeballs aren't bouncing on the ground. "What?"

"So go ahead and hit me," he prods Steve.

Steve stares at him, his eyebrows pulled down low over his eyes. "You fell for her?"

Jax lifts his chin and clearly says, "Yeah."

Steve looks at me. "Are you two still together or not? You said it was over."

My bottom lip quivers. "I don't know what's going on," I whisper. I twist my fingers together. My gaze bounces back and forth between the two men. Steve seems to be calming down. Jax is…unruffled.

"I don't either." Steve scowls.

"I do." A slow smile slides over Jax's face.

Someone appears around the corner of the tent. "What the hell are you doing back here? You guys are up. Get out here and sign some autographs."

"Oh my God." I press the heel of my hand to my forehead.

"Be right there, Modi," Steve says. He steps away from Jax. "Are you okay, Molly?"

"I'm…" I float a glance Jax's way. "I'm not sure."

Steve turns a glare on Jax. "She's not sure."

"It'll be okay." Jax moves to me. He cups my face in both hands and, nearly nose to nose, he stares into my eyes. "It'll be okay. Got that?"

I nod slowly, mesmerized by the affection and heat I see in his dark eyes.

He presses his lips to my forehead in a long, tender kiss, then draws back. "We'll talk when I'm done. Okay?"

"Okay."

I'm blinking rapidly. My heart thuds against my ribs and my hands are shaking. I glance at Steve, who has looked away, his jaw tight, then I follow him and Jax back to the table where fans are waiting.

Blade returns with an ecstatic Josh and Cam, who are carrying T-shirts and pennants.

"We need to get these autographed!" Cam says.

"You guys have Steve's autographs," I remind them, tapping the big number of the back of Cam's jersey where Steve signed it last year.

"We'll get Jax Wynn's, then!"

"Okay." I get in line with them.

The boys are bouncing with excitement, and I'm vibrating with nerves and uncertainty. What did he mean, he fell for me? What, what, *what*?

When we get to the front of the line, the boys hand their pennants and shirts over to Jax.

"These are my nephews," I tell him. I set a hand on Cam's head. "This is Cam. And this is Josh."

"Good to meet you, guys."

"You too!" They both nearly shout. "You're a great right-winger!"

"Thanks, guys."

"I can't wait till your first game!" Josh says.

"Yeah, same." Jax grins. "The start of the season is exciting."

"I'm so glad you're playing," Josh says, aware that Jax almost missed training camp.

"Me too." Jax's smile turns wry. He meets my eyes over the heads of the boys.

Once again, our gazes hold. I'm a buzzing ball of nerves and confusion. I don't know what's happening.

Steve's signing a jersey for another fan, and he glances up. He gives me a wry smile and a nod.

"I'm done here in twenty minutes," Jax says. "Can you stay?"

The boys look up at me. "We're staying longer than twenty minutes, right, Aunt Molly?"

"Er, yeah." We haven't actually seen much of the festival yet. There's also an open scrimmage we could go watch with about half the players trying out for the team this year. "We'll be here for a while."

"I'll text you when I'm done," Jax says.

Steve's mouth twists up overhearing this, then relaxes. "You two have some stuff to sort out, apparently."

I'm so frickin' grateful to Steve for not making this a hundred times worse than it already is, although I don't condone his threat to break Jax's nose. I shoot him a grateful smile as I shepherd the boys away so the people behind us can get autographs.

We pass a face painting session and the boys want the Aces logo painted on their faces, so we do that. Then Cam and Josh want mini donuts, and how can I say no to that when I love mini donuts myself? We're munching on those as we enter the practice facility to watch the scrimmage.

We've just found our seats when my phone buzzes. I pull it out of the cross-body purse I'm wearing. It's Jax.

Where are u?

Watching the scrimmage.

I'll find u.

I don't know if this is a good idea with my nephews here. What are we really going to be able to talk about?

I can't sit still, shifting on the hard bench in the stands, my muscles quivery and twitchy. I see him enter the rink area, looking around. I lift a hand, and he spots us and heads our way.

There's room for him on the bench if we shift over, so I nudge Josh and Cam to move down. They're big-eyed as Jax bumps fists with them.

There's a buzz of excitement around us as everyone realizes who he is.

"Mini donuts," Jax says. "My fave."

Cam wordlessly hands him the paper bag, and Jax takes one solemnly. "Thanks, man."

I'm shivering, both because of the cold in the arena and my nerves. I've barely had time to process what's happening. Why did I say what I did? Why didn't I lie? Why did Jax say that? I don't understand any of this.

"So," he says in a low voice near my ear, "we're busted."

I clap a hand over my mouth to stop my startled laugh. "I guess so, yeah."

"Sorry about that."

"Why are you apologizing? You didn't do it. I should be apologizing to you. You're the one who has to work in an, um, awkward situation."

"Seems like Steve is more pissed about me hurting you than about us being together."

I suck on my bottom lip and turn my eyes up to him. "That's what it seemed like."

Steve's already shown he's not in love with me anymore, but it seems like maybe he still cares. That's…nice.

"When do you get rid of the tadpoles?" he murmurs near my ear.

"Their parents get back around six tonight. I guess seven-ish by the time they get home from the airport."

"Can I come see you after that?"

I swallow. "Okay."

"I need your fucking address."

Thankfully, he's talking in a quiet voice on the side opposite to where Cam and Josh are sitting. "Why do you sound angry about that?"

"Because I don't even know where you fucking live. I should know that."

Oh. I give him my address and he enters it into his phone.

He says goodbye to the boys and leaves, everyone around us watching all of this take place.

What is even happening?

25

JAX

What the fuck just happened?

I try to smile and focus on the fans as I sign autographs and make small talk, aware of Chucky next to me doing the same.

I thought Chucky was going to deck me, and I was ready to take it like a man. But maybe I should be thanking him. Haha.

All I know is, when Molly said she fell in love with me, I was done.

Done. Finished. Dead. My heart cracked at what she said. I can't bear that I hurt her. I didn't know.

Okay, maybe I did.

I sign another jersey and pose for a photograph, smile in place.

I knew it was hard for us both to say goodbye at the end of her stay. I knew I was a miserable bastard after she left. I guess I didn't realize how hard it was for her.

Then she was crying and apologizing for falling for me, and fuck! That's not right!

She said she can't get over me. Christ. What have I done?

I think I fucked up big time.

All I know is, I can't lose Molly again. She's what's been missing in my life. She's why I haven't been interested in seeing other women. She's why signing this contract hasn't felt that celebratory. I need her to celebrate with. I need her to commiserate with. I need her for every damn thing.

I'm still not sure what happened there with Steve getting pissed at me for hurting her, when he's the one who broke her heart.

When Modi finally tells us we're done, we push back our chairs and stand. I meet Chucky's eyes and jerk my head to the back of the tents where we were earlier. "We need to talk."

He narrows his eyes, lifts his chin and follows me.

Behind the tent, I turn to face him, my shoulders hunched. But I hold his gaze steadily when I say, "I'm in love with Molly."

"I got that," he says quietly.

"I'm sorry, man. I know it's weird and awkward and I never meant for it to happen." I suck air into my lungs. "We both agreed we'd just have fun over the summer, but it turned into more."

"For her too, apparently."

He's remarkably calm. Although there is a vein pulsing in his forehead.

I swallow. "I have to find out. If she really feels the same." I still hold his gaze.

He stares at me and I start to think he's going to try to hit me again. Then he says, "I get it."

"We have to play together. I don't want things to be…weird and awkward," I repeat lamely.

"Oh, it's going to be weird and awkward."

My gut tenses.

Then Chucky sighs. "We'll get over it. Go do what you have to do. Just…don't be an idiot. Like me."

Shared understanding vibrates between us.

Maybe this will be okay.

I give him a short nod and turn to bolt.

In my vehicle, I sit for a moment before starting the engine. It's goddamn bizarre, but whatever. It feels…right. Like this had to happen.

I grip the steering wheel of my SUV. Okay. I got this.

No. I don't. I don't know what the hell I'm doing.

I don't know what to do. I've never been in this position before. I'm always the one making a quick exit, and this time… well, I tried, thinking that was what we had to do. But I screwed up.

I tip my head back and let out a long stream of breath.

Who can I talk to? I need help.

Fuck.

I don't have friends I can talk to about this. I mean, Rico and Heart are my two best buddies still left on the team, now that Gander is gone. But I don't share all my deepest secret crap with them. That's not me. I haven't said a word to them about Molly, out of fear it would get back to Chucky.

Too late for that, though. Rico apparently saw the Instagram post that led to this shit show.

I remember my mom lamenting that I don't talk to her. And Molly commenting about all the time I'd lost with my dad because of not talking about what happened.

Shit.

Welp, if Mom wants me to talk to her, she's about to get an earful.

I put my SUV in gear and leave the parking lot.

I wait for my mom to say, "I knew it!" or "I told you so!"

Luckily, she doesn't. Because I don't really want to have my stupidity rubbed in my face. My mom's pretty great.

"Remember what I said at the lake?" she asks, in a calm voice.

"That I don't talk to you enough?"

"Well, that too. But I told you men aren't programmed to cheat. There are many reasons that they do. But it's always a choice."

"Right." I rub my face. "I get that. But…I'm afraid I'll screw up. I want to believe in love. I want to believe in happily ever after. After this summer…I guess my eyes were opened. I thought Chelsea married Grandpa for his money. Turns out they really love each other. I thought Dad cheated on you. Turns out he didn't. I want to believe I can be faithful to one woman for the rest of my life."

"That's not good enough for Molly."

"What?" My jaw slackens, and my gut goes hollow. I stare across the room.

"You can't go to her *hoping* you can be faithful. You have to *know* it. You have to know that every day, you'll make that choice not to cheat. *Every day*, Jax. You have to believe in yourself."

I close my eyes.

"Is she worth it?" Mom asks quietly.

I nod slowly, even though Mom can't see me. My eyes burn.

I think about Molly. About how much I've missed her. How much I need her. How empty my life has felt since she left. I think about how good she makes me feel and how I want to be there for her. Always. "Yeah," I rasp out. "She's worth it. I can do it."

"Good." Mom pauses. "Jax. Your dad and I didn't want to talk to you about what happened in our marriage, because we didn't want to point fingers at each other. But part of the problem was not talking to each other about how we were feeling."

I remember sitting on the deck in Catalina with Dad. I wasn't great at talking about my feelings, he'd said.

No shit. I guess that's where I get it from.

"He said it wasn't your fault."

Mom laughs softly. "That's admirable of him to say that. Maybe he's learned something. But the truth is, I wasn't good either at expressing what I needed from him. I thought he should know. I let the resentment build. Don't be like that."

I frown. "Resentment?"

"Not that specifically, just whatever you're feeling. Tell Molly. Tell *someone*, but especially Molly. I wish you'd told your dad and me how you were feeling."

Another memory of that conversation with dad. Because I'd blamed him for cheating on Mom, never asked him about it, never told either of them how much it wrecked me that they split up. *What a lot of wasted years.*

Wasted years between Dad and me. Wasted years between him and his own father. Wasted years between Dad and Mom, too, I guess.

I don't want that for me and Molly. I don't want to regret not being brave enough to tell her how I feel. About everything. Ever.

Yeah, she's worth it. She's all that I want in the world.

***

Molly

I can't dash out the door the minute Travis and Erin get home, much as I want to. I dutifully wait to admire the gifts they brought the boys, listen to all the things they did in New York, then make my escape.

As soon as I'm home, I text Jax to let him know.

My apartment is a disaster, since I was staying at Travis and Erin's place the last few days. I left dishes in the sink, clothes piled on the chair in my bedroom, and a basket of laundry in the hall. I have more laundry to add to it now, and I need to get ready for work tomorrow.

I start in the kitchen, frantically loading the dishwasher and scrubbing a pot that's been soaking for days. Gross. I scrub out the sink and wipe down the counters, then pick up the laundry basket and carry it into the bedroom. I manically sort through the clothes on the chair, tossing some into the laundry basket, others onto the bed to be hung up. Do I have something to wear to work tomorrow? I find an outfit and swiftly hang the rest in my closet.

And never mind my apartment; *I* look like a wreck. I'm still in my Aces T-shirt and jeans. I felt hot when I was cleaning the kitchen, so I scooped my hair up into a ponytail without even looking in a mirror. My hands smell like bleach cleaner. Ugh. I run to the bathroom to get cleaned up.

I'm still rubbing my favorite pink grapefruit lotion into my hands when the apartment buzzer sounds. I let Jax in and pace until he knocks at the door. My apartment is on the second floor so that doesn't take long.

My heart hammers in my throat when I open the door. "Hi."

"Hi."

His smile is so, so gorgeous. I've missed it so much.

"Come in." My hands are shaking as I close the door.

He walks into my living room. My apartment is old, in a three-story brownstone, but I like it.

"Nice," he says, taking in the old hardwood floors, the bay

window overlooking the street, the wide, white-painted base-board and door trim.

"Thanks." I'm dying. "Would you like something to drink?"

"Uh. No. I'm good."

I move past him and take a seat on the couch that sits in front of the bay windows. "Have a seat."

He sits next to me, but with a bit of distance between us. He's holding a small cardboard box in his hand that I only now notice.

"What's that?"

He looks down. "It's a trivia game."

I tilt my head, a smile tugging my lips. "Seriously? You want to play trivia?"

"Yeah." He meets my eyes and his are glinting. He sets the box on my coffee table and opens it.

I can't believe this. I'm about to have a stroke, and he wants to play trivia.

He picks up a card. "Okay. What arouses men more than any other scent in the world? Your choices are: a. lavender; b. lilies; c. woodsmoke; d. beer."

I choke on a laugh. "The scent of beer is arousing?"

He grins. "Is that your answer?"

"No, I'll say lavender."

"Correct."

He sets the card down, picks up another and hands it to me. "Your turn."

"Wait. How does this game work?"

"Just follow along."

Smiling, I say, "Okay." I read the card. "What arouses Jax more than any other scent in the world?" I blink and look up at him. "You?"

"Yes."

I keep reading his choices. "A. Molly's grapefruit perfume."

I pause. What is this? "B. Molly's grapefruit lotion; c. Molly's grapefruit body wash; d. Molly." My insides soften and warm as I meet his eyes.

"All of the above," he says softly.

I swipe a hand under my nose. I think I see where this is going and it's amazing.

He picks up a card. "What chemical is responsible for making my heart race when I see you? A. dopamine; b. norepinephrine; c. adrenalin."

My throat is squeezing up. "Adrenalin."

"That's right."

"Your heart races when you see me?"

"Yes." He holds my gaze steadily.

"Me too," I whisper.

After a protracted silence, he says in a gruff voice, "Your turn."

"Oh. Right." I take the card he hands me. "Which bonding chemical is released in my brain when you make me orgasm?" I lower the card. "Where did you get this game?"

"Never mind that."

I keep reading. "A. estrogen; b. oxytocin; c. vasopressin."

"Oxytocin."

"Yes."

Jax is next. "What are my favorite parts of Molly? A. Smile; b. butt; c. breasts; d. legs."

My eyes widen. "Uh…" He has commented a lot that he likes my ass…

"Never mind, it's all of the above. Your turn."

I choke on a laugh, shaking my head. "Okay. What is the best sex position for me to have an orgasm in?" I look up. "Me, as in *me*?"

"Yes. You."

I clear my throat. "A. missionary; b. girl on top; c. doggy

style; d. the bridge." I look up. "I don't even know what the bridge is."

"We'll work on that. The answer is c, doggy style."

"That's right." My cheeks heat up as I lay down the card.

"What makes Molly the most loveable? A. her sense of humor; b. her belief that everything will be okay; c. her PMS; d. her love of hamburgers; e. her generosity; f. her incredible trivia knowledge." He pauses. "Although being a know-it-all can be a little annoying at times."

"Hey!"

His lips twitch. "In life, it's important to know when to stop arguing with people."

"And let them be wrong," I finish.

He barks out a laugh, shakes his head, then continues reading. "G. her sexpertise; h. her—"

"Stop!" I press my hands to my mouth, trying not to laugh. "You're crazy!"

"That's not the answer."

"Oh my God."

"Okay, fine, the correct answer is all of the above."

My bottom lip quivers. "Jax."

"Your turn."

Shaking my head, I pick up a card. "Why is Jax an idiot when it comes to relationships?" I roll my eyes. "A. He's just an idiot; b. He's a coward; c. Both A and B." I pause and add my own answer. "D. He's not a coward and he's not an idiot. That's my answer."

He grins, but ruefully. "Yeah, I am. I've always believed marriage is for suckers. That real long-term relationships don't exist. I've always been afraid that if I get into a relationship, I'll hurt her because I'll do something stupid like cheat on her."

I knew he didn't believe in relationships. I knew part of that stemmed from his parents' divorce. But believing he would do the same thing he thought his dad did? I didn't know that. "Do you still believe all those things?"

"No." He meets my eyes and holds them with a steady, open gaze. "That was the idiot part. Then there's the cowardly part."

I blink at him.

"I talked to my mom earlier." He lowers our clasped hands to his thighs. "I needed advice. I've never felt like this before. I've never screwed up like this before. I didn't know what to do about it. My mom…always used to tell us that if you make a mistake, the first thing to do is admit it. Then learn from it. And don't do it again."

"Good advice," she murmurs.

"I don't want to make that mistake again…not talking about things." He bends his head. "I've never been good about talking about my feelings."

"I know."

He lifts his head, his lips twitching. "Yeah. You told me that. I missed years with my dad because I didn't want to talk about it. After he left, I pretended everything was fine. I was strong. I could handle my dad leaving, no problem. I kept telling everyone I wasn't worried about my contract. But talking to you about that…helped. The way you listen and don't judge… you never made me feel weak."

I swallow, my heart rising to lodge in my throat. "You're not weak. It's not weak to have feelings."

He nods. "That's what Mom told me. Keeping myself closed off that way just deprived me of connecting with other people. Kept people distant. Even my parents." He pauses. "Even you."

My bottom lip wobbles.

"It left me all alone," he rasps out, his fingers tightening on mine. "When I signed the contract, I didn't have anyone to share to the good stuff with. And that's important too."

"Yes." I blink rapidly, my eyelashes damp.

"I want you in my life. So I have to be brave enough to tell you how I really feel. Even if it scares the hell out of me. And I'm not scared anymore. I *will* be faithful to you, Molly. I know it. I don't want anyone else. And I will never hurt you."

We share a slow, heated smile, warmth blooming inside me and spreading from my chest outward.

He reaches out and picks up another card. "Who typically says 'I love you' first? Men? Women? Or both equally?"

When he looks up from the card, I gaze at him. I open my mouth at the same time he does and we both say, "I love you."

Then we burst out laughing.

Except my laughing is almost crying because I'm so emotional and I fling myself into his arms. He wraps me up in a tight hug, my face pressed to his shoulder. "I love you. So much.

His hand strokes my hair. "I love you too, Molly."

26

JAX

Only inches separate our faces. I drag my gaze away from Molly's wet eyes and look at her mouth. The plump bottom lip parts slightly from the top just so I can see the edge of her white teeth. I can't believe she's in my arms and she loves me and I'm so fucking relieved and elated and hot for her I can barely think.

I hear her indrawn breath, feel the tremors of her soft body in my arms. Her scent surrounds us, intoxicating me. I feel her breath whisper on my lips, her heart knocking against me. I see her pulse, just as quick, beneath the fine skin of her throat.

Then our mouths meet, in an agonizing, excruciatingly beautiful kiss. Her mouth is heaven, sweet and soft. I stroke inside with my tongue, and she opens for me, meeting my tongue with hers. I kiss her again and again, long, slow, clinging kisses, our tongues brushing as we draw apart in slow, lush licks. She moans deep in her throat, slides her hands around my neck and pulls me closer.

I lift her onto my lap, turn her, tipping her back against the arm rest of the couch, leaning into her. I need to taste more of her, more of her sweet mouth. I thread my hand into her hair, twist it around my fingers and give a little tug, eliciting a whimper from her that has my blood sizzling through my veins.

I draw back to look at her face. The love shining there punches me like a fist in the gut, spreading warmth and relief and gratitude through me. I kiss her again, deep, open-mouthed kisses, eating her up, trailing my fingers down the side of her neck, over her collarbone. I rub the top curve of her breast. Heat sparks, ignites and grows between us as our kisses deepen, as I cup one breast in my hand and rub my thumb over the nipple. My throat aches and my heart lurches with overwhelming emotion. I can't get close enough to her.

Without words, I stand and pull her up from the couch, and she leads me to her bedroom. There, she winds her arms around my neck and presses against me. We stand like that, foreheads together, noses side by side, just breathing in each other. Then Molly shifts her mouth closer to mine, and I take it in a long, hungry kiss.

"Want you out of these clothes." I pull her T-shirt up and over her head, and she reaches behind her back to undo her bra, a sweet little barely-there pink lace number. I flick open the button of her jeans and work them down over her hips, along with her panties. She steps out of them, one foot at a time, then I move her to the bed and lay her down gently. She smiles up at me, her hair spread around her face, her smooth skin glowing, her eyes shiny.

As I take off my own clothes, I study her curves, her perfect breasts, the shallow indent of her navel, the swell of her hips. My eyes return to hers to see her watching me too, a look of avid longing in her eyes. I fucking love that.

I lie down beside her, hand on her stomach, elbow bent, my head propped on my hand.

Luminous green eyes turn to me and I'm lost. "I love you."

"I love you too."

I press my face between her breasts, breathe in her pink citrus scent, then kiss the inside curve of each breast. I take a nipple into my mouth and suck, then rub my tongue over it. She tastes so sweet and her whimpers tell me how much she loves that. I move to the other nipple, taste it too, play with it with my mouth while my fingers pluck the other. I test the weight of her breast, squeezing it gently.

"That feels so good." Her fingers sifted through my hair, her body twitching and writhing against me. "So good."

I move over her and she reaches for my cock. Her hands feel sublime, soft yet firm, stroking me in long pulls that send pleasure licking over my skin.

"Inside me. Please."

"I need to get a condom."

"Do you?"

I lift my head and peer down at her. Our eyes meet. I swallow. Her trust hits me like a puck in the chest. "Do *you?*" I ask quietly.

"I'm on the pill. And I went to the doctor when I got back to Chicago. All good."

"Me too."

"Okay then."

I press a hard kiss to her mouth as she guides me into her. Her heat and wetness surround the head of my cock, then more as I ease in, hot velvet squeezing me. A low, rough sound tears from my throat. I've never been bareback and I'm so fucking glad it's with Molly.

I hold my weight on my elbows and she parts her legs wider. I push in deeper, all the way, and the air rips out of my lungs. "Molly, oh, Christ."

"I know." Her hands clutch my ass, pulling me deeper. "Fuck me, Jax."

My groans mingle with her sighs as our bodies come together, perfect, easy and right. I surge into her, our connection so intimate, joining not just our bodies but our hearts. Something even more than that. Our souls? Something touches me inside, a searing, exquisite sensation, an overwhelming desire to protect and take care of her, to be with her forever. My eyes sting and my throat closes up.

I frame her face with my hands, my gaze holding hers. I see a reflection of my own devotion, my own longing, my own hope in her eyes, and it draws me in, so deep, like I'm falling over a cliff. "I've never felt like this before."

She stares back at me steadily, meaningfully. "Me either."

Christ. I know she's been in love before. But those words mean so much to me. Emotion swells inside me and I'm overflowing with everything good and right and dazzling. "I love you, Molly. I love you."

Her hands stroke over my back and I feel the tenderness in her touch, hear her pleasure in her muffled whimpers, feel her love in the brush of her breath against my mouth. "I love you, too, Jax."

Her body tightens beneath me and around me as she climaxes, squeezing me inside and out. She cries out and I watch her face, humbled by her beauty, by the ecstasy I see there because of me, awed and gratified by her trust and her belief in me and her love.

Pressure builds at the base of my spine and in my balls, building to my own exquisite peak of pleasure. Her hands grip my hips as I drive into her one...more...time...and explode. Lights flash as my lids squeeze shut against the intensity of my orgasm, and when I pour myself into her in long, hard, almost painful pulses, I'm joined to her like I've never been with anyone.

We settle beneath the soft warmth of her duvet, curled into

each other. I press my cheek against the top of her head and smile. I loved her arms around me, stroking my back, down over the curve of my ass, dragging her fingers up the crevice there. Jesus, I'm going to be hard again in two minutes if she keeps that up.

"I tried to get over you," she says quietly as we snuggle together. "But I couldn't." She strokes up my back. "My friends told me I should go out with other guys, try to move on. It didn't work."

"I was so fucking pissed seeing you with that guy."

"Yeah?"

"Yeah." I sigh. "Again, time wasted because I was afraid to say what I needed to."

"I didn't say anything either," she points out. "I mean, I told you I missed you."

"I thought you meant as a friend."

"No. But I wanted you to think that. I didn't think we could be together because of Steve."

"Okay, how fucked up was that that we told each other how we really feel about each other while he was standing right there? And after that, I think he was actually *less* inclined to clock me."

"I know!" She shifts against me. "That was so…weird. But…good."

"I talked to him."

She draws back and stares at me. "What?"

"After the autograph session. We talked again. I don't think he's totally happy, but he didn't punch me in the face, so there's that."

She chuckles.

"I think it'll be okay. He knows he fucked up." I pause. "He told me not to do the same."

She nods slowly.

"I won't, Molly. I promise you."

Her lips tip up into a trembling smile and she touches her fingertips to my cheek. "Remember what you said, the night of the wedding? I mean, the non-wedding?"

"Uh…no."

"You said sometimes not getting what you want can be a good thing."

"Fuck, I am so smart."

"I know." She laughs lightly and presses a kiss to my chest. "You were right. Things worked out so much better. For all of us."

I slide a hand into her hair and press her face to me. "Yeah. Things did." I roll her to her back and rise up over her to peer down into her eyes. "I promise I will never cheat on you, Molly. If I've learned anything, it's that I need to talk. If I'm ever feeling…I don't even know, fuck, I can't imagine wanting anyone but you, I love you…but if I'm not happy, I promise I will talk to you about it instead of doing something stupid."

She nods, her eyes wide and glowing with love. "Thank you."

"And if I don't, you have my permission to smack me across the back of my head with a hockey stick."

She smiles.

"Telling my dad I thought he cheated on Mom was hard. But it was worth it, to find out the truth. And to have a relationship with my dad, to be able to respect him again."

Her eyes go glossy, her smile tremulous.

"Telling my mom I'm in love with you after I denied it to everyone was hard. But it was worth it too." I kiss her. "*So* damn worth it. Telling *you*…was surprisingly *not* hard." I smile wryly. "I hope I know now that even if it's hard to talk about something, it's worth it."

Her throat works as she smiles and gives a tiny nod. "Thank you." She touches my face.

"My whole family is crazy about you." I nuzzle her ear. "Everyone's been asking me about you."

"Really? That's so sweet."

"You're sweet." I nibble her ear lobe and she shivers. "And I want to taste you. Everywhere."

I proceed to do so.

27

———

MOLLY

"It's the fuckening."

Jax's silence greets my comment. "What?"

"The fuckening. You know when things are going too well, and you don't totally trust it's going to last and shit goes down? That's the fuckening."

Jax falls over on his couch laughing. "Jesus."

"It's not a laughing matter." I could cry over what I just read online. About me. I press my fingers to my mouth. "We thought things were okay with you and Steve about us being together. But we didn't take into account the rest of the world."

I found a blog online that posted about Jax and me being a couple, one of those "Hottest Wives of the NHL" things, and some jerkface commented and called me a hockey whore because I'd been engaged to Steve and left him at the altar to run off with one of his teammates.

It's true, though.

"I'm sorry I'm embarrassing you. Both of you."

The comments also implied that there was bad blood between Jax and Steve now, causing tension in the dressing

288

room and on the ice. That part is *not* true. I think? Unless Jax hasn't been honest with me…

"Christ, Molly. It's not you. Haters are gonna hate. People will say all kinds of shit. You have to get used to it."

"Are things really okay with you and Steve?"

"Yeah. It's weird, but we weren't best buds before all this. We're both professionals."

"Okay." I pout, still unhappy about what people are saying and thinking about us. "You're right, I know. We can't pay attention to this stuff."

I knew that when I was dating and engaged to Steve. But I never really gave people anything to gossip about; I'm just a midwestern school teacher who loves kids and trivia. Then I did a crazy thing. I guess I deserve the backlash for that.

"Ignore it," he says. "All that matters is us."

My eyes fall on the framed photo sitting on a shelf in his living room. The first time I came here after we got together, I nearly cried seeing it. It's one of the photos he took on the whale watching cruise, but it's of me, rosy cheeked, bright eyed, beaming a smile of pure joy directly at him, the ocean glinting behind me. The fact that he had printed that image, framed it, and put it up in his condo brought me near to tears again. It nearly matches the photo I took of him, capturing his happiness as he took pictures that day. I had it on my phone and kept looking at it. After I'd decided not to date anymore, I got a print made of it, just a small one, and I too had framed it and set it in my bedroom, a bittersweet reminder of the summer I learned what love really is, in case I never found it again.

Now our pictures sit side by side, as do we. Hopefully for the rest of our lives.

EPILOGUE

MOLLY

I'm not wearing a princess dress. There are no beads, no layers of tulle. My dress isn't even white; it's ivory. It's plain satin, fitted to my body, spaghetti straps leaving my shoulders bare, and the trumpet shape hugs my butt.

Because Jax loves my butt.

This time, the wedding is small, family and close friends. Okay, Jax has a sizeable family, but still, there are only about thirty-five people here. We're at the Tarragona Resort, where we stayed almost exactly a year ago. I pause before walking across the terrace toward Jax, the Pacific Ocean shimmering behind him. He's dressed casually—narrow beige pants, a white shirt open at the collar, and a dark jacket.

I let Jax pick the music for me to walk down the aisle. When it starts, I drop my head forward, trying not to laugh. Led Zeppelin? Oh. My. God.

I walk alone, this time. Nobody has to give me away. I'm giving myself to Jax.

I catch Jax's eye as I walk and listen to "All My Love." Okay, it's a pretty good song. We're both grinning like crazy.

Unplanned, he comes to meet me, picks me up and swings me around, laying a big smooch on my mouth. Well, we didn't want this wedding to be traditional.

Everyone claps and cheers for us.

I'm so happy I can't stop my feet from dancing the rest of the way down the aisle toward the officiant, who's also smiling. As we stop in front of him, Jax turns to me and holds out his fist. We do our secret good-luck trivia handshake, still beaming at each other. This arouses more chuckles in our audience.

The ceremony is short and sweet, including the vows we each wrote. Then we're husband and wife.

A pop and a hissing sound comes from behind Jax, and his best man, Brian Erhardt, hands him a can of Budweiser. To my surprise, Grace places one in my hand also and I can't stop laughing as Jax holds his beer up to toast me. I tap the cold aluminum against his and take a gulp of the fizzy lager. Then he leans over and kisses me again, long and lingering.

Our friends and family clap and cheer again.

Grace takes my beer and hands me back my bouquet, a small arrangement of white roses and eucalyptus. Jax clasps my other hand and smiles at me as we turn to walk back down the aisle together.

The music starts, another Jax choice and again, I'm dying. It's Gary Glitter's "Rock and Roll Part II." How many times have we heard this song in hockey arenas? We both start bopping to the rhythm, then half-dance down the aisle. It's an appropriately triumphant, celebratory tune. When the band yells "Hey!" all the guests also yell "Hey!"

Joy bubbles up inside me as effervescent as the beer I just drank as we sign the legal documents, then mingle with our guests, exchanging hugs and kisses and smiles.

We've been here in California for a couple of weeks, following the Aces' deep playoff run. They lost to the Condors, who went on to play St. Louis in the final. Sadly, the Condors lost, but they've come a long way in the last couple of seasons under new leadership.

Last weekend, we attended Taylor and JP's wedding. Everly and Wyatt are now engaged too, so there'll be another Wynn family wedding soon. Tomorrow, we fly to Winnipeg, where we'll rent a car and drive to Clear Lake for our honeymoon. I can't wait.

We eat a lovely dinner in a small private dining room, then dance a little. Our first dance song was my pick, Al Green's "Let's Stay Together."

"Good choice." Jax smiles into my eyes, then twirls me.

"Thanks."

"Having fun?"

"So much fun."

"Me too."

"I think I'm going to hyphenate my last name."

After a beat, Jax's eyebrows shoot up, and he says, "Molly Flynn-Wynn?"

I laugh. "Doesn't it sound great?"

"No."

"I'm kidding. I'm happy to be a Wynn."

We smile into each other's eyes, then I jerk my head across the dance floor where couples are joining us. "Your mom and dad are dancing together."

His eyebrows fly up as he follows my gaze. "Whoa. And they don't even look angry."

His mom just moved to Los Angeles for a new job. She's a bestselling author now. I love her so much. I really like Mark too. And I'm so happy for Jax that he and his dad have been keeping in touch.

I look over at Bob Wynn, sitting at a table near the small

dance floor, surrounded by family. He's smiling and it's wonderful to see him happy, Chelsea holding his hand.

Over the past year, Jax and I started doing trivia nights to raise money for charity, specifically for the Alzheimer's Association. It seems a small thing, but at least it's a way we can contribute and draw attention to the fight for research and a cure. We've met so many people affected by the disease and have heard heart-breaking but also awe-inspiring stories.

"Hey guess what?"

I focus back on Jax. "What?"

"There's only one bed in our hotel room."

"Oh no!" I widen my eyes dramatically, then we both burst out laughing. We have so much fun together, even when we're doing nothing. A year ago, I was broken hearted and sorry for myself because I thought my beautiful life had been ruined. But now I know Jax was right…sometimes not getting what you want is a good thing.

ACKNOWLEDGMENTS

As I finish the final edits of this book, the world is deep into the COVID-19 crisis. I re-read lines like "we mingle with our guests, exchanging hugs and kisses and smiles" and I screamed inwardly, "Nooooo!" But this story happens in a different world, where we don't have to worry about hugging and kissing the people we love, and I hope that we are soon back to that kind of world. In the meantime, let's remember that love is the most powerful force in the world, even if we're stuck at home in isolation or socially distancing ourselves.

I know that Bob Wynn's story has been hard for some readers. Alzheimer's affects so many people with our aging populations. I too am affected by it in my family. Like Jax and Molly, I hope in my own small way I've brought attention to the need for research and a cure. You can learn more here https://www.alz.org/ and here https://alzheimer.ca/en/Home.

Mega huge thanks to my assistant, Stacey Price who does so much for me. Also thanks to my publicist, Heather Robertson for helping people find my books, because that's pretty important. Thank you to all the bloggers and bookstagrammers who read and share my books—your love of books and reading makes the world a better place. And most especially, thank you to my readers, I am so deeply grateful to everyone who buys and reads my books.

ABOUT THE AUTHOR

Kelly Jamieson is a best-selling author of over fifty romance novels and novellas. Her writing has been described as "emotionally complex", "sweet and satisfying" and "blisteringly sexy." She likes coffee (black), wine (mostly white), shoes (high heels) and hockey!

Sign up for updates about her new books and what's coming up, follow her on Twitter @KellyJamieson or on Facebook, visit her website at www.kellyjamieson.com or contact her at info@kellyjamieson.com

With Strings Attached

How to Love

Slammed

Windy City Kink

Sweet Obsession

All Messed Up

Playing Dirty

Brew Crew

Limited Time Offer

No Obligation Required

Aces Hockey

Major Misconduct

Off Limits

Icing

Top Shelf

Back Check

Slap Shot

Playing Hurt

Big Stick

Game On

Last Shot

Body Shot

Hot Shot

Bayard Hockey

Shut Out

Cross Check

Dancing in the Rain

Love Me

Friends with Benefits

Love Me More

2 Hot 2 Handle

Lost and Found

One Wicked Night

Sweet Deal

Hot Ride

Crazy Ever After

All I Want for Christmas

Sexpresso Night

Irish Sex Fairy

Conference Call

Rigger

You Really Got Me

How Sweet It Is

Three of Hearts

Loving Maddie from A to Z

Firecracker